Buddy System

A SMALL-TOWN, MMF, MILITARY ROMANCE

HONEYBEE HOLLOW

ARIELLA TALIX

Ariella Talix

Ringmaster Publishing

Cover Design by Dar Albert, Wicked Smart Designs

E-Book ISBN: 979-8-9895156-3-9

Paperback ISBN: 979-8-9895156-4-6

Dedicated to all of the brave veterans who have selflessly given up so much to serve our country—especially my father.

Do your best. One day, you will be someone's hero.

—Anonymous

CHAPTER

One

I DON'T KNOW IF I WAS SHIVERING MORE BECAUSE OF THE freezing cold or nerves. As I faced the open doorway, heart pounding, I tensed at the sound of incoming bullets and saw the silhouette of a small advancing form. Before I could grab my firearm, a heavy, bellowing body nearly flattened me by flinging itself onto me facing outward.

"What are you doing, Levi?" I shouted at him over the sounds of rapid fire and agonized screams. The lousy intel on this place had led us into a trap. I was immobilized for a moment both by his weight and by the shock of having him cover me in such a way. Levi fired off a series of shots at our intruder, and the shooter fell. Just a kid. My heart felt heavy, and I fought the urge to be sick, but then Levi moaned in pain and his body shook. I felt a warm wetness and knew it had to be Levi's blood. His rifle dropped out of his grip and onto the dirt floor of our crude refuge.

I mentally prepared to die with my best buddy in a spray of bullets. There had to be more gunmen on the way—or a smarter, more efficient attacker with a grenade. Afghanistan was filled with people who'd like to see us dead. We were sitting ducks now that we'd been erroneously sent into this deathtrap.

Just then, an explosion shattered the area somewhere outside of the hovel that sheltered us, and its reverberation thundered through my body as pieces of debris shook loose and fell from the ceiling. It was a wonder we weren't crushed, but the roof and walls held. The shooting stopped; the attack was over. I smelled gunpowder and dirt. And blood.

I had to get Levi off me to assess his state. Carefully, I shoved him to the side, mightily relieved to hear him scream in pain. He was alive! For now, anyway.

"Don't you fucking *dare* die on me Levi Spencer, you hear me?" I shouted at him. He had taken some painful shots to the chest where he was protected by body armor, but below the armor, he was bleeding profusely. I did my best to apply pressure. I shouted over and over for medical assistance, but it was like the world had gone deaf. Finally, *finally*, someone squawked in my headphone and requested our location. After rattling it off, the answer I got was grim.

"We're fifteen minutes out. We'll do our best. Anyone else hurt or…?"

I looked around and saw that I was the only one left in one piece. "All dead except for me and Sergeant Spencer," I answered, trying to keep my emotions under control. *All dead.* They had been my friends, the guys I counted on and joked with. I knew about their wives and kids, their pretty girlfriends and the beloved dogs they'd left at home so they could serve our country. All of them were gone just like that. I continued into my headpiece with a badly shaking voice, "And I don't know how much longer he'll be able to hang on. We need you ten minutes ago!"

"We'll do our best."

"Do better than that, or he'll bleed to death!"

"Roger that."

In the middle of crabbing to myself about how shitty it was that we were both supposed to be getting *out* of the Army when we got sent on this fucked-up mission, I heard a sickening noise. With an ungodly screech, the roof collapsed on us, driving a splintered timber nearly through my shoulder. The crushing pain was so intense, I could barely breathe. Terror washed through me that our rescuers would show up and find nothing but a pile of rubble and dead bodies. Then I wondered what it would be like to live with one arm if we made it out somehow. It would be better than if the wooden beam had landed on my neck. No one lives without their head, but an arm was doable. My last ridiculous thought before passing out was, "Raise high the roofbeam, Carpenters." I always was a Salinger fan—ever since our Honeybee Hollow librarian Mrs. Lassiter introduced me to his books.

CHAPTER
Two

Brooke

When I met Levi, I knew in my heart I could be happy for the rest of my life. He made me laugh, he was brave, handsome, and charismatic, and he was as smart a man as I'd ever encountered. He was a soldier, and one with a strong sense of pride in his country and an even stronger sense of duty to uphold his ideals.

Levi was coming to the end of his enlistment, but I never counted on Afghanistan. I thought things there were winding down…boy, was I naive.

Levi and I married only six months after we met. We were positive we were destined to be together. I knew he was a military man, and I got used to him having to be away for a few weeks at a stretch. But each homecoming was sweet and laden with pleasure. We could make love for hours, wrecking each other with our words of devotion and our divine lovemaking. He could be a gentle lover when the mood struck him, or he could burn me to a crisp with his passion. He was always unpredictable except for letting me know that I was cherished and adored. We were both insatiable and desperately in love. Most of all, I knew his loyalty to me was as strong as his loyalty to his country.

But five months after our wedding, he was deployed, and I felt like a wreck. I was so lonely for him—my best friend in all the world, my lover, my protector, the father of our future children. I was sad I wasn't pregnant; then at least I would have had that bit of him with me. I tried to hide my fear before he left, but I know he knew.

We went from daily interaction to virtually no communication at all. I couldn't call him or text him, so I wrote daily letters telling him about regular life, not knowing if he'd ever even see them. My job as a data analyst was going fine and paid well, so I had no complaints other than I missed Levi and hoped he would stay safe. When my friends asked how I was doing, I would thank them for their concern and say I was worried for Levi, but I always downplayed the absolute nightmare my nights had become. I was used to Levi's large presence in bed—his soft snores and a body that warmed me like a sauna. It had been a pleasure to work remotely for the past few years, but now our house felt oppressively quiet except when jets flew over, and they were a cruel reminder of the military that had taken my beloved Levi into danger. We didn't even have any pets I could dote on. I routinely lay awake for hours trying not to worry.

Often during that time, I thumbed through our wedding album. He was dashingly handsome in those photos, and his happiness and pride were obvious. But it was a candid shot of him that was my favorite—one I'd snapped when he was sitting on his sister Kate's couch talking to his four-year-old niece Louisa. He called her Lulu the moment he met her, and the nickname stuck. His earnest expression and the sweet look in his eyes just flattened me. So I blew up and framed that picture and carried it with me from room to room. He would eat dinner with me that way. He watched over me as I did my work, and I could say goodnight to the Levi I loved each night.

I counted the months, the weeks, the days, the hours of his deployment. Time passed too slowly, but I tried to stay positive. After all, the longer he was gone, the sooner he'd be home. The idea bolstered my spirits tremendously—especially when I knew it was less than a month away. I started going back to the gym and spruced up the house for his return. All of the household projects I'd planned to do finally kept me occupied so I wouldn't fixate on his return. I wanted everything to be perfect for him. I cleaned the carpets, painted the kitchen, planted some flowers, and got rid of a bunch of junk from the garage. Our little house in Hopkinsville, Kentucky gleamed with readiness for his return. In the back of my mind, I decided it was time to talk about starting a family when he came home.

But a week before he was supposed to arrive, I got the word that his deployment was extended for another unspecified length of time. I understood this was often the case, so I wasn't overly worried…just really frustrated. It was so unfair!

Though, I reminded myself, no one promises that life will be fair. I squared my shoulders and waited.

Anyway…it got worse. Three weeks after that, I got a call that made me want to faint. Sergeant Levi Spencer had been injured in the line of duty and would be treated in a military hospital in an undisclosed location.

I was crushed and terrified. What had happened? How was he? When could I see him?

All I knew was that he'd been in a "skirmish." Facts were scarce. I thought my world would fall apart. Calls to his parents didn't afford me any relief. They were just as freaked out as I was. No one knew what kind of shape he was in or if he'd come home draped with a flag. His dad had been in the Army too, and he tried to keep a stiff upper lip, but the poor man was losing it with worry. He vowed he'd make some calls and try to get more information, but he didn't know how effective he would be. We promised each other to call the minute we had any more news.

Levi's dad surmised that the next step for Levi would most likely be a transfer to Walter Reed, "Depending on his condition." No one would give him any more specifics than I already knew. I had to ask him where Walter Reed was and found that it was in Bethesda, Maryland. I didn't grow up in a military family, so my knowledge of things like this was lacking.

Time ground to a halt. I lost weight from not eating and worrying myself into a stupor, and each time my phone rang, I thought my heart would beat right out of my chest. Finally, I got a call telling me that Sergeant Spencer's surgeries (yes, plural) had been successful, and he would be transferred to Walter Reed as soon as he was able to be moved. I asked if I could speak to him, and the caller had no idea what to tell me about that. He was just the messenger, he told me, and had many more calls to make. "Have a good day, ma'am," he said and hung up. *Good day*? I wanted to scream.

At least I knew Levi was alive.

I waited one day before calling Walter Reed. I called every morning and every evening to see if Levi had been admitted. A week went by, and then, finally, I got an affirmative answer. I asked to be transferred to his room so I could speak with him, but I got absolutely nowhere. Nor would they tell me anything about his condition. "HIPAA rules prevent that," they said. Caregivers would only be given information upon the patient's discharge if it pertained to their well-being. I called his parents, and we all booked flights to Reagan Airport.

Although my imagination had come up with every scenario I could dream up, I was not in any way prepared for what I found.

CHAPTER
Three

Levi

Life sucks. You try to do the right thing, and it all goes to shit.

I tried to serve my country and ended up getting my men *killed* in a mission that accomplished nothing.

I married the love of my life, and now I might be worse than useless for her.

I tried to save my best buddy's life and almost got him killed too. He probably hates me for it.

It's all my fault. My parents are going to be so disappointed in me. I love them so much. I've tried to be a man they could be proud of.

This is the way my mind goes—day in and day out. Rationally, I understand there are reasons these things happened that are beyond my control, but not everything. I didn't plant bombs or purposely lead my squad into what turned out to be a slaughter. We had intelligence that we'd be able to liberate hostages, so we infiltrated the area with caution and high hopes. We wanted so badly to accomplish something good, but my people were mowed down and bombed instead. Our soldiers were trying to protect the perimeter while my special team went in with me to grab the prisoners, and immediately it became obvious that we were trapped. There were no hostages, just gunfire and a huge explosion. I can't hear too well out of my right ear now. But that's just the tip of the iceberg.

The mission was such an epic failure, I'm not even allowed to discuss it. I acted on orders, but somewhere along the chain of command, the information was either intercepted or pure crap from the get-go. That knowledge won't bring back all the brave soldiers who died that day.

I can't sleep at night. I can't walk or even sit up. I can't even take a decent piss. I can't stand myself.

I hear the door open, and it's the one person I love more than life itself. My beautiful Brooke came all the way from Kentucky to see me in Bethesda. I'm so sick of myself, I can barely face her. She looks up and down my body with tears streaming down her cheeks—no doubt checking to see if I'm all here, and then she smiles. Why? My voice sounds shattered even to me when I croak out, "Brooke."

She rushes toward the bed. She probably senses what a wreck I am. When she gets close enough, she leans in and puts her hands on my face. I want to reach out to her, but I feel so unworthy. I'm a mess. I can't help it though. Without consciously willing them to, my arms wrap around her, and I hold onto her for dear life. It's more than a little awkward with my arm connected to an IV and a bunch of monitors. At least the bruises on my chest aren't painful anymore.

Now she's kissing me and hugging me and telling me, "I'm so happy to see you, Levi. It's wonderful you're going to be okay! I'm not sure what treatment you had, but they said your surgeries were successful."

Who is she kidding? I don't think I'll ever be okay again.

I turn my face away. Fuck, I love this woman. She could do so much better than me. "I should send you away," I tell her. "I'm no good for you. You need someone who's whole. But I love you too much to make you leave." I turn back to her. "Don't leave me, Brooke. Please?" A blasted tear rolls out of my eye, and I feel like a stupid wuss as I stare into her silvery blue eyes. She's always been striking with her dark hair, pale eyes, and those full lips I've dreamed about night after night. She's the most stunning creature I've ever imagined—tall and lithe with all the right curvature, and I feel so selfish for wanting to keep her instead of setting her free like a better man would do.

Before Brooke can answer me, a doc knocks once and

enters the room with a brisk step. He's smiling as he looks at us. "Ah, Mrs. Spencer, I presume?" he asks.

Brooke straightens up and answers, "Yes, I'm Levi's wife, Brooke Spencer." She shakes his hand politely as he introduces himself as Dr. Winslow.

"Sergeant Spencer, I'm sure you're still exhausted from your long trip here, but you're doing quite well, I'm happy to report. I just reviewed the X-rays from this morning, and we can see evidence already that the bone fragments are beginning to knit together just as we'd hoped." He looks at Brooke and then at me and continues, "Once we can get you started on a physical therapy regimen, you'll be back walking in no time."

"Would you mind explaining a little about his injury, Dr. Winslow?" my wife asks. I'm embarrassed to say I haven't told her anything myself. I know I should have written to her or called before this, but I didn't know what to say. At first, I was afraid of losing my leg or getting stuck in a wheelchair for the rest of my life. I saw so many horrendous injuries when I was in the hospital in Germany. At least all of my limbs are still attached, and I can see. That made me happy for a little while…but then I realized that my body wasn't working the way it used to, and I worried myself sick about Brooke's reaction. I didn't have a clue what to tell her, so I took the coward's way out and stayed silent. One more reason she ought to turn tail and run.

Dr. Winslow looks at me questioningly, so I nod to him

and say, "Tell her." Someone has to break the news to her that her husband is useless. I can't find the words. Anyway, she can probably see the bag I'm pissing into and can figure out some of it herself.

Brooke scoots a chair close to my bed, sits, and grabs my hand. She looks at the doctor with her shoulders straight and posture erect. She's bracing herself—I can tell.

"There isn't a lot more to tell, actually. The surgeons in Germany removed the bullet that shattered his pelvis and had to do some repair work to veins and muscles. It's going to look rough for a while, and there will be a certain amount of swelling around the nerves. However, Levi was lucky, and the bullet missed his important parts. That's always a worry in pelvic wounds. But, as I said, the bone is beginning to heal nicely as evidenced by calcium deposits we see in the X-rays. He's a healthy young man and should make an excellent recovery. I'm glad to report this kind of result because we often have such drastic, life-changing things happen to our brave young soldiers."

Brooke clears her throat and asks in a small voice that grows in volume as she speaks, "So…we shouldn't expect any alteration to our normal…uh…activities…eventually?"

"You mean can he eat normally and have sex, right? Just to be clear."

"Well, yes." She's blushing. "Those things."

"He luckily didn't have any major damage to his intestines or other organs. So don't worry, he won't need to poop in a bag, and we'll get rid of the catheter as soon as he's ambulatory. As far as sex goes, it isn't going to happen right away. I'm sure there is significant pain right now, and his muscles will need to restore to their previous strength, but his penis and testicles will work just fine."

"How long?" she asks. I can't bring myself to look at him.

"That's hard to say. We'll see how he does in physical therapy. Everyone is different in how quickly they heal. I want to stress to you that the men we worry about in this regard are the ones who've had actual trauma to their bladder or genitals. Those men may end up unable to urinate normally or achieve an erection due to scar tissue that we can't do much about. We also worry about ruptured intestines. That kind of injury can lead to infection quickly."

"But not Levi?"

He smiles gently at her. "Your husband will make an excellent recovery. The lost bone and muscle will regenerate. Both of you just need to have patience. Often men with this level of injury re-enlist for another tour because they heal so well, but that's entirely up to the two of you." He looks at Brooke and then at me and asks, "Do you have any more questions?"

I don't, and I sure as hell have no desire to go back into combat. I also think he's wrong; I'm pretty sure my dick is dead. Serves me right.

"No, I'm clear about things now. Thank you." Brooke has

better manners than I have. She smiles at him as he turns to leave.

As soon as the door closes, I grit my teeth and tell her the truth. "He's wrong."

"What are you talking about, Levi? You'll be out of commission for a while because of your shattered pelvis, but they were able to repair it, and you'll get better. You're going to be fine."

"You don't know that. I might never be able to…you know…perform."

"Levi! You're looking at the worst-case scenario. Yes, the doc explained that some men have lasting problems, but he said *you* had no damage there. You'll be fine."

"I'm not fine. I can't feel anything."

"Levi, honey, give it time. You'll be back to normal. It's not like a simple pelvic fracture—yours was shattered. You have tiny bone fragments that still need to fuse, and you have surgical trauma. I have faith. You need a little. But even if it never works, I still love you, and you're still my husband. I'm not going anywhere." She gives me a thoughtful look and asks, "Have you talked to a therapist?"

"No." They offered to send one in, but I declined. I don't need someone telling me to cheer up.

"Maybe you ought to. But listen, your parents should be here in an hour or two. They've also been worried sick, and your dad's been hollering at everyone he could think of to find out anything about you. Why didn't you contact them? Or me? Surely you had access to a phone at some point."

Why is she being so nice to me about this? She ought to be pissed off and yelling at me because I know I should have called. I'm a loser, and she needs someone a lot better. Someone brave like my buddy Skyler. I wonder how he's doing. I'm afraid to ask, but I know one thing for sure, if Skyler hadn't been on top of me when the roof caved in, I'd be dead. I'm just sorry he took so much of the brunt of the collapse. He looked awful when our rescuers dragged him off of me, and I haven't seen him since we ended up in the hospital. I should have tried harder to locate him, but I was too into my own issues, I guess. Instead of answering Brooke, my mind goes down a rabbit hole thinking about Skyler Colfax—the most amazing friend I've ever had—besides Brooke, of course.

She's still talking, and I'm not listening until I hear, "Levi? Did you hear me?"

"Oh, uh. No. Sorry. Actually, my ear on this side doesn't work as well as the other." That's a pretty lame excuse. It rings a lot, but it's getting better.

She blinks and speaks up a bit. "I said I need to go rent a car and check in at the Fisher House. They have a free place for me to stay because of you being a patient here, and they're expecting me soon. It sounds nice—with good Wi-Fi, a kitchen, and everything I'll need to cook, if you want me to make any of your favorite foods."

"Why are you being so nice to me?"

Her jaw drops. Maybe that was the wrong question. I see tears in her eyes again, and she's struggling to not cry. "What?" she whispers.

"I'm a useless asshole, and you're planning to bring me things I like to eat. I don't get it."

"Levi, you're not thinking straight. I'm guessing you're on pain meds, and you're probably still in a good deal of pain, so I'm going to ignore most of what you say for a while if it's all the same to you. Your parents might be kind of emotional when they get here. This has been hard on them too, you know."

My heart breaks a little as I watch her trying to keep it together, so I reach out to her. "I'm sorry, Brooke. I'm sorry I've failed everyone, and I'm sorry I scared you and my parents. It's a lot to deal with, you know? They're all *dead*." She flinches at that word as my voice cracks. "I was in charge of them, and everyone but Skyler and I got mowed down like worthless junk. I can't stop thinking of *their* loved ones now. I was responsible for them."

"I'm sure you did everything you could to keep them safe and follow orders. It's not in your makeup to do anything else. And I'm happy and relieved to hear that Skyler is alive. I was honestly afraid to ask." She squeezes my hand gently. "Levi, I love you so much. I'm proud of you and know you're not a failure. Whatever happened was not because you made a mistake. You must have had bad orders, or there was a breakdown somewhere. Were you ambushed?"

"Something like that. I can't talk about it."

"I'm so sorry. I know how hard you always try to do your best."

"This was a giant fuck-up, and good men *died*. I'd have died too if Skyler hadn't protected me."

Brooke stays with me long enough to make sure I've calmed down some, then makes her excuse that she has an appointment at this place that's giving her housing for a while. I wonder how long it'll be before she gives up and goes home. I can't stomach my own company, so I sure can't understand how she does.

CHAPTER
Four

It turns out my arm is still attached to my body, even though my shoulder was pretty much crushed, and there is some permanent nerve damage. They did extensive repair surgery, and I may face more later depending on how well it heals. One thing's for sure: I won't be fighting in Afghanistan anymore, and that's a relief. I was glad to serve, and now it's time to figure out what to do with my life. They call this a million-dollar injury—bad enough to get you sent home, but not serious enough to kill you. I wouldn't be able to shoot anyway since my right hand is mostly numb. I wonder if that will ever go away.

I got sent here to Walter Reed a few days ago, and today I found out that Levi is here too. So I'm standing outside his door. I hear voices inside, and I'm not about to interrupt him because the other voice is female, and it doesn't sound like a nurse. I can't wait to see how he's doing though. Probably pretty banged up. I am too, but at least I can get up and walk around. I'll be going home pretty soon, but I'll have to find somewhere that will handle PT for me. It would be nice if I could do it at home, but I'm not holding my breath. Someone will probably need to drive me to a bigger city for a while. We'll see.

The door finally opens, and my eyes take in the amazing sight of Brooke Spencer. Just like every other time I've seen her, I'm struck speechless. This woman is a goddess, even with her clothes rumpled from travel and tell-tale dark worry shadows under her eyes. Those eyes! She's ethereally beautiful. It takes me just a little too long to gather my wits and extend my left hand, saying, "Hi, Brooke, it's good to see you. I owe everything to your husband, you know. He saved my life by risking his own."

"He says the same thing about you saving him. You're both heroes, if you ask me."

I've always thought she was beautiful, but when she smiles, oh my ever-loving God. I think about that smile all the time; I've never seen anything like it. That lucky bastard has the most incredible woman in the world. We exchange pleasantries for a moment, and her voice is low and sexy. I need to stop thinking this way because she's *Levi's wife*. But damn, if I'm not fighting a boner. Maybe I need to find a woman when I get out of here.

Levi and I became friends right after we enlisted, and we were lucky to be able to stay together the entire time we served. We clicked right away. I don't know Brooke anywhere near as well, and that might be a good thing considering my reaction to her. Since their wedding—where I served as Levi's best man—Levi spent every possible moment he could with her. Can you blame the guy? I missed his company but didn't begrudge him one moment of happiness with her. They moved into a crappy little house off-base, and I've only been there a few times.

Eventually, she says she has to scoot out to an appointment and tells me how great it was to see me. I'm sure she's just being nice. Being around her is like talking to a celebrity. I am painfully aware that I'm standing in the hallway in a hospital gown and robe—probably looking like I got hit by a semi. Oh well.

"I hope to see you again soon, Brooke," I tell her, and off she goes. I slowly push open the door to Levi's room.

He looks like crap. He faces me and gives me a hollow smile, so I joke with him. "Sorry if I don't salute. The wing's kinda banged up." I tip my head toward my shoulder.

Relief floods Levi's face, and he grins for real. "You doing okay?" he asks. "I'm so glad to see you up and about."

"Of course I'm doing okay. You saved my life, Levi. If

you hadn't gotten in the way, I'd be full of holes right now and six feet under. I'm so, so grateful, but I'm also sad you got hurt so badly on my account." I sit in the chair that Brooke must have just vacated next to his bed. Just the thought of her makes me warm inside. I need to nip that shit in the bud.

"Well, you returned the favor, man. They told me later that you protected me from bleeding out by keeping pressure on me—"

I interrupt him with a humorless laugh. "The pressure was because the roof fell on us!"

"And having you on top of me also kept the wooden beams from impaling me. I think we're square on who saved whom that day. I will forever think of you as my hero." He bows his head, breaking eye contact, and mutters, "For what my miserable life is worth, anyway."

"What do you mean? You'll be able to walk again, won't you?"

"Yeah, but I don't think my junk works anymore."

I blink at him a few times before asking, "How would you know that? Haven't you reacted to sponge baths by cute nurses or something?"

Levi snorts. "Whenever anyone messes around with the catheter, it's like I'm completely numb down there."

"Oh! Um…sorry, Levi. Have you asked the docs about it?" *My God, it would suck to be numb!*

"They say there is nerve trauma from the surgery, but it's

just temporary swelling. I think they're full of shit and just won't fess up to the real deal."

"Wow, so when Brooke was just here…?"

"I kissed her and…nothing. You've seen her." He clenches his hands into fists. His face twists in torment. "I'm not a real man anymore! She needs to move on."

"Levi, no. Brooke loves you, and she wouldn't do that. I think you need to give it time and talk to someone."

"Everyone thinks I need a shrink. I need a functional dick!" He looks devastated, and I don't know what to say, so I switch the conversation to sports. That seems to relax him, and for a while it's like we're back to normal.

After half an hour or so, an older couple rushes in—obviously Levi's parents, so I give him a squeeze and pat him on the shoulder, but he responds with a funny look on his face. I tell him, "Don't be a stranger. I'll be going home in a couple of days." I leave him to visit with his parents.

The next morning, I find myself discharged first thing. My parents, who'd already been staying in Bethesda, arrive to take me home. On my way out, I knock on the door to his room, but no one answers. I try to call, even send a few texts, but there's no reply.

In the end, I don't get a chance to say goodbye to Levi before I go.

It's an eight-hour drive from Walter Reed to my hometown, but I'm grateful for the trip. We pass countryside, cities, and many, many little towns on our way from Maryland to Kentucky. I breathe a little easier when familiar scenery appears out my window.

Finally, our truck turns the corner, and we're driving down Main Street in Honeybee Hollow, where I was born and raised.

The town has always been filled with great people—the kind who'd give you the shirt off their back if you needed it. In the past several years, however, the town has had something of a renaissance. We're on the map! We're known throughout Kentucky (if not the whole country) as the best small town to live in. This is mostly thanks to the Lassiter family. Their son became our tremendously popular mayor and then the youngest-ever governor of Kentucky, and their daughter brought industry back to the town when she bought an abandoned factory and gave people jobs again—making *hats*, of all things! Those fancy hats of hers sell all over the place now, and with the Kentucky Derby fashion tradition, her original designs are sought after by all the ladies.

But it wasn't just Madison and Tanner Lassiter who made our town the best. Town pride soared when everyone saw what those two talented young folks could do, and others started figuring out how they could make a significant difference by giving back to the community. We now have a small but thriving business district that includes all the regular stores like Piggly Wiggly, a hardware store, hair salons, Sock Hop—the best hamburger joint in America—plus a nice hotel, a fancy art gallery, restaurants, a coffeehouse/bakery, antique shops, a couple of bookstores—one just for kids—and a whole slew of trendy boutiques. People have opened up bed and breakfasts in historic buildings and older homes. We have a couple of popular bars where you can listen to live music. One features rockabilly and bluegrass, and it's frequented by the older residents of the community who've been here for generations as well as a younger crowd looking for "authenticity."

The other tavern is more eclectic with a mix of rock, pop, country, and Friday night karaoke. We even have a nature camp just outside of town where corporations send their employees for retreats. Tour buses bring people to town for day trips once in a while, and some of the day trippers end up moving here. Our economy is booming. But even with all this new stuff going on, we're still a small town; maybe the greatest small town in America, but a small town, nonetheless. Everyone supports the high school's sports teams, and we have very little crime.

One of the best things about Honeybee Hollow, in my opinion, is its sheer beauty. Sitting at the foot of the Appalachian Mountains, the scenery is incomparable. The air is pure and just makes you feel healthy—even if your head may be filled with demons trying to snatch away your happy thoughts. The best mood enhancer I know of is taking a hike on one of our nature trails. Or fishing. I love to fish right in my own back yard. That might be a challenge for a while with only one functioning arm, but I'll get better. As for my other hobby…well…I don't want to think about my artwork. I may never get to do that again.

My family runs a garden center, and it's been thriving now that town pride is at its highest ever. Except for the years I was in the Army, I've worked for them since I was a teenager and enjoy being outside, doing the heavy lifting, and advising people on what to grow.

That is, I used to do the heavy lifting. It's a lot harder now. I don't mean to sound like a whiner. I'm as happy as can be that I made it home after that fiasco in Afghanistan.

So why was I itching to leave such an idyllic town in the first place? My parents are uber patriotic and even named me for an obscure vice president they admired. Schuyler Colfax (they made my name easier to spell, thank heaven) served under President Grant and was one of the original abolitionists with an interesting life our history books have mostly ignored. I don't think my family's actually related to him though. Anyway, my daddy inspired in me a strong love and duty to country, so I enlisted in the Army after graduating from college. I'd never been out of Kentucky, so I thought I could see the world and maybe learn a trade that I'd enjoy.

I did not learn one. I don't regard shooting people as a marketable skill. So thank heaven for my grandparents and the property I own. I won't ever go hungry thanks to their generosity.

Like a dumbass, I didn't count on us being shipped off to Afghanistan so late in the game. We could have been deployed anywhere at any time, but this was a shock after believing the war there was over. Levi and I were supposed to be almost done with the Army! I'm both thankful he was there with me and sad about it at the same time. I owe him my life for his strategic maneuver that shielded me from gunfire, but I'm sorry as hell he got himself shot because of it.

♡♡♡

Months go by. I settle back into life in Honeybee Hollow. At first, it's rough with my arm and the slower pace of my small town, but I get through it. The biggest issue isn't my injury, or the PTSD, or even the feeling like everyone else around me has moved on with their lives and I'm still stuck in the same place. No, the biggest pain for me is the absence of Levi. He hasn't called, texted, or written. I've tried everything I can think of to get in touch with him, to reconnect, but it's been radio silence.

I just wish to God he was still in my life. I miss him so badly, it's a physical ache. I was worried for a time that I'd lose my arm, but the loss of Levi is like phantom limb syndrome. Pain in what is gone.

Finally, after about six months of silence, I can't take it any longer. Fort Campbell isn't so far away, and he lives in Hopkinsville, which is just north of the base. I call my parents to let them know I'll be gone a little while and won't be available to help them at the garden center. They're totally understanding considering what I've been through. My parents are the best.

I leave at the crack of dawn the next day, armed with a thermos of coffee for the drive.

CHAPTER
Five

BROOKE

LIVING WITH LEVI ISN'T LIKE IT USED TO BE. AFTER HIS
discharge from Walter Reed, we came back to our little house
in Hopkinsville and tried to act as though we were fine.

We weren't. We aren't.

Levi can still be his sweet self—mostly. He spends a lot of
his time at physical therapy appointments and is religious
about his exercises when he's at home, so he's looking good.
He's affectionate to a point, but he makes me feel more like a
loyal pet than his wife. By that I mean the passion has dried
up, and we're not having *any* kind of sex. I've tried talking to
him about it and not talking to him about it. I've tried sexy
clothes and lingerie. I've tried creating a "mood." Once I even

tried jumping his bones pretty aggressively in bed; that pissed him off more than anything. I wanted to die of embarrassment when he rebuffed me.

I know we have to alter some of our "activities" while he's still healing, and I'm perfectly happy to cater to those needs by lowering expectations and changing positions. But I just… need…him.

He claims he's not in much pain, or we could chalk it up to that. Maybe he's in more pain than he wants to admit. Probably.

I've researched everything I can think of, and finally—when Levi refused to go—I saw a therapist myself. By all accounts, Levi's trouble appears to be psychosomatic. I've seen a little evidence of morning wood, though Levi wouldn't admit it. He's definitely suffering from PTSD and depression, and there is very little I can do other than try to maintain a healthy atmosphere for him so he can relax, and I pray that he eventually gets over this phase of his life.

"You need to move on, Brooke," he tells me when his demons are hounding him. "I'm no good for you as a husband. You need someone better." Then other days, he clings to me like I'm a marsupial mother, and he breaks down and begs me, "Swear to me you'll never leave."

And I promise him. Because I'm *not* leaving him. I love this man with every bit of my heart, and I know that somehow we'll get through this and be better when we get past it. I just wish I could get him to discuss more of what's eating him up inside. Also, we're both thirty-three, and I'd like to have kids before too long, but I sure don't see that happening at this rate.

"Why don't you contact Skyler? Talking to him might be exactly what you need. I'm sure he understands what you both went through better than anyone."

"I don't want you leaving me for him," Levi snaps, rather incongruously. *What?*

"Why on earth would you even think that, Levi?" I have to admit, the guy is a major hottie, and I couldn't help but notice how attractive and polite he was whenever we've spoken. But seriously? Levi is worried I'd leave him for his best friend? I wrap an arm around him and lay my head on his shoulder. "I love *you*, Levi," I tell him.

"I know you do. So maybe you should just fuck him, since that's all you seem to want lately."

Hot tears burn my eyes, and I struggle to keep them at bay as I jerk back. "That's not a very nice thing to say, Levi. It's not crazy to want to make love to my *husband* so I can show you how much I love you."

Immediately, he hangs his head, "I know, babe. I'm being an asshole." He gets up quickly and clomps into the kitchen with the aid of his cane to grab a beer. I don't stop him or tell him it's a little too early in the day for a drink. I don't have the energy. What happened to that man in my favorite photo? The one with the smiling eyes? Levi has big brown eyes that can look so sweet. Lately, though, they're devoid of any emotion.

I get up and grab my purse out of the bedroom, then I head

through the kitchen to the back door to the garage. On the way I tell Levi, "We're low on a few things, so I'm going to go buy groceries." He barely looks up from the beer bottle label he's studying. When he gets like this, it's like living with a ghost. We're not actually low on anything, but I think we both need some space for a little while. I know I do.

As I start to back out of the garage, a truck pulls into the driveway. It seems to be from some garden company. That's odd. We're not planning to have any work done to the yard, but maybe the landlord has plans I don't know about. I pull the car back into the garage and get out to ask him what he's doing here, immediately realizing he looks familiar.

He heads toward me with a bright smile on his tanned face, and it hits me. "Skyler! What are you doing here? I mean, it's good to see you. You look so different...and so much better!"

Wow. This guy fills out a t-shirt and jeans like nobody's business. His thick blond hair is a lot longer now, and he looks *way* better than he did in a hospital gown with cuts and scrapes all over him. I need to stop perving on him. If I can't get Levi to have sex soon, I may go nuts.

"Hi, Brooke. I hope I'm not interrupting you guys. The fact is, I can't get Levi to return my calls, and I'm concerned about him. I can't help but worry...did I do something wrong? This seems so out of character for Levi. Is he okay?"

I bite back a sigh. "I'm sure you did nothing wrong, Skyler. Levi's going through a rough time. We were actually just talking about you, if you can believe it. Why don't you go on in and visit with him? I can leave the two of you alone for a while because I was heading out to the market for a few things." I see the concern in his eyes, and it guts me. I don't want this kind man to feel like he's done anything bad. I reach out and give him a quick hug, regretting my action immediately as we hear the kitchen door open.

"I thought I heard voices out here. Well, if it isn't Skyler. It didn't take the two of you much time, did it?" Levi steps back in and slams the door.

Skyler looks at me with a baffled expression and asks, "What's going on?"

CHAPTER

Six

Levi

What is going on? I have a gorgeous wife, and I can't respond to her no matter what she does. Fucking Skyler shows up out of the blue, and for the first time since I saw him at Walter Reed, I start to get hard? All he did was touch me, and I chubbed up, and now I see him hugging Brooke, and it happens again. This is so weird.

No sooner do I think this when both of them follow me into the kitchen. Brooke looks about as pissed off as I've ever seen her. I guess she has good reason.

"Levi Spencer, you apologize this instant! I'm your wife, and I love you more than anything in the world, and this is your best friend. You saved each other's *lives*, for heaven's sake! And you have the audacity to accuse us of something in our front yard? In broad daylight? As if either of us would? Have you lost your mind?"

"I probably have." I look up from studying my feet. "Hi, Skyler. Sorry."

Skyler approaches me like he's going to hug me too, so I quickly sit down, putting a stop to that. He looks so good. I'm sure he's had a lot to recover from, and his right arm has scars that show below the sleeve of his t-shirt, but he's clearly been working out. Oh my God, I have to stop staring at him.

"Want a beer?" I ask.

"Oh…not really, but I could sure go for a bottle of water after I use your bathroom, if you don't mind. It was a long drive up here."

"I'll show you the way," Brooke tells him. I guess her shopping trip is on hold for a while.

Less than a minute later, she comes marching into the kitchen glaring at me. "Is this how you treat your best friend?" I don't answer that, and she's on a roll, so she goes on, "I was merely saying hello to someone I admire and I'm certainly thankful for. Without his intervention, you wouldn't be sitting here. You need to do better than that lame-ass apology to him. He just told me he drove *nearly six hours* to see you." I don't answer that either, and she has a full head of steam going. "I'm going to run out to the deli and bring back some lunch since he says he hasn't had anything to eat. I hope by the time I get back you two have worked through what's going on." She picks up her purse and stomps out the back door again.

I reach into the fridge for some water and hand it to Skyler as soon as he returns. "Here. Sorry I'm such an asshole."

"Do you want me to leave? If I've come at a bad time…"

"No, stay, please. It's good to see you. But I have to admit we don't have much other than bad times lately. It's all because of me. Brooke is her normal sweet self—even if her present attitude is the exception. I know she's trying, but I'm still a wreck."

"Where is she?" Skyler looks around.

"She went to get us all some lunch. I hope you like whatever she picks out."

"That was nice of her. I guess I left enough room in the driveway for her to get out. You know I'll eat just about anything. I'm not picky."

"Yeah, I remember—all except for mushrooms."

"Well, true. They're gross. I've seen too many nasty toadstools in the garden to ever enjoy a mushroom. I'm always sure I'll eat a bad one."

"Are you back working for your mom and dad's business?"

"Part time, yes. I'm not sure for how long, although I do love it in Honeybee Hollow. You guys ought to come down for a visit. It's beautiful and relaxing there. The people are great too."

We shoot the breeze for several minutes, talking about

Honeybee Hollow and nothing of much consequence until I can't stand it anymore. I look at Skyler's earnest expression and ask, "So why are you here?"

He frowns and snaps, "Because you won't answer your fucking phone! I've been worried about you and…I missed you."

"Oh."

"Oh?"

"Um, oh…sorry?"

"Levi, what in the hell is going on with you? Are you still in a lot of pain? On drugs? Something else?"

"I just…I don't know. Nothing sits right with me. Every little weird noise makes me want to jump out of my skin. The planes and helicopters flying over from the base all the time make me want to dive under the bed, and I have terrible dreams and flashbacks. I just want to disappear."

"That's pretty normal after being in combat and especially after being wounded, you know."

"Yeah, I know. But I feel horribly responsible for our guys who didn't make it back." My voice cracks, and that makes me feel even worse. "I was in charge, dammit!"

I wait for Skyler to tell me how it isn't my fault. I wait for him to say all the things that everyone else says about how I just have to be positive, be patient, give it time. But instead, Skyler just nods. His eyes are sad and resigned, as if he really understands. I blow out a breath, my body relaxing just a little bit. "How are you coping?" I ask.

Skyler shrugs. "Some days are better than others, but I don't try to put up a good front for anyone, and I don't live near a base that reminds me of stuff all the time. When I have a bad day, I go fishing or watch too much brainless TV. Sometimes I hike on the nature paths around town." He pauses for a second and then adds, "I think about you a lot too. That always makes me feel better—except when you treat me like I'm a stranger by not answering my calls. Have you asked for help on the base, or do you know any other vets around here in town you can talk with privately?"

"I haven't tried." I scowl. "Brooke has been after me about that."

"Then you're lucky I showed up," Skyler tells me with a big grin. "Even if you haven't answered your damn phone."

"How long are you planning to stay?"

"I guess until you either throw me out or come back to the Hollow with me."

"Why would I do that?"

"Not just you, Levi. You and Brooke. For some time off and a change of scenery."

"Hmm…"

"Do you like this house?" he asks, looking around.

"Not particularly. Brooke and I rent it month-to-month. I'd like to buy something though. Maybe a little bigger than this, but this place has been fine for us."

He shrugs. "This place is okay, but I bet houses are way cheaper and lots nicer in Honeybee Hollow. And we don't have military aircraft annoying the shit out of us by flying over."

"Are you the Honeybee Hollow ambassador now, or did you just get your realtor's license?"

"Neither one. I just think you'd like it there. Didn't you tell me Brooke works remotely?"

"Yeah."

"Then what's keeping you here? Do you have more family I don't know about?"

"Nah. My parents went to Florida to retire a few years ago. I'm not sure they like it though. And my sister and her husband live in Lexington."

"That's only a couple of hours away from the Hollow. You could see her more often than you do now, I bet."

I sigh. "It would be fun to watch her kids grow up."

"You planning on having any of your own with Brooke?"

I snort. "Not at this rate. I'm pretty sure I can't."

Skyler raises an eyebrow. "That's *still* a problem? Levi, I saw the hole that got blown into you, and it sure as hell didn't rid you of your balls. What's going on?"

I take a long pull on my beer. "I don't know. I'm afraid of letting Brooke down...maybe? Or I'm afraid I can't be the same kind of lover I used to be. It was amazing before Afghanistan, but since then, I can't...oh crap." I drag my hand over my face in frustration and feel the unwanted sting of tears looming. "I'm self-conscious because I'm all scarred up, but worse...I have visions of making love to her and then in the middle of things, something might trigger me—like a car backfiring, and I'll lose it. The house creaking, or a flashback, or any of a million other things. I just can't…uh…find myself. You know? I can't get it up for her anymore! And that scares the shit out of me."

"I doubt the scars would faze Brooke unless she's worried about hurting you. But…so *nothing* gets you hard? Have you been to a urologist? Or a shrink?"

"I haven't wanted to see anyone because I keep thinking it'll go away. But I'm also afraid to try too hard in case it doesn't work, and we'll be disappointed. The only…uh…*semi* I've had was a few minutes ago when I saw you hugging Brooke. God, I can't believe I admitted that." I take another gulp and drain my beer. Skyler has always gotten me to open up like no one else could—even Brooke, if I'm honest with myself. Probably why I've avoided his calls for so long. I just couldn't bring myself to discuss anything with him, and I knew he'd get it out of me. And now he has.

"Huh. Interesting," he tells me with an inscrutable look on his face. Then he gazes out the window at our typical urban neighborhood with small to medium houses. Some are in fair shape like ours, and others look like crap. He turns back to me and surprises me by asking, "So what's this neighborhood like on the Fourth of July?"

Humorlessly, I snort. "Deafening. I hate it. Any day now, the neighbors will start shooting off cherry bombs and fire-crackers and keep them going for as long as a month afterward. I'm sure this year I'll want to hide under the bed like a three-year-old who's afraid of monsters, and I'm scared I'll flip out and accidentally hurt someone."

Brooke comes back in then with a couple sacks that smell delicious. My stomach rumbles. "Meatball subs?" I ask her.

"Yes, among other things. I wasn't sure what you guys were in the mood for, so I bought some choices, but the meatballs are hot, so I'd recommend those, and I can refrigerate the cold sandwiches for later." She sets down the bags and grabs some plates and napkins.

"Sounds delicious," I tell her. "Thanks, babe." I look at Skyler and grin. "No mushrooms, I promise." He looks relieved. "But I like to sprinkle these hot peppers on mine."

CHAPTER
Seven

"I WANT TO TELL YOU TWO ABOUT SOMETHING YOU MIGHT FIND interesting," I say this between bites of a spectacular sandwich. "This is delicious, Brooke. Thank you!" I down some water and begin my sales pitch for what might just nudge Levi out of his mental issues…at least somewhat.

"The Fourth of July is just around the corner, and I understand how someone suffering from PTSD reacts to the noise of fireworks. I dread being around them myself. Some of our dogs also hated them when I was growing up.

"Several years ago, Madison Lassiter, the sister of our recently retired Governor Lassiter, who started his political career—as you probably have heard—as the mayor of

Honeybee Hollow, went to a fancy Independence Day party given by that famous author Gunnar Dahl. Rumor has it she met her husband at that party too. He's Dahl's younger brother and pretty famous himself. But I digress. Madison and Tanner Lassiter were the children of Honeybee Hollow's town veterinarian, and Dr. Lassiter had been trying to get an ordinance in the town for years banning fireworks because they were so upsetting to the local pets and the wildlife in the surrounding mountains.

"So when Madison saw that Gunnar Dahl had this huge celebration with *silent* fireworks, she got her brother to work really hard to get the town to adopt the noiseless fireworks displays. All we can buy there is stuff like sparklers for private use, but Tanner secured a grant that's good for I don't know how long—probably at least fifty years—so the town itself has a celebration of beautiful fireworks that are silent. It's fantastic. First, there's a big community party in the middle of the high school football stadium with games and stuff for the kids, and sometimes the school band will play, or the school glee club will sing together with some of the church choirs to entertain everyone. It kinda depends on who's available each year. Then, when it's finally dark, we have this amazing silent fireworks display that's synchronized with music. Everyone can have a good seat to watch from and be safe. It's loads of fun and really patriotic, and it's probably one of the best places in the country to celebrate."

"Wow, how wonderful!" Brooke exclaims.

Levi gives me a thoughtful look. "There's fishing, you say?"

I laugh and nod. "Yeah, there's a good-sized creek at the edge of my property that separates my land from the neighbor's. We have catfish, bluegill, bass, and trout that are so delicious, you won't believe it. I think the two of you need to take some time and get out of town. Come back with me to Honeybee Hollow, at least over the Fourth, and stay as long as you like. I have a big old rambling farmhouse that was built by my grandparents, and I get awfully lonely in it by myself. It's a far cry from living in Army barracks, that's for sure, but there's way more room than I need. And don't worry, Brooke. I have excellent Wi-Fi if you need to keep working."

Brooke looks at Levi and quirks an eyebrow. "It sounds amazing. When can we leave?"

"I…uh…well, I guess a change of scenery couldn't hurt. How soon do you want to head back, Skyler?"

"It's a long enough drive that I'd like to wait at least until tomorrow."

"Of course," he tells me. "When we're done eating, you can bring your stuff in, and we'll put you up in the spare room. It's kind of a combination bedroom and office for Brooke, but it has a comfortable bed."

Brooke leans over and plants a kiss on Levi. "This is the best thing I've heard since we got back from Maryland." She looks at me. "What kind of clothes should we pack?"

I laugh. "It's a pretty casual town. Whatever you're

comfortable in is best. If you want to go out to hear music and dance or sing karaoke, you can bring something for that, but there are a bunch of local boutiques that the ladies seem to love, so maybe you'd prefer to find something there. Oh, and pack a bathing suit. I have a hot tub out back. It wasn't there when Granny and Pawpaw lived there." I can't help chuckling at the mental image of my grandparents in a hot tub. "It was my addition."

Brooke looks at Levi and says with a smile, "I bet a hot tub will make your hip feel better."

He nods and grumbles, "Yeah, but I won't be dancing much. I'll leave that to Skyler if you feel the need."

Levi

SKYLER HAS THE NERVE TO WINK AT MY WIFE AND SAY, "MY pleasure!"

I fight the urge to kick him under the table. A trip to Honeybee Hollow sounds really good though, so I'm trying to be on my best behavior. I know that logically, staying here over the Fourth would be bad for me…and therefore bad for Brooke.

Just then, a car with a super-loud engine goes vrooming by out front, and I cringe at the noise. At least the stupid thing didn't backfire. We can't leave soon enough if it's as idyllic as he claims.

Skyler's eyes light up. He adds, "Levi, you should also

bring your combat uniform. People like it when anyone in the service or honorably discharged wears theirs to the celebration. It helps remind folks that this country was founded on blood, sweat, and tears."

I'll comply with taking the clothes, but I'm not sure about wearing them. I'm about to say that I'll *think* about it when Brooke exclaims, "Ooh, I love a man in uniform!"

Well, I'm not letting Skyler get all of the attention.

It takes us all of the next day to finalize our plans and do stuff like having our mail held and whatnot since the length of our visit is up in the air. Brooke even hired a neighbor kid to water her flowers. We've decided to take our car and caravan down there with Skyler. Brooke and I will have to share the driving so my body doesn't cramp up on me and cause a problem. Who am I kidding? She'll do most of the driving. I can change the seat position around as we head down there if I'm the passenger. It would just be my luck to be driving and have my foot go numb on me.

We're almost packed up and ready to go early the following day when Brooke zips back into the house. When she returns, my jaw drops. "Why are you bringing that?" I ask her.

"You haven't touched your guitar since we got back, and I hate to see it gathering dust. I thought maybe you'd like to play it again," she tells me with a beautiful, optimistic smile. She carefully places the case and a beat-up leather satchel full of my music onto the back seat.

"Humph. Maybe," I grumble. I haven't exactly felt like singing or writing any music lately. Maybe something will change. I'm sure not going to tell her to put it back when she looks so hopeful. I know I've been an insufferable grump, and I need to make an effort. "Okay, yeah. It sounds like a good idea. Ready to go?"

On the drive down, I try not to fidget and look too uncomfortable, but Brooke has a sixth sense about when I need to stand up or stretch. About an hour into the trip, she says, "Honey, would you give Skyler a call and tell him to stop at the next place where I can use a restroom?" Sly, Brooke. I know she's doing this so I can move around. It's one of the things I love about her. She's always been careful of my feelings without being super-obvious about it.

Skyler seems relieved too. I've noticed that he does exercises for his arm and shoulder a couple times a day. Yesterday, while we were packing and planning, he would stand up and start moving around in repetitive patterns like it was completely normal behavior. He had small barbells he'd brought to build up his muscles again too. We haven't spoken about our injuries much at all. Fine with me. I've noticed a look of strain on his face more than once, though, and Brooke has been careful not to ask him to lift anything heavy. His hand is pretty stiff, and his arm doesn't seem to straighten out completely. I wonder if that will fix itself eventually. I bet he isn't lugging around hundred-pound sacks of topsoil anymore for his parents' customers.

We take lots of breaks' after that and find a great little country café where we stop for lunch. They advertise their peach pie as the best in the country, so even though we're all stuffed, we have to sample it. And oh, man, is it ever delicious. What a treat.

After lunch, my mood is so good, I offer to take over the driving for a while, and Brooke thinks about her answer with a shrewd look on her face before she says, "Sure, but promise me you'll speak up as soon as you start to feel any pain or need to get up and move around, okay?" She knows if she says no, it will make me feel useless. I try to look as upbeat as possible, but I doubt I'm fooling her much.

"I will." I probably won't. I know how I'm built too.

It feels good to be back in the driver's seat for a while, but that joy wears off in about twenty minutes when my ass starts to go dead, and my leg wants to twitch. My hip is throbbing, but I don't say a word. I squirm around as much as I can and still drive as I ignore a pointed look from Brooke. Pretty soon she asks, "You doing alright? Be honest."

I sigh and tell her in a grumpy voice, "Call Skyler and tell him to pull off at the next available stop. I'll keep it together until then." I think better of my attitude and add, "Thanks, babe." The next ten minutes are pure torture trying to hold my body still enough to manage the gas pedal and brake. I've learned my lesson. I can barely get out from behind the wheel to let Brooke drive, even though she's there to support me and hands me my cane immediately.

She looks at me with love and whispers, "You did really well, Levi." Then she plants a big kiss on my lips and helps me into the passenger seat after I've had a good, long stretch. When she gets back into the car she suggests, "Why don't you take a pain pill? That was a lot for you." No recrimination and no I-told-you-so. I love this woman to death.

CHAPTER
Nine

BROOKE

THE CLOSER WE GET TO OUR DESTINATION, THE MORE SCENIC IT is. I wasn't aware of how much I needed to relax and see beautiful surroundings. It was easier to look around while Levi was driving, but he was in terrible pain, and it took all the fun out of rubbernecking. I couldn't wait to get the poor guy comfortable again. He took something after that and conked out, so that was a relief. I hate to watch him suffer. At least after taking his pill there was no question about him driving again. I wonder how Skyler is feeling since we haven't stopped in quite a while, but I don't want to disturb Levi by calling him. I have to trust Skyler to stop when he needs to.

I know we're getting close because the road signs proudly

proclaim that we're approaching "Honeybee Hollow: The Best Small Town in America." The town pride the residents have is not only cute, it's impressive. I can't wait to see the place.

Skyler leads us through the middle of town, so I nudge Levi awake and tell him, "Honey, we're here. You want to see the town? It's really pretty."

Levi blinks his eyes open, looking spaced out for a moment until what I told him registers, then he raises his seat-back, stretches, and looks around with a grin. "Wow. Skyler was right. This place is gorgeous." The shops along Main Street are colorful and trendy, and everything seems fresh and clean with plenty of flower boxes beneath shop windows. American flags are everywhere, underscoring the town's sense of pride and patriotism. I wonder how many of the shoppers on the sidewalks live here and who is a tourist. I see folks of all ages.

As we pass through town, I take note of places I want to come back to visit. Eventually, we exit the commercial district and turn down a country road where huge trees make a shady arch over us. Skyler slows down and then stops to allow a small herd of deer to nonchalantly cross the road. After they pass and we're on our way again, Skyler stops at a couple of mailboxes and fishes a thick pile of mail out of one of them. He turns right, and we follow a gravel driveway that goes on for quite a distance. The drive ends at a roundabout, and I'm not at all surprised to see a flagpole in the center of it where Old Glory ripples in a light breeze. We pull up in front of a gorgeous, large white house that has the most fantastic landscaping around it I've ever seen—trees, shrubs and flowers of all sorts of textures and colors. I can't identify most of them, but everything is bursting with vitality, and the sight makes us both smile. The house itself has an old-fashioned wrap-around porch with several rockers and a swing. Hanging baskets full of flowering plants adorn the porch here and there. The house looks like it's ready for a huge family or a party. Skyler pulls his truck around one side of the house where he opens a garage door remotely and then waves us in to park alongside him. The garage is spacious enough for several vehicles and is sparkling clean. One end is full of yard equipment of all kinds, including a tractor mower. I certainly didn't expect this. When he said "farmhouse," I was picturing something worn down and simple. This place belongs on the cover of *Southern Living Magazine.*

"Are you doing okay?" Skyler asks Levi as my husband ungracefully extracts himself from the car. "I figured you'd call if you needed another stop."

Levi laughs good naturedly and says, "I'm fine. I just woke up when we hit town, actually. Pretty place!"

"It's good you're rested, and I hope you guys are up for it. I called my parents and let them know I was back in town, and my mother insisted we all head over there tonight for supper. She knows I need to buy groceries, and she said this way I could do that tomorrow and still feed you like a proper host."

Levi smiles and shrugs, looking at me. He still seems a

little groggy, so I tell Skyler, "How nice of her. We'd love to. Thanks, Skyler. And tomorrow, I can help you with the shopping." I start to grab some of our stuff and say, "You were right about this area. It's breathtaking. How does anyone ever leave?"

"Well, not everyone is cut out for small-town living. But lots of folks leave and eventually come back like boomerangs." He smiles broadly, and frankly, it's devastating to see. Those sparkling hazel eyes of his seem to see right into my soul. "Come on, I'll show you guys to your room."

Levi picks up his guitar and music. I'm glad he isn't trying to carry anything heavy and stress his hip. Skyler also seems to be carrying big things with his left arm only. At least they aren't trying to be overly macho despite their injuries.

Skyler leads us through a truly beautiful house with gleaming wood floors and comfortable, colorful furniture. Between the large windows, art and photographs line the walls, and some of the drawings and paintings have the name "Skyler" scrawled in the corner. A few of those are clearly from his childhood, and I have to believe it's what his grandparents hung on the wall. But there is a progression of talent that shows he's been working on his art throughout the years.

I stop in front of a magnificent landscape and gasp. "Skyler, you didn't mention you were an artist. This is amazing." It has a modern, almost impressionistic quality to it—only edgier with more detail. You can feel a storm brewing and wind picking up, even though the scene is idyllic.

He shrugs his left shoulder and answers in a way that sounds deceptively blasé, "Thanks. It's just something I did. Before. I can't control a paintbrush too well now."

"Oh, I'm sorry. I hope you get your strength back enough to keep painting. Do you ever sell any of your work?"

"Not for a while now." He turns away abruptly and continues through the house. Levi and I look at each other, and Levi gives me a look that says he clearly understands how Skyler is downplaying his sense of loss. It's no wonder these two creative guys were so drawn to one another and became such great friends. I hope they can both reclaim that creativity once more. I also thank God they both still have all of their limbs.

Skyler leads us into a ground-floor master bedroom that is airy and bright. There's a big king-sized bed and an en suite bathroom. It's positively gorgeous.

"You're not giving up your room for us, are you?" Levi asks. "I can try to make it up the stairs…"

Skyler chuckles and answers, "Nope. There are a bunch of bedrooms upstairs, but my grandparents wanted a big suite on the ground floor, so they built it this way many years ago. My room is similar, and it's right next door to this one. We share the master bathroom, so I hope you're both okay with that. The toilet is private, but you may catch me brushing my teeth if you barge in." He smiles. "Pawpaw would never admit it, but they ended up in separate beds a lot of the time due to his snoring. No one wanted to sacrifice their comfort." He smiles again. "At first, it made me wonder how on earth they're getting along now on their big adventure."

Levi furrows his brow quizzically, and I have to ask, "What big adventure?" I thought they'd passed away, and that was why Skyler ended up with this great house, but that seems like a funny way to describe the hereafter.

"They wanted to see the country while they still have their health, so they sold a huge chunk of land to a company that built a corporate retreat camp and protected the environment with their project. This gave my grandparents more money than they knew what to do with. They put this house in my name, handed me the keys, and bought themselves an amazing tricked-out motor home. And before you worry about my eighty-two-year-old Pawpaw out on the open road, they also hired themselves a full-time driver whose wife does their cooking and is sort of a housekeeper for their home on wheels. From what I hear, they're having the time of their lives. I asked Granny how she manages Pawpaw's snoring in close quarters, and she said age has its benefits. He probably still sounds like a motorboat, but she just removes her hearing aids and sleeps like a baby."

I exclaim, "How wonderful for them. You must have a terrific family, Skyler."

He laughs and says, "You'll be able to determine that for yourselves tonight, I guess."

"Maybe I'm off-base, and I hope I'm not being rude when

I say this, but this isn't the picture I had of Appalachian living," Levi adds.

Skyler chuckles. "We get that a lot. Honeybee Hollow is unique to say the least. I hope you can grow to love it here." He winks at Levi, and my tummy does a little dippy thing for some reason. I hope the guys don't see that I'm blushing.

After a tour around the house and grounds—about five acres of magnificent creekfront land—we all have showers and dress to meet Skyler's parents. He ushers us into a snazzy new and obviously very expensive car he unplugged from an outlet next to his truck. I'm getting a completely new picture of Levi's country-boy buddy. The gardening business must be booming.

"Why didn't you drive this on the trip to our place?" I can't help asking.

"I didn't want to draw attention to myself around the base," he answers simply. "No one pays any mind to a work truck."

I've never been in an electric car before, and the silence is odd. It's even odder though when Skyler punches something into the dashboard screen, sits back, and lets the car drive us most of the way to his parents' house without his intervention. We get there just fine even though it freaks me out a little.

The house is reminiscent of Skyler's with its porch and general appearance, but it's smaller and there's a basketball hoop by the garage and a large treehouse that looks more like a raised, covered deck about five feet above the ground in an enormous tree with a sturdy staircase going up to it. The tree is festooned with cheerful strings of lights, and the whole thing makes me smile.

As soon as we get out of the car, we're surrounded by three shiny black Labradors with big doggie grins and tails waging so hard, their bodies sway with them. "Sit!" Skyler commands them, and they all obey immediately. "Good girls! The one with the gray on her muzzle is Martha, the taller one is Eleanor, and this little sweetie is Mamie," he says by way of introduction. "They're good dogs, but watch your food." He laughs as he bends to pet them and scritch their ears. Their tongues loll out of their mouths in pleasure. It's a happy sight.

A lovely blonde woman comes out of the house to greet us, and I can see immediately she is Skyler's mom. They have the same expressive eyes and smile. She hugs her son and turns to us. "Welcome, Levi and Brooke! We're so glad you both decided to come for a visit and hope you plan to stay a while. I'm Tracy Colfax, and my husband Mike is around back fiddling with his grill. I hope no one is a vegetarian." She leads us into the house and into a huge country kitchen where she has Skyler pour drinks while she sets out a tray of appetizers.

A smiling, barrel-chested man comes through the backdoor wearing an apron that proclaims, "My meat is delicious!" I try not to snort my drink out of my nose. He grabs Skyler in a hug and then shakes Levi's hand. He has a booming voice when he says, "Levi, we are so happy to know you and your beautiful wife." He smiles at me and looks back to Levi saying, "I think the Lord put you on earth for a special reason, and that was to save the life of our son. We seriously can't thank you enough for your service and your bravery."

I can see tears welling in everyone's eyes, and I have to steady myself so I don't lose it. Skyler and Levi came so close to not coming home, and when I think about it, I can barely breathe. I can imagine Skyler's parents feel much the same way.

Instead of dwelling on this topic, Mike Colfax just asks, "How does everyone like their steak? I tend to go with medium rare, but if you want anything different, speak up."

I'm thrilled to find out we'll be having dinner in the tree-house. What fun! There is a dumbwaiter contraption with a manual pully system that they use to take the dishes and food up and down. The treehouse is screened in to keep the bugs out, so we have a wonderful, mosquito-free evening and a delicious meal with Skyler and his parents. They are so warm and inviting, it's easy to see how they raised such a caring, thoughtful son. We're all pretty tired from the long drive, though, so we don't stay terribly late.

The last thing his parents tell Skyler is to take a couple of weeks off from the garden center. "You need the time to spend with your friends and relax," his mom tells him. "And the height of the planting season is past, so we can easily spare you now. Take as much time as you all need—the rest of the summer if you want to."

It's obvious she knows it's not just Skyler who needs a break from worry and pain. He probably needed to work when he felt up to it so he had a purpose, but now these guys need to find themselves. It's also pretty obvious that Skyler doesn't *need* a job at his parents' business. He's doing quite well on his own. I wonder how that happened. It certainly wasn't from a soldier's pay.

CHAPTER
Ten

Levi

When we get back to Skyler's house, he asks us, "Anyone feel like a quick soak in the hot tub? I know I do."

Brooke sees me smiling at the idea. "Sure," she tells Skyler. "Let's go get changed."

"Anyone want a beer or a soda? It can get kind of warm out there."

We both opt for a beer, but when we get some privacy, Brooke asks, "You're not on any pills right now, are you?" I shake my head, wishing she wouldn't baby me. I can't be mad at her though. I know I'm not supposed to mix pain pills with booze.

By the time we are changed and make it outside, Skyler is

already in the hot tub with three bottles of beer in an ice bucket on the table alongside him. The jets are bubbling, and he looks relaxed with his head back and his eyes closed. When he hears us, he looks up and smiles like he's the most contented man on earth. I can see him checking out Brooke in her bikini, and I see that she's blushing. I'm a little turned on by this, to be honest. She's chosen her skimpiest bikini, which is actually a thong, so her amazing ass is totally on display.

There is a short ladder to get into the tub, and I'm a little worried about navigating it well, so I let Brooke hop in first and offer me her hands to steady my climb. I noticed Skyler taking in the sight of her behind before she got into the water. I make it up the steps alright, but as I stretch my leg over the top and into the tub, even as I hold onto Brooke's hand, I lose my balance for a split second. Skyler hops up to assist us, but I correct myself enough to get in without incident. Brooke, however, completely loses her balance as I sit down. She crashes backward into Skyler, trying to break her fall by putting her hand back, and by the look on his face, she plants it right on his dick. Then she winds up somehow sprawled across his lap. Did I mention her bikini is a *thong*?

She laughs as Skyler automatically puts his arms around her, asking, "Are you okay, Brooke?"

I'm sure they're wondering about the look on my face as Brooke starts to disentangle herself from Skyler. I say to them in a soft voice, "Stay there for a minute, Brooke. You two look so beautiful together."

Brooke immediately asks, "Are you sure you didn't take a pill?" She's terribly confused, but I can see she's unconsciously settling into his embrace. I imagine the feel of his warm, hard chest, his slippery skin against hers, and…oh wow! I'm getting hard. This is great!

"Do you like being in Skyler's arms, Brooke? Tell me honestly."

"Levi! He, um, feels nice, but I'm kind of awkward with this. I'd like to come over and sit on *your* lap." Then as she sits up straighter, she gets a surprised look on her face and exclaims, "Oh!"

Skyler looks embarrassed and says, "I haven't had a mostly naked woman on my lap in ages. Sorry."

"Nice," I tell them with a grin. "So why don't you let him give you a kiss before you move away?" Skyler is shocked. I nod at him in what I hope is an encouraging way, so he gives her a polite peck on the cheek and helps her up. He does give her butt a quick pat as she steps over to me. She looks over her shoulder and gives him an unreadable look.

I reach for her and drag her between my legs. She feels so good. I'm also hard, and I know she feels it because she gives a little gasp, she grinds on me, then turns and wraps her arm around me, whispering in my good ear, "There you are. Welcome back." I wish my hip were up to having her sit on my lap, but this closeness is almost as good.

Skyler is unusually quiet for the rest of the time we're soaking. I don't know if I pissed him off or he's tired from our long day of driving. For some reason, I can't take my eyes off of his chest and arms. He looks fantastic, even with a messed-up shoulder. There's no doubt he's a great looking guy, though I've tried hard not to think about it before.

Brooke wisely scoots away and sits on the bench beside me. It's not like we could do anything in front of Skyler, even if this is the first complete erection I've had in forever. But when that idea pops into my head, I find myself feeling things below the belt again. Finally, I say aloud, "Skyler, thank you. This is the most relaxed I've been since coming home from Walter Reed. I'm starting to feel more like myself again, and we've only been here for a few hours."

He smiles kindly and answers, "Honeybee Hollow will do that to you."

"It's more than that," Brooke adds. "Being around you has a lot to do with it too, I imagine."

He just nods, leans back, and takes a swig of beer. Then he tells us, "If you like, we can all have breakfast in the morning at Hot Stuff. My friend Juni owns the place, and she makes incredible coffee and pastries. I think you'll like her."

A stab of jealousy zings through me. Where did that come from? "Girlfriend?" I ask, trying to keep the snark out of my voice.

Skyler laughs and answers, "Hardly! She's *very* taken. They're building a house on the land next to us that I sold them recently—and made a killing on the price, I might add." He gestures vaguely in the direction of the construction site. "I didn't need that much property, but I wanted some funds to make investments. Anyway, they'll be neighbors when the house is done—not that you'll be able to see the house from here. There's plenty of space in between." He doesn't elaborate anymore about it but says instead, "Guys, I'm exhausted. I'm going to have a quick shower and head to bed. Your room ought to have everything you need, but let me know if I've forgotten anything. And there are tons of clean towels in the bathroom cupboard. You can turn off the hot tub jets with that blue switch over there."

He climbs out, and I find myself checking out his legs and ass as he makes his exit. What is wrong with me? Then I realize Brooke is doing the same thing, so I smirk at her, and she mouths at me, "What?" Sure, honey. Take in the sight. He has all the goods in all the right places.

"Hey, Skyler, do you want me to do anything special to lock up the house?" I ask as he wraps a towel around his waist.

"Nah. I usually don't even bother. But if it makes you feel better, you can lock the door. Night. I'll see you whenever you get up."

CHAPTER
Eleven

Skyler

What the fuck was that? Levi wants me to *kiss* his wife? And he wants her to sit on my lap in basically nothing?

I couldn't get rid of this stiffy after Brooke grabbed my junk by accident and then squirmed around on me. Then they both started checking me out like a couple of hungry predators. I guess if they haven't had any sex in forever, that's at least understandable—at least for Brooke. But Levi too? Who am I kidding? I haven't gotten laid in ages either, and I'm a horny mess around them. I hope I managed to make it out of the hot tub without being too obvious, and I was glad I had some big towels handy to wrap up in. I can't wait to get into the shower and take care of myself.

I make a beeline through the house to my bedroom and strip quickly. I'm sweaty and stiff—in more ways than one—so I turn on the shower and brush my teeth as fast as I can while it heats up. I can barely bend over the sink to spit out the toothpaste with this monster boner in my way.

Finally! I get under the spray and start to stroke myself. Visions of Brooke's ass fill my head, and I try to think of something more appropriate. Unfortunately, I've always been an ass man, and good Lord, would I love to plow that one. Suddenly, my fantasy takes hold and won't go away, but another element creeps in—I'm fucking that fine ass of hers while Levi has her too. I've never done DP or shared a woman in my life, but now the idea has me by the balls, and I can't see straight I'm so turned on. It only takes a dozen or so yanks on my dick, and I'm coating the wall of the shower with ropes of cum. I let out a long moan as I shoot over and over. I hope they aren't in the house yet. I'm afraid that was kinda loud. At least I'll be able to sleep well after this.

I hope.

My routine is to plug in my phone before turning in, and I realize I left it outside. Damn! The darn thing is almost out of juice again, so I really need to charge it up. The bathroom is empty, so I listen at their bedroom door, but I don't hear anything. They must still be out in the hot tub. I grab a pair of shorts and head out again.

As soon as I open the back door, I hear Brooke mention

my name. At first, I think she heard me coming and asked me a question, so I step outside.

Oops. I can't take my eyes off of them. Levi is naked, and they are both stunning. I wish I were closer to them, but I don't want to interfere. I stand there transfixed, feeling like a creeper, but I can't make myself leave. Brooke is out of the hot tub and bent over Levi. That amazing ass of hers is just begging me to grab it, and Levi looks like he's in heaven. His head is tilted back, and his eyes are closed. I can feel the ecstasy flowing through him as though it were mine.

And…now I'm hard as a rock *again*.

Twelve

BROOKE

LEVI IS FINALLY RESPONDING SEXUALLY. THIS IS HUGE. I don't want to rush him though because as soon as Skyler left us to take a shower, Levi got that worried look that I'm getting used to seeing on his face, and it usually isn't good news. I've promised myself that I won't ever push or make him feel as if he needs to perform for me. I need to be careful with what I say.

"Can we make sure *all* the doors are locked up tight before heading to bed?" I ask him. "I'd feel better that way." I hope I'm not too transparent, but I think that may have been the trigger that undid him a little. He's afraid of bad surprises.

"Sure, babe. Whatever you need."

He seems to be rallying a little, so I try to deflect by changing the subject to something more fun before we head to bed. "Have you ever had any crazy fantasies? I mean sexy ones."

"Uh, well, maybe."

"So? Will you tell me one?"

"I…um…" He stops speaking and looks away.

"Okay, I'll go first then. I have sometimes fantasized about having sex outdoors in the woods. It's the middle of a gorgeous day, and anyone could walk by on a hiking path. I get turned on by the element of danger and the idea that someone might see us from far enough away that they stop and watch without bothering us. But when we're done, they approach us and tell us we're incredibly sexy."

"What does everyone do after that?"

"Oh, I have no idea. It's not a long fantasy. Just enough to make me horny," I tell him with a laugh. "Your turn now."

"I'm kind of embarrassed."

"Don't be, Levi. I told you mine, now tell me…all about how you want to share me with Skyler."

Levi's eyes flash, and his jaw drops. "You knew?"

I smile. "Just a guess."

"I'm sorry. I don't mean any disrespect."

"I don't feel disrespected. It's actually a turn-on. I'm not sure I could ever go through with it, but it's a fun fantasy. Better than mine." I look around and say, "But since no one is out here, why don't you take off your trunks, sit up on the step, and let me blow you. I'd hate to waste that nice erection you've had going."

"Well, we can try, I guess."

The worried look is back. I need to hurry. "Here, let me help you." I pull him into a standing position and start to yank down his pants. I'm a bit sorry to see the current state of his dick, but at least it's a partial at this point. I can work with that. I hop out and get a folded towel to stick under his butt on the top step and help him into position with his back to the tub, facing out so I can stand on the deck.

I hear the back door squeak open behind me. I don't know if Levi heard it over the jets because he has his attention riveted on me, and I'm still not too sure about his level of hearing damage.

"Now…think about sharing me with Skyler as much as you like," I say as I stroke him. It's helping, and I'm talking louder than normal to be heard over the jets. "Think about the sounds Skyler and I might make if we were all three in bed together." Hmm…better still. I slide his dick into my mouth and start to blow him like my life depends on it. I'd love to have an orgasm tonight too, but it's far more important to get Levi out of his funk. But then…he's responding so well, I stop for a second and tell him, "You're turning me on, and I can't take it! I need to do something to myself too." I quickly drag my bikini bottoms down and start circling my clit with vigor. "Mmm," I moan as Levi starts to move his hips. This is promising! He likes it if I play with myself, so I shouldn't worry about taking away from his experience now. I really turn up the heat, both with my hand on myself and my mouth and hand on his dick. I can't help moving my hips around, clenching and unclenching my butt cheeks. Faster and harder I go, and finally, I can tell by his movement and breathing that Levi is about to blow. "Give it to me, Levi!" I beg him and latch on for a last few final sucks.

Victory!

Levi lets out a primal holler that sounds like some kind of woodland creature in distress, and I have to keep myself from laughing just because I'm so happy. This is the best thing that has happened in months for both of us. As I swallow, I give myself another hard tweak on my clit and feel the rapture of an orgasm blast through me as I groan in satisfaction. We didn't fuck, but I'm calling this a total success.

I hope our audience enjoyed it as well.

As I think this, I hear a thud, a quiet male voice muttering, "Ow! Fuck!" and then the back door clicking shut. I'm immediately turned on again knowing that Skyler stood there and watched everything.

Skyler must have forgotten something out here. I look around and see that his phone is sitting next to the empty ice bucket. I guess we ought to take it in so he can charge it up. I wonder how he felt about what we just did, and I can't help whispering, "Skyler just went back into the house. He saw us. I didn't see him because I was…you know…busy. But I heard him." I don't add that I was giving him a wiggle show with my butt.

"I saw him, but I don't think he knew I knew he was there. It got me going like crazy," Levi mutters into my neck. "It turned you on too, didn't it?"

"Definitely. One of us needs to give him his phone that he left out here. You want to, or should I?"

"You do it. I'm too embarrassed," he tells me, but he's laughing softly.

"There's no reason to be. We were just doing our thing, and he was the peeper. Anyway, I'm thrilled that you came for me. Well…for us."

Levi's chest is still heaving gently, and he has the dreamy, satisfied look I feared I might never see on his face again. I hand him a dry towel and kiss him. Then I tell him, "I love you so much."

After we turn off the jets and the outdoor lights, I grab a towel for myself, and we make sure the house is securely locked. Then we head to the shower. I have Skyler's phone, so, still wrapped in my towel, I knock on his door to the bathroom. In seconds, he opens and peeks around the door looking slightly flushed. It makes me suddenly aware that I may have interrupted some "self-care" time.

"Oh, I'm glad I didn't wake you." *Hah, as if!* "I saw this outside and thought you might want to charge it."

"Yeah, right. Thanks. Uh…see you in the morning." He takes the phone and starts to close the door.

I can't resist telling him, "You might want to put some ice on your forehead. It looks like it's going to be quite the bruise." I have to stifle a smirk before climbing into the shower with my gloriously handsome husband.

Later, as I drift off to sleep, I wonder if Honeybee Hollow has some kind of magic to it. I'm already seeing the beginning of a transformation in Levi, and we've only been here for a matter of hours. Whatever it is—the town or being with Skyler again—I'll gladly take it.

CHAPTER
Thirteen

In the morning, I see that my forehead bruise is a good one, so a baseball cap is going to be featured in my wardrobe today. It's either that or makeup, and I sure as shit don't have any of that stuff lying around. As soon as Brooke sees me, she raises her eyes to the cap and gives me a wink. Levi pays no attention to it. Maybe I can get through the day without answering any questions about it.

We're all early risers, and that's a good thing if we're going to snag the best selections at Hot Stuff. I've been disappointed a few times when I've gotten there to miss out on one of Juni's giant cinnamon rolls or her amazing orange cranberry muffins.

Levi seems a little embarrassed this morning, but he also seems more relaxed than I've seen him since before Afghanistan. I guess there's nothing like a great BJ from your wife. I have to get the image of them out of my head! Brooke bent over his dick with her luscious ass on display and both of their toned bodies glistening with water droplets in the soft outdoor lights.

I've always thought men have beautiful bodies, but I've never had any particular desire to have sex with one of them. But hearing that Levi might possibly be open to a three-way with Brooke and me? Holy moly. What a turn-on that was. And Brooke was encouraging him to think about it. Wow.

We pull up to Hot Stuff, which is right on Main Street, and I'm gratified to see that Juni isn't too busy yet. She has a few customers, but she's currently drinking coffee at a table with her two partners Jack and Asher—two terrific guys who adore her as well as each other. Her employee, whose name I always forget, is managing the counter. Juni sees us coming and jumps up to say hello with a huge smile.

I introduce everyone and explain to my guests, "These are the people who are building the new place next to my property. We'll be neighbors soon." I can see the questions in Levi's and Brooke's eyes, but I let Juni explain.

"We're all so happy you're here visiting with Skyler," she says politely, and she also sees the questioning looks, so she grins and says, "Asher, Jack, and I need a bigger place where we can live together comfortably. We're in a triad relationship that we expect to last always."

There is no defensiveness or challenge in her tone; it's merely a statement of fact. The guys are holding hands on the tabletop, making their part of the relationship obvious.

"Nice!" Levi mutters almost inaudibly.

"Oh! Interesting," Brooke says with a smile. "I'm happy for you, and it must be an exciting project to build a house."

"It is! Please, sit down and join us," Juni tells us. "I'll bring you all a coffee, if that's what you're here for." We all nod our thanks. "And I'll get you all your pastries. I know how hungry Skyler can be when he shows up here in the morning. Any preferences? I have a new blueberry muffin recipe I'm trying out, so I won't even charge you if you try one of those. I've added a new secret ingredient, and I want to see how folks like them." She looks pointedly at me and adds, "Don't worry, Skyler. You'll get your regular."

"I'm game for the blueberry surprise," Levi answers with a big grin, and I wink at Juni. She knows my passion for a good cinnamon roll.

The pastries are amazing, and the coffee is robust. We all sit around and chat for about an hour. As the shop fills with customers, Juni has to hop up and take care of business a few times. From the way they interact, it's clear that she has a deep affection for her two men and they for her. And I must say, Levi can't take his eyes off of them. He looks like he's taking mental notes.

As Jack and Asher make noises about needing to leave, Jack says, "If you're not in a rush, you all ought to pop over to my gallery. I have a new exhibit by a young Kentucky artist I'm trying to promote. She's quite talented, and I'd love to show her off to you. I'm just around the corner on Third Street; the gallery's called Imagine."

Now, I love art as much as most folks love music, movies, or books. But I'm feeling pretty crappy about it lately since I can barely hold a paintbrush well enough to even sign my name, so I speak up and say, "I hope you don't mind, but we have a ton of groceries to buy today, Jack. I don't want to wear out Levi's hip, so can we take a raincheck?"

"Oh, I'm okay," Levi tells us. "If it starts to hurt when we get to the Piggly Wiggly, you can put me in the cart and push me around like a toddler." He gives me a playful shove and a dumb look like he's about to suck his thumb. "Let's go look at Jack's art gallery, and maybe it'll inspire you to do more hand exercises so you can paint again."

Jack looks mildly surprised. "You're an artist? Why didn't I know this?"

"Uh…" I splutter.

"He's a *wonderful* artist," Brooke says. She sounds like my mother.

"I'd love to see some of your work," Jack tells me. "You know I'm always on the hunt for Kentucky talent, and if I had someone from Honeybee Hollow, just imagine what the turnout might be for your art opening." He studies the expression on my face and adds kindly, "No pressure, Skyler. Let me know when you're ready." Jack is a perceptive guy.

I can't back out now, so I answer, "Sure, let's all go take a look." I turn and say, "Asher, it was nice seeing you. I hope we can all get together again soon." Then I get a great idea. "Maybe we can all meet up at the Fourth of July celebration."

Everyone looks enthusiastic about that and agrees, so we all have a "date."

We hug Juni and tell her to keep the secret-ingredient blueberry muffins on her menu, even though not one of us could identify why they seemed so different and special— they just were. Juni kisses her men goodbye, and then they kiss each other before heading in opposite directions.

I feel Levi's eyes on me after the guys kiss, and I don't return his stare. I can't deny I have a bit of a reaction to them. I feel warm. I'm also aware that appearances mean nothing. I'd never in a million years have guessed either of those guys were queer when I first met them. But their chemistry with each other as well as with Juni is undeniable. They're so happy and natural with one another; they're fun to be around.

Before we leave, Juni asks Brooke, "I'm planning to do a little bit of retail therapy one afternoon this week, and if you're interested, I could show you around to the various boutiques in town. It's always more fun shopping with a friend."

Brooke laughs and answers, "Thanks, Juni. I agree, and I

always want to shop with someone honest enough to tell me if my butt looks too big in whatever outfit I'm trying on."

"Impossible," I mutter under my breath, and Brooke gives me a funny look. I can't resist winking at her.

"I promise complete honesty," Juni says with a laugh. "How about tomorrow then?" she asks. "Meet me here around two, and we'll hit the shops."

And just like that, Brooke says, "Perfect!" and has a new friend in town. She looks quite pleased about it.

I look at Levi and tell him, "While the ladies are shopping, you and I can go fishing." Levi's eyes light up, and he readily agrees. I tuck that happy expression away in my mind. It looks so good on him. He's losing that haunted appearance bit by bit. I just knew he could be happy here.

The next thing I know, I'm heading to look at art in Jack's gallery with my friends.

CHAPTER
Fourteen

Brooke

Overall, the art gallery is terrific, but the special exhibit pales in comparison to what we've seen of Skyler's work. I can tell immediately that he's aware of it and way too polite to say so. I can also detect a bit of longing in his eyes as he wanders around the gallery.

"Where did you learn to paint?" Jack asks him as they stand in front of a colorful still life.

"Oh, um…I had an art teacher here at the high school who added an after-school class for people who were interested. Fortunately, she waited until football season was over. At first, it seemed like a good way to get to know some of the girls better, but the teacher was so great, I pretty much gave up flirting and focused on my work. I'd always loved to draw, and this class helped me look at things in my own individual way. When I went to college, I majored in business, but I minored in art. I had some wonderful professors, and eventually I was sorry I hadn't gone for the major in art. But I was afraid I needed more of a serious education, so I went with the more practical route. Then I joined the Army and…well…I guess I'm glad I didn't put all my eggs in one basket."

Skyler stretches out his hand at his side and then squeezes it into a fist. I wonder if he even realizes he's doing it.

With a thoughtful look, Jack asks, "I'm no doctor or physical therapist, Skyler, but have you ever considered trying to paint again? There are several ways to go about it. I doubt you've lost your vision for how you want to convey your ideas on canvas, but perhaps some strengthening exercises or a special paint brush grip might help. I hate the idea of you giving up on it."

Skyler answers, "I still go to physical therapy once a week and practice lots of stretching and strengthening exercises, but I could look into using some kind of grip. Thanks." He turns to Levi and adds, "There is a terrific PT clinic right here in town. I meant to tell you that."

Levi chuckles, "The Honeybee Hollow Ambassador is at it again. You're not going to rest until Brooke and I move here permanently, are you?"

"It's crossed my mind."

Jack also smiles and adds, "I've never been happier since I

moved here. It's a great town. And now I'm in love, have a thriving business I created for myself, and I'm building the house of my dreams with the partners of my dreams. I highly recommend this place."

After a tour of the gallery, Levi is getting a look on his face like he needs to sit down for a bit, so I suggest, "Guys, we need to hit the Piggly Wiggly before too long. Are you about ready to go?" We all say our goodbyes to Jack and promise to make plans for the Fourth with them. He really is a great guy.

On my suggestion, we leave Levi in the park under a shady tree, happily equipped with his Kindle and a new book (I had it in my purse just in case), and Skyler and I make the grocery run. I couldn't force Levi to wander around the market when he's obviously starting to hurt.

Once again, I find myself marveling at Levi's transformation since we arrived here. Just a few days ago, if I had mentioned the possibility that he needed a rest, he would have spiraled for hours. But when we finished shopping, we found a well-rested Levi greeting us with a smile.

After an easy dinner, we curl up on Skyler's comfy couch to watch a movie, but we all end up falling asleep about halfway through. I wake up to the realization that both men have their heads on my shoulders, and I'm getting pretty toasty between them. As soon as I stir, they both wake up, and Skyler looks embarrassed. I kiss him on the cheek because he looks so sweet and bashful and then help Levi up.

In bed, we don't have anything like the night before, but Levi is cuddly and sweet before he falls asleep again.

♡♡♡

Shopping with Juni is more fun than I've had in a long, long time with a girlfriend. She has a great sense of humor as well as a terrific sense of style. We hit all the boutiques—including a vintage clothing store—and try on everything under the sun. After three hours and a few purchases, Juni asks me if I'd like to relax with a margarita or a beer before heading home to Skyler's place.

"Sounds good," I tell her, and she leads me to a popular watering hole called The Hive. It turns out they have the best salsa and chips I've ever tasted. The margarita goes down pretty easy too.

"We'll all have to come back here for some music and dancing one of these nights," Juni says. "They always have really good bands play." Then she shoots me a questioning look and asks, "So…you and Levi *with* Skyler, eh?"

It takes me a moment to process what she's asking, and I sputter, "Oh, no. I mean, not…uh…not…"

"Not yet? Not ever?" She laughs. "Not officially? Look, it's none of my business, but I see the way he looks at you and Levi, and we heard a *lot* about Levi from Skyler before he went and dragged you guys down here from Militaryland, or wherever you were. He clearly adores your husband. And Levi couldn't take his eyes off my men and the way they were treating each other. You have to admit there's an interest there, even if it hasn't been acted on yet." She pauses and takes a drink while I ponder what she's said, before adding, "Just tell me to butt out if I'm making you uncomfortable."

"No, it's fine. You're not at all. I'm just surprised it's obvious. We haven't talked about it with all three of us together, and nobody has actually done anything, but the idea is intriguing, and it's certainly something Levi has mentioned to me." Realizing I'm rambling, I clear my throat and lower my voice to a whisper. "Apparently, he's fantasized about sharing me with Skyler, and I think it sounds pretty interesting. I have no idea how it would work, but having all the attention on me is a little too much for me to imagine."

Juni gives me a big smile and says, "That's the beauty of it. Have you ever heard of compersion?"

"No."

"When three or more people get together in a relationship that is based on more than just sex, and each participant is equally attracted to all of the members of the union, they all get as much satisfaction in seeing their partners enjoy one another as they do for themselves. When I see my men together…God, it's such an amazing rush, and a total turn-on. They're beautiful together. And then they turn that same attention on me, or one does while the other is pleasuring him, and it's like nothing you've ever experienced. Compersion is that sense of completeness and joy you have in seeing your partner give and receive pleasure. And believe me, it can be just as powerful as physical pleasure."

"Do you think that's why Skyler wanted us to come stay with him so badly?"

"It might be part of it—even if it's not something he thinks about consciously. The other part could also have been that he missed Levi horribly and wanted him to get far away from the Army base, so he'd get over his PTSD. I know Skyler has suffered from it. He's a lot better than he was a few months ago, and he's definitely having fewer migraines. I see that same strain in Levi's eyes. Those poor guys are never far from those terrible memories that bombard their thoughts."

"So you think I ought to encourage having a three-way with them to get them to be more relaxed?"

Juni smiles and shakes her head. "I'm not saying it's a cure-all, Brooke. And I'm only suggesting it if you're willing to work at it and interested enough in it to begin with. Not everyone is cut out for polyamory. And just like with any relationship, not all of them work out. Asher and I both had failed three-way attempts a long time ago. We learned, and this time it's been wonderful."

"Oh. Wow. Were you looking for another…what did you call it…triad?"

"No. That wasn't a priority of mine at all, but when I saw them together, it was like magic. I knew Jack a little, and Asher not at all, but we immediately gelled and had to try it. I've never been sorry. I highly recommend it if you're open to it." She winks at me, and I get all fluttery inside—not from her but from what she's been saying.

Just then, my phone buzzes with a text from Levi asking when I plan to come home and eat the wonderful trout dinner Skyler is preparing. I laugh and tell Juni, "Thanks for everything today. I had a great time, but I'm being summoned to dinner, and I don't even have to cook." I grab the check, take care of it, and give Juni a big hug. "I'll see you soon, and thank you for your…um…encouragement!"

CHAPTER

Fifteen

Since Brooke is gone for the afternoon, Skyler and I decide to do some fishing. He has a great setup out at his creek. There's an easy path to get there, so we wheel our tackle box, poles, and a cooler out there in a wagon. At the water, there's a comfortable bench his grandfather built where we can set up. Someone has trimmed the lower branches of a graceful willow tree so we can sit beneath it, shaded from the hot sun. And best of all, the sky is brilliant blue with not a single noisy aircraft marring the peace of the day. I could get used to this.

Skyler does have some dexterity issues with his right hand, so I tie our hooks to our lines and load them up with bait. He busies himself with putting our chilled beers in koozies and opening them. Skyler's grandfather must have enjoyed his beer as well because the arms of the bench have built-in drink holders. It's not a terribly large bench, so we keep brushing our arms against one another. I'm finding that I don't mind this at all; his nearness is a comfort.

While we're getting set up, Skyler says, "I've always meant to ask you, how did you meet Brooke?"

"Oh, uh…" I try not to look embarrassed. "During one of our block leaves, I was babysitting Lulu for Kate when she had a doctor's appointment, and we ran out of snacks. So I took Lulu to the market and ended up buying a whole bunch of crap. By the time I made it to the parking lot, Lulu was having a meltdown because it was way past her naptime, and I couldn't get her into the car seat. While I was struggling with her, my shopping cart rolled away, and this lovely, helpful angel ran and got it and brought it back before it crashed into someone's car. Then she talked Lulu down out of her fit while I unloaded the cart. I had a terrible time convincing her I wasn't some scatterbrained new dad, and I was only the scatterbrained uncle. She finally agreed to having dinner with me when she heard Lulu call me Uncle Levi."

He cracks up and says, "Smooth. Why didn't I ever know this before?"

"I dunno, but hey…she married me! So I couldn't have been that awful."

After his laughter peters out, Skyler lapses into silence.

We've been fishing for a while with no bites at all, but he doesn't seem too focused on catching anything. He clearly has something on his mind. He starts to speak a few times and then stops himself. After a long silence, he finally asks me, "Why did you jump in front of me?"

A chill runs down my spine despite the heat of the day. "In Afghanistan?" I ask like a dope. Of course that's what he means, and I'm stalling. I hate thinking about that day. And I hate that I can't stop thinking about it.

He turns and looks at me with those expressive eyes of his. "Yes, Levi. In Afghanistan. The shooter was mowing people down, and you took it upon yourself to shield *me*. I'm happy you did it but…why?"

My hands start to shake, so I quickly reel in my line and grab a gulp of beer while he patiently waits for my answer. "I've thought about that day a million times. I had to do it. It was like everything was in slow motion after we got in there and realized it was an ambush. That little shit blasted holes in the two guys at the other end of the room before he even made it through the door, and he was working his way toward us. I saw that your rifle was on the ground for some reason, and I knew you couldn't defend yourself. I instantly thought of what it would be like to go home without you…" My voice catches, and I stop for a moment. I have to clear my throat before I can go on. "Instinct took over. I jumped in front of you, hoping like hell you didn't shoot me in the back by mistake, and I started firing. I know I made a fuck-up of the whole thing because I should have shot sooner to possibly save more guys. They were caught off-guard because the shooter came in with his rifle spraying bullets, and the sun was right in their faces through the doorway. Even though the open door was blocking him from my view until he was pretty far inside…" I pause and take a breath so deep my chest hurts from it. "I feel like I killed them myself some days. It's hard, Sky. It's really hard to take."

He nods at me and says softly, "I like it when you call me Sky."

"That's how I think of you in my head. I guess it kind of slipped out."

"You know you don't have to feel guilty about any of what happened." He puts his arm around my shoulders, and it feels so good.

"Rationally, I know that, but my heart has a hard time with it."

Skyler looks pensive a moment and adds, "My PT guy here in town hooked me up with an online therapist who really helps me with the memories and nightmares. The guy is terrific. I'll give you his contact information if you think you'd like to talk to him. If not, I won't bug you about it. But you should also know he encouraged me to drive over to your place and seek you out. He thought seeing you would be healing. He's not wrong."

I nod and tell him, "Thanks. I should probably talk to him. I just haven't been ready. You know?" I turn to look him in the eye and ask, "So why was your gun on the ground?" I'm sorry I turned toward him because his arm slips away, and I miss it immediately.

"I was adjusting my headset. It was loose and kept bugging me. I guess that was a bad move, but obviously, I didn't have any idea we were going to be shot at right then."

"No, it makes sense, and the headset was crucial in the long run. You got the rescue party to us as quickly as possible." I place a hand on his shoulder and say, "Thank you for sticking with me and bringing us down here. I'm not sure Brooke and I were going to work the way things were going. I know I was being an asshole to her. And I apologize for shutting you out. I just felt like such a worthless shit. I was afraid to face you, even as much as I missed your company. Even though you seemed pretty cool when I saw you at Walter Reed, I was still scared you'd think more about that day and blame me for the other guys, and as long as I didn't have to hear it from you, it might not be true."

"Well, I can't tell you how to feel, but I can tell you that I certainly *don't* blame you for what happened, and I doubt Brooke would leave you for any reason. She's crazy about you. You're a lucky man, Levi. She's special for sure."

"You want to fuck her?"

Skyler's eyes widen. "Levi! Knock it off. Just because I can give her a compliment doesn't mean I'm trying to steal your wife."

"I know that. You're the best friend there is. But I think seeing you and Brooke together would be amazing."

"What are you saying? You *want* us to get it on so you can…watch?"

"I wouldn't say no to that." He stares at me wide-eyed, so I continue. "Look, the reason I got hard the other night was because I was thinking about Brooke being with you. That's the first time I've managed to come since before we were deployed."

"Well, shit."

"Sky, I see you ogling her all the time. Tell me you haven't fantasized about her."

"Uh…"

"Right. You can't. You want a piece of her. And I could talk her into it, I'm sure."

"Jesus, Levi! I'm shocked. It's just…I'm…"

"Just what? Are you actually more interested in someone else, and you just like looking at her?"

"Um…I'm totally attracted to Brooke, but…yeah, kinda. There is someone I sorta think about sometimes. Not that I know what to do about it."

"Oh. That doesn't sound like you. But…look, I didn't know you had someone in mind already. Maybe you could just try to man up and say something. Sorry to butt in."

"Nothing to be sorry about." Skyler fiddles with his pole, not looking at me.

"So who is she?"

Instead of answering me, Skyler jumps up and whoops, "Caught one!"

For the next couple of hours, we bring in a whole string of trout, not talking about anything other than our prowess as fishermen.

Finally, we head back to the house and clean the fish. We both agree that it's the worst part of fishing, but it's worth it. We get cleaned up, and Skyler grabs a bunch of ingredients that mystify me. He tells me to call Brooke.

"Dinner will be ready in about forty-five minutes," he announces. "You have plenty of time for a shower if you want one before we eat. I'm just going to get the initial prep done and then I'll go shower. I'll do the last part when she gets home…er…I mean when she gets *here*."

I smile and tell him, "It feels like home, Sky. I texted Brooke a little while ago already." Then I add with a grin, "You can forget the ball cap now. Brooke told be about you smacking your head on the door when you made your hasty retreat."

"Oh, uh…yeah. Sorry about last night. I was just out there looking for my phone, and…well…"

"No apologies are necessary. We both knew you were there."

"You did too?"

"Yes, and if it had bothered me, I'd have either asked Brooke to stop—hah! Fat chance! Or I'd have politely asked you to head back indoors. The fact is it turned me on having you there." He doesn't say anything and just stares at me, so I go on, "Look, I don't know why that is, or what it means. I've sure as hell never felt that way in my life before. I've always been fiercely protective of Brooke, but I also strangely feel possessive about you. I don't know if it's the hero thing, if it's because you're my best buddy, or it's some new kind of feeling. I just…" I exhale deeply. "I just feel *things* about you and Brooke. It's not that I need her any less, but I need you too for some reason. Does that make *any* sense?"

Skyler doesn't meet my eyes for a while, but when he does, his look is penetrating. "Okay, Since you're spilling some…stuff, I'll give you pure honesty. Like I said, I'm not trying to interfere in your marriage. I think Brooke is gorgeous and a remarkable woman. I like everything about her and think you're a lucky bastard to have her. I pray that the two of you never mess up what you have because you're both special. That said, I'd take her to bed in an instant if my conscience didn't keep me away from her. But…it does. I'm not sure I could ever get past that."

"Even for me?" I ask.

Brooke comes waltzing into the house and stops to look at us. I'm sure we have strange expressions on our faces. She looks so pretty and puzzled, I can't resist going to her and wrapping my arms around her. I nuzzle her neck and nibble on her ear because I know that's always gotten her going.

"I'm glad you're back, babe," I whisper in her ear. "Did you have a fun time with Juni?"

"Yes, loads of fun. Did you guys have a good day?"

"We did. We caught lots of fish and talked about some interesting things." I look sideways at Skyler who has a nervous look on his face, so I stop talking before I embarrass both of us. "I'm heading to the shower before dinner. Want to join me?"

"I think in all fairness I ought to help Skyler with dinner since the two of you caught it, and I've done nothing."

Skyler grins and says, "You can set the table. Indoors or out? It's up to you."

"I choose outside," she says with a grin and proceeds to set us up on the screened porch.

CHAPTER
Sixteen

How am I supposed to keep it together around these two? Brooke is the sexiest woman I've ever known. She *exudes* sex appeal even doing something as mundane as setting the table, and I don't think she's aware of it. Sure she takes good care of herself and dresses to show off her incredible…assets, but beyond that, she's not particularly flirty or anything. She's just…Brooke. Maybe I was nuts to bring them down here to Honeybee Hollow. Looking at her, hearing her voice, even smelling her is torture.

But I had no choice, I remind myself—I had to invite them. I missed Levi like crazy, and the longer it took to communicate with him, the worse I got. It was like I had an itch I couldn't reach or…no, it was way worse than that. I'm sorry he feels so responsible for what happened on our crappy mission, but he's not to blame. I wish I could make him believe it. Oh crap. I wish a lot of things.

I'm preparing a salad and getting the trout ready to pan sear, letting my mind get caught up in these thoughts, when Brooke breaks into my reverie.

"I haven't properly thanked you yet for everything, Skyler. You've done so much for Levi by being a great friend and hauling his ass out of the house to come down here for a visit. He looks so much better than he did even just a few days ago. It's like I can finally get through to him."

"Maybe you two could consider staying here indefinitely. What's there back in Hopkinsville for you?"

"Oh! Well, a few friends, I guess, but I'm not all that close to anyone really. I feel like I have more in common with Juni after a couple of days, actually," she says with a smile. "I'll talk to Levi about it. It's sure a beautiful place. And the company is wonderful." She gives me a dazzling smile.

I have to duck my head to hide my blush. "I saw that you brought Levi's guitar. Does he sing too?" I'm curious about this side of Levi that I know nothing about.

"Oh, absolutely. He writes songs and has a fantastic voice. I'm sorry he's never tried to pursue it as a career beyond selling a few pieces, but I guess the Army has been a bigger priority until now. His songs are amazing, and his voice is all raspy and emotional." She chuckles, "He sounds a little like

Jelly Roll if I had to compare him to someone. Levi's voice is deeper, but it has that same kind of quality."

"Wow. That's quite a compliment."

"It's true. I just hope he feels up to playing again; he's been such a wreck for months. It might be a good release for him emotionally." She looks at me closely. "And what about you and your painting? You clearly have some serious talent there." I start to interrupt, but she keeps going. "I know you've lost some fine motor skills with your hand, but that might come back gradually. And even if it doesn't, it shouldn't mean you give up on art. Maybe you can't make intricate drawings the same way you used to, but I bet you still have the eye and an amazing sense for color. Maybe it's time to develop a new style. Create something more expressive and less detailed. You seem to be managing around the kitchen just fine, so your hand obviously still works—just maybe not the way you're used to."

I look at her thoughtfully, and she turns pink.

"I'm sorry, Skyler. I didn't mean to butt in."

I smile as warmly as I can. "It's fine, Brooke. I'm just surprised at how intuitive you are. There's definitely something to your way of thinking. Painting has always been a stress reliever and a good way to express myself, but I've frankly been afraid to try since I was injured." Just then, Levi wanders in with damp hair, smelling less fishy, so I take the opportunity to duck out before this discussion gets too intense. "I'm going to hit the shower now, so help yourselves to drinks, and I'll be back in a few minutes." I look Brooke in the eye and tell her, "Thanks for giving me a lot to think about."

As I leave the room, I hear Levi asking, "What ideas did you give Skyler to think about, babe? Anything fun?" He must have grabbed her ass because I hear giggling as I head down the hall.

THE NEXT COUPLE OF DAYS ARE KINDA WEIRD. DESPITE OUR great conversation about my art, I'm uncomfortable around Brooke because I'm afraid to look at her. I'm even more attracted to her now than ever, and I hope she doesn't think I dislike her because that couldn't be less true. Levi seems to be watching me like a hawk, and I don't know if it's because he wants me to be interested in her or if he's worried I'll make a move. I'm not sure what to do, so I try to play the good host and show them around the town.

So far, we've toured the hat factory—which was a lot more interesting than I'd imagined—and I've taken them to have the "Best Burger in the World" at Sock Hop. Brooke especially got a kick out of that place with their 1950s decor. Tonight, we're having dinner at the Honeybee Hollow Inn, and afterward, we'll hit karaoke night at The Hive.

AFTER SETTLING OURSELVES AT A TABLE IN THE BAR, WE TRY for a while to coax Levi up on stage. He isn't having any of it, so we shut up instead of making him uncomfortable. I even offer to sing (not that I can), but that doesn't persuade him. However, his attitude switches somewhere around his third beer or so after some guy sings a terrible rendition of "Sweet Caroline" that gets the audience involved, and Levi can't help singing along with the rest of us. Levi goes and puts his name on the list after all! Maybe he feels like he warmed up his voice or something. I don't know.

But then…when it's Levi's turn, he makes his way up onto the stage with the help of his cane and belts out "Creep" by Radiohead. My chin drops at the emotion that man packs into the lyrics, and I look over at Brooke to say something. She has tears rolling down her face. Levi seems to be singing the words right to her.

The people sitting at the table behind us get into a noisy conversation about how Levi belongs on *The Voice,* and I have to agree. One of them finally shushes the others so they can hear better.

Levi's talent is remarkable. The rasp in his voice breaks my heart, and the roundness in its quality gives me goose-bumps. All I can think is, *Why isn't he famous?*

I guess if Levi can get up on stage and sing like that, I can certainly tackle some paints and a canvas. We're on! I make a mental note to thank him for the inspiration when it's less noisy and he can hear me.

As he ends his song and takes a bashful bow to the thunderous applause, the guy sitting at the table next to us bellows to his partner over the cheers, "His body looks pretty perfect to me. He can creep all over me any day."

His partner snickers and says with a pout, "I thought you loved me!"

"Oh honey, I do, but haven't you ever heard of a hall pass?"

I have to bite the inside of my cheek to keep from cracking up.

Levi slowly makes his way back to our table amid back slaps and handshakes and probably a few cocktail napkins with phone numbers shoved into his pockets. When he gets to us, an audible "Aww!" and a few whistles and catcalls go through the room as Brooke stands up and throws her arms around him. She kisses him like he's her oxygen, and she's out of breath. Not to be outdone, I also stand up, and as soon as they unlock their lips, I grab him in a bearhug. I'm so proud of him!

Levi is all smiles, but he says, "Ready to get out of here?"

Before we can make it outside, an older guy stops us and introduces himself as the owner of The Hive. He asks Levi, "Do you ever do anything besides messing around with karaoke?"

Levi smiles and answers, "Sure. I've never actually sung karaoke before, but I do play guitar and write music. I'm just a little rusty right now."

"Well, practice some and then come see me with your guitar. I'd love to sign you up for a regular gig once a week or so. You have real talent, son. And if that's what you sound like when you're rusty, I'm in for a treat! Here's my card. Name's Buford Wallace. If you need backup musicians, I know all of them around here. Give me your name and number, if you don't mind."

"Oh, well, thank you, sir. I don't exactly live here…"

Brooke immediately interrupts and interjects, "But we're seriously thinking about it."

Laughing, Levi continues, "I guess we're considering making the move. Thank you for your interest. I'm Sergeant Levi Spencer, and here's my number." He grabs a napkin and writes it down for Buford.

"Military, eh?" Buford's eyes drop to Levi's cane for a second.

"Yes, sir. Army. Up until a few months ago. Sorry, it's just a habit to introduce myself that way."

"Nothing to be sorry about. Thank you for your service. How would you like to sing the national anthem at the Fourth of July celebration coming up? I was tasked with finding the right person because I'm on the town council and know a lot of singers, but the one I had is having a family issue and won't be in town for the Fourth. We'd love to have a soldier do it."

"That would be an amazing honor, sir. I'd be delighted. Thank you."

Buford turns to the room and sticks two fingers into his

mouth. He makes a shrill whistle that stops everyone from talking immediately. "Listen up, folks! This here is Sergeant Levi Spencer, and I'm sure you're all planning to make it to the Fourth of July shindig at the high school. Levi is going to be singing our national anthem for us, so be sure to get your tickets if you haven't yet, and we'll see you there!" A raucous cheer goes up amid clapping and stamping of feet. He turns to Levi and says, "You'll be on the stage right before the fireworks go off."

"Do we need tickets?" Brooke asks me quietly while Levi and Buford shake hands.

"Nope. Military personnel and their families get in free."

What a night. I was already excited about the celebration, and now I can look forward to watching Levi perform again too. I'm glad he agreed to bring his uniform.

CHAPTER
Seventeen

It turns out we're not just joining Juni, Jack, and Asher for the Fourth of July extravaganza. Skyler also asked his parents to meet us there, and I invited Levi's sister Kate to bring her family down and surprise Levi. They arrive an hour before we plan to leave, and Levi looks so happy to see them he has tears in his eyes. Everyone swamps him with hugs and kisses, telling him he looks great.

We all head over to the high school football field that is barely recognizable as a sports venue. Red, white, and blue is the color scheme of the day for everyone's dress as well as the decorations, and flags of all sizes fly proudly wherever someone has been able to attach one. There is a stage at one end with constant entertainment—everything from a kid doing a magic show to a barbershop quartet to baton twirlers to the local ballet school giving a recital. The little ones are adorable, and Levi's niece Lulu announces immediately to her parents that she wants to learn to "Do ballet and wear a pink tutu."

The rest of the area is populated with games, food trucks, and booths filled with local Honeybee Hollow crafts. The Sewing Bees seem to have a booming business going with their fine needlework projects, and there are several booths selling t-shirts of all kinds. There are delicious-looking baked goods, jams and preserves, and more flavors of honey and beeswax products from local beekeepers than I ever imagined possible. Kids are getting their faces painted in patriotic designs, and a guy dressed as Uncle Sam is handing out balloons non-stop. The lawn in front of the stage is covered with blankets and yard furniture where people are sitting with their families and enjoying the festivities. No matter who performs on that stage, the applause is raucous and enthusiastic.

You have to love small-town enthusiasm.

It's a little weird, I have to admit, to see Levi and Skyler dressed like they're almost ready for combat, even though they aren't the only ones in uniform. They toned down their uniforms to the basics—meaning they aren't wearing Kevlar vests or helmets, and they certainly aren't armed. But they do look official to me at least, all decked out in boots and camou-flage. As the day progresses, and the temperature rises, they both take off their jackets. Skyler's scars are visible this way, but so are the impressive muscles on both guys, earning them some—well...a *lot* of stares. I admit they're desperately handsome.

Levi is still using his cane, so the two of them spend most of the day explaining things about being a soldier to curious kids and accepting thanks for service from grateful citizens. I'm so proud of them and wish I had a nickel for every time a pretty girl hugs them.

I've also noticed that a lot of friends and acquaintances are making a point to visit with Skyler, and he's happy to talk to them. He's apparently popular in this town. That's understandable with his affable personality and good looks.

Finally, we all sit down with Skyler's parents to have dinner. They had already staked out a large area for us to gather. I can't help noticing that Levi doesn't eat much. "Butterflies about singing?" I ask him quietly.

"Hmm, not really, but it's hard to sing on a full stomach. Maybe I can save something and have it afterward." He may not admit it, but I'm positive Levi's nervous. His eyes are darting around like he's looking for an enemy or an escape. I try to catch Skyler's eye to alert him, but I find that he's already keeping a very close eye on Levi. Maybe he's been acting jumpy for longer than I realized. There isn't a lot I can do, so I reach over and stroke Levi's back. His muscles are tight. Maybe the large crowd is starting to get to him. The number of people gathered for the fireworks has grown quickly.

After a while, Juni, Jack, and Asher join our group with exhausted smiles. As they sit down, Juni explains that she had been running a food stand with Jack and Asher's help. The three of them had been serving coffee and pastries all day. About a half-hour ago, they sold their last red-white-and-blue berry cupcake and closed up shop. "We grabbed the first food we could find and headed this way!" Juni says, leaning against Jack's shoulder with a happy sigh.

We introduce everyone, and they quickly become part of the family. Lulu immediately makes her way over to Asher, tells him he looks like a giant, and grills him about his tattoos. He takes it all in stride and answers her with good humor, smiling the whole time. I wonder idly whether they plan to have children after they move into their new house. I'll have to ask Juni privately; that's certainly too nosy of a question in a large gathering.

As expected, Lulu tells her parents she wants to get tattoos like her friend Asher. "He's pretty!" she exclaims, and I have to squelch a giggle. He's a ruggedly handsome guy who has that massive Samoan look going on, and "pretty" doesn't do him justice.

The grassy area where people are eating is getting more and more crowded. I'm glad we brought chairs because I couldn't see Levi trying to be comfortable sitting on the ground and getting up again gracefully. He's getting better all the time, but some things are still a struggle.

And speaking of struggles…as Skyler explained, there are no noisy fireworks planned for later, but you just never know what to expect in a large crowd.

A group of rowdy teenagers has congregated right behind us, and they seem to be getting more and more boisterous. Suddenly, there is a series of loud bangs when one of the kids pops a whole bunch of balloons in rapid succession, making a couple of the girls with them scream.

Levi loses it. He flies out of his chair and hits the ground, grabbing me on his way down. I shriek in bafflement and then realize he's having a PTSD episode from the bangs and screams behind his head.

I try to let him know everything is okay and we're safe. I try to haul him up into a sitting position, and then Skyler wraps him in his arms. We both speak to him in soft voices, telling him over and over what the noises were. Levi has a wild look in his eyes, and he's completely unfocussed. It amazes me that even in his panic, Levi's instinct was to protect me from harm.

Jack scoots closer to us saying, "Man, I can't stand those stupid things either. I've hated balloons ever since my parents hired a terrible clown for my fifth birthday party and we had the Balloons of Doom disaster." He lowers his voice and adds, "I peed my pants." I try not to snicker, and I appreciate Jack's attempt at lightening the situation.

Somehow, the message finally gets through to Levi, who says, "Thanks, guys. I think I need to go take a walk and find a quiet spot for a while." We help him up, and I see that Asher —who is at least six-foot-five or more—is having a quiet chat with the kids who thought popping balloons was a fun thing to do. With a no-nonsense look on his face, Asher looms over them and points out the various servicemen and women around them. The only word I can make out is "respect."

Before Levi can settle himself enough to take his walk to calm down, one of the kids approaches him looking mortified. "I'm sorry, sir," he says. "I didn't mean to make you upset."

"I know you didn't," Levi says and shakes his hand. "No lasting harm done. It's just an ingrained reaction that I hope to eventually be able to get rid of." He smiles at the kid, but it's wobbly, and he's still trying to control his breathing. I haven't let go of him yet.

People around us were obviously aware of what happened. They're all subdued and trying not to stare. I guess it's a learning experience for a lot of them.

Skyler takes Levi by the arm, helping him navigate out of the crowded area. Levi seems to be limping worse than he has in several weeks; it makes sense—crashing to the ground must have hurt like hell. I decide to let them handle this themselves since Skyler knows better what to talk about with Levi—if they talk at all. Instead, I give Jack a quick hug and tell him, "Thanks for sharing; your story seemed to help bring him around."

"Hey, it was true. I was traumatized for years after that experience. I can't even imagine what those guys went through in *combat*. Their shit was real."

About half an hour later, Levi and Skyler return to our group. Levi is walking a little better, but I'm still worried about his pain level. The sun is setting, and the guys both look calm now. They're smiling as they sit back down, and soon the mayor takes the stage which is now lit up with spotlights. He welcomes everyone and tells them all how proud he is to serve as mayor for this wonderful community. He tells a bit about the history of the town and thanks the sponsors for the event. It's a typical mayor-type speech on a patriotic holiday that goes on just a little too long.

As he speaks, the high school band quietly fills up the stage behind him with the band director. Finally, the mayor winds down his talk and asks, "Will all of the military personnel please make their way up here and line up in front of the stage?" He waits as they file forward, during which time the band members make a bunch of squawky noises as they tune up.

When everyone, including Levi and Skyler, stands at attention in front of the crowd, the mayor says, "On this most patriotic of days, please everyone, show your appreciation for these brave men and women who have given so much of themselves to serve and fight for our beautiful country." Cheers go up, and the applause is deafening. As it dies down at last, he says,

"Now if you would all please join the Honeybee Hollow High School Band and sing

'America the Beautiful.'" He steps to the side of the stage as the band director takes over.

The band isn't the best I've ever heard, and the voices are a mixed bag, but the whole thing is so enthusiastic and genuine, I'm on the verge of tears throughout the song. I look over at Skyler's parents, and they are singing arm in arm—just as moved as I am.

When the applause subsides, the mayor takes the mic again as the band files out. "Thank you, kids, that was just wonderful. And now we have a special treat, I'm told. We have a brand-new Honeybee Hollow resident among us who is going to sing our national anthem, and I've heard from several people that he's exceptional. Please once again put your hands together and welcome to the stage US Army Sergeant Levi Spencer."

Well, our new residency is news to me! I guess the community already wants to claim Levi as their own. The thought makes me warm inside.

Skyler carefully helps Levi up the stairs to the stage. I feel awful that I hadn't even considered how he'd manage the eight or so steps. Once they reach the top, Skyler lets go and stands proudly at the edge of the stage. Levi approaches the mic, shakes the mayor's hand politely, and thanks him. The mayor asks everyone to stand and then steps away.

I've heard Levi sing many times. But his a capella rendition of "The Star-Spangled Banner" cuts me to my very soul. He looks so brave and handsome, and his voice doesn't miss a trick. He's impassioned, proud, and utterly amazing. I chance a glance around at the crowd, and jaws are dropping everywhere. Tears are streaming down Levi's sister's face, and I'm sure I look the same. His brother-in-law seems to be capturing the entire performance on his cell phone, as are a few hundred other folks in the audience. I want to kick myself for not recording him too.

I look over at Skyler, who is standing proudly at attention with his hand over his heart, and I can see pure love in his eyes as he watches Levi and listens to the magic of his voice. My heart pounds as I wonder, *Why didn't I realize it before? He's* in love *with Levi just as much as I am.* Well…he has good taste. I think back to what I've been told about their horrible experience in Afghanistan and how they risked their own lives to save each other, and I understand the dependency and respect they have for one another, but I also see that it runs deeper than that. If those two aren't in love, I'm nuts. Part of me wonders why I don't feel threatened or jealous, but I'm okay with it. No matter what kind of love it is, it's beautiful and to be respected. I don't feel as though anything is being taken away from me, only added. Levi can have two people who love him. He's a lucky man for it.

As soon as Levi sings the line, "And the rocket's red glare, the bombs bursting in air," the silent fireworks begin in the sky, and the crowd gasps and points. Levi continues the verse to its end like a champ, and finally waves to everyone with a big smile before exiting the stage to thunderous applause—and with Skyler's help.

The crowd settles into their seats, and the magnificent fireworks show continues with a rousing musical soundtrack that begins as soon as the guys are off the stage. The display is breathtakingly beautiful and inspiring, but I know the most memorable part of the entire celebration was Levi.

When the grand finale fades away, and the last crescendo of the music is nothing but a memory, everyone claps once more, but this time it's more of a polite applause. It feels to me like clapping in church. Everyone is smiling and happy—but subdued. Several people come over to thank Levi and welcome him to the community. When he can get a word in edgewise, he introduces me to well-wishers, but they truly only have eyes for him. I can tell he's drained by all of this, and I could not be prouder of him.

We're all exhausted and half asleep by the time we make it back to Skyler's house. It's been a long, emotional day. Kate and her family are taking over the upstairs tonight, so they don't have to drive home so late. After quick showers, Levi and I fall into bed, and I snuggle into his warm embrace. I can't help but whisper, "So…we're officially moving here?"

Chuckling sleepily, Levi answers, "Guess so. At least that's what everyone tells me. You okay with that?"

"Absolutely." He squeezes me tighter. "Levi? I'm pretty sure Skyler is in love with you. Did you know?"

Dead silence. But I feel a certain *stirring* in his boxers. Smiling to myself, I pull the covers away, scoot down, and slide his pants out of the way to show Levi how much I love him too…with my mouth. He doesn't have any objections, and soon I feel him tensing and thrusting and finally releasing into me.

"I love you so much," he mumbles. "Tomorrow…" and he falls asleep. I understand. It's been quite a day.

Eighteen

SKYLER

WHAT AN EXPERIENCE THAT WAS YESTERDAY. EVEN THOUGH some of what happened was tough, Levi managed to pull himself together and wow everyone. I was so proud of him, and I could tell Brooke was relieved as well as thrilled.

I'm beyond happy that I asked them to come down here for the Fourth celebration, and okay, I did have an ulterior motive and hoped to get them to stay. But thanks to the town gossip chain that never gets the facts quite right and spreads like wildfire, my friends were made to feel like important new *residents* of the town already. I don't know if it was because Levi and Brooke felt obligated to be polite or because they love it here that much already, but I'm not going to argue with their announcement that they plan to stay. It'll be good for Levi, and anything that's good for him is good for Brooke. And good for me.

It's still early in the morning, but when I wander out to the kitchen and head for the coffee maker, I see that someone already made a fresh pot. Levi and his sister are sitting outside in the relative cool of the morning, and they seem to be having a serious conversation over their steaming mugs. I don't know whether to join them because I'm hesitant to interfere in a family matter. My decision is made for me, however, when Levi notices me, smiles, and beckons me to come out and join them. I nod and grab a stack of plates and a box of muffins and scones that I load onto a tray with my coffee before I head out.

Levi grins and thanks me, then tells Kate, "Try the blueberry muffins. I don't know what Juni does to them, but they're amazing."

Kate's expression remains somber and concerned, but she does go for a muffin saying, "Juni's nice. She and Brooke really seem to have hit it off." Looking at me, she asks, "Tell me, Skyler, does what happened to Levi last night happen very often?"

"You mean, does he blow everyone's socks off with his singing?" I ask with a cocky grin. "It's getting to be a habit."

She narrows her eyes at me. "I'm referring to his reaction to stress. His PTSD. He doesn't seem to want to open up about it with me, but I promised our parents I'd find out how he's really doing."

I don't want to shrug it off; I know she's concerned. But Levi's response makes sense to me. I try to explain, saying, "Levi and I both have issues with it. His reaction was understandable last night. He was already tired and obviously experiencing significant pain from walking around all day—as well as feeling nervous about getting up and singing. Add some thoughtless kids to the mix who startled him, and it's a perfect storm for a bit of a meltdown. His immediate reaction to protect Brooke from possible danger was noble and actually pretty endearing."

"I agree that he was noble. He always is. But…shouldn't he be over all this by now?"

I give a humorless laugh, shaking my head. "Seriously? There aren't any rules or timelines, Kate. Levi's doing great." I know she's concerned, but I wish she'd butt out. "Excuse me for saying this, but he sure doesn't need any more pressure to hurry up and get back to what *you* think is 'normal.' I know you love your brother, but let him be. Please."

Levi reaches over and grasps my hand, giving both Kate and me something to look at, and I'm just as startled by it as she is when he says to her, "I was about to explain—just when Skyler showed up—that he knows of a great therapist I can talk to. And now that Brooke and I are sure where we want to settle, I'll take care of that soon." His hand slips away, and I miss it.

Kate looks at me and then looks at Levi with a quizzical frown, but her expression clears, and she forces a smile at her brother. "That's all I can ask, and I'm glad you told me. Are you planning to buy a house?"

Levi squints a little and says, "Hmm, not sure. We haven't discussed it yet."

She nods and asks, "Do you think you're finally going to pursue your music seriously?"

He smiles in my direction, rolling his eyes slightly. "Big sisters. What are you gonna do with 'em?" I shrug because I'm an only child, so what do I know about siblings? He looks back at Kate and says, "We have a lot of decisions to make, sis. I've thought about it some, but we'll see. Please relax." He's certainly polite and patient with her. I'm ready to tell her to keep her nose in her own fucking business, but I stay silent. I've said enough. The music business is a tough one to break into, and I don't know how much stress he needs, no matter how talented he is.

With that, a tiny pink-clad tornado comes whooshing out of the house hollering, "Uncle Levi!" She runs to him, followed by her father—who looks a little frazzled—carrying her baby brother. Lulu reaches up to hug Levi, who swings her up carefully onto his lap, and I notice he positions her on his good side. Lulu begins a long-winded and completely one-sided conversation about the pretty pink tutu she's going to wear when she becomes a "ballaweena." Then she hops down, throws her arms over her head and attempts to spin around a few times, only to end up landing on her behind in a fit of giggles. Levi is charmed by the whole thing and has a huge grin on his face.

Brooke also joins us, greeting everyone happily. She looks radiant as she gives Levi a blinding smile. I wonder if things heated up for them last night. Then I chastise myself. It's none of my business.

We all settle into a conversation about the amazing fireworks show they put on last night, and the pressure seems to be off of Levi for now. I'm relieved for him and promise myself to give him the therapist's contact information later today after Kate and her family are gone.

A couple of hours later, the extra guests are all packed and ready to get back to Lexington, promising to visit again soon. It was great to have them, but I'm also happy to have Levi and Brooke to myself again. We all wave goodbye, and as their car pulls out of sight, we each look at one another, and the air seems charged. I glance up at the sky, and there is no evidence of a summer thunderstorm, but there is definite electricity in the air.

"So…Skyler…" Levi says, looking me straight in the eye. I wonder what's on his mind because it seems to be something momentous. "Brooke has an opinion, and when she voiced it to me, it made me think about what you said the other day." He pauses, but I stay silent. I'm not sure where this is going, but he looks serious and far from angry. When I say nothing, he continues softly, "It's me, isn't it?"

"You? What is you?"

He smirks. "The 'other person.' The one you're attracted to the same way you're attracted to Brooke."

"I, ah…" Suddenly, it's hard to look at him, and I feel my cheeks burning.

Levi isn't finished. "I'm flattered. I'm happy you think Brooke is amazing, and I've also come to realize I'm attracted to you." Brooke's eyes widen at his admission.

"You are?" I can't answer above a choked whisper.

"Of course. So is Brooke. You and I are both a couple of hunks, man! Nothing but the best for my gorgeous wife." All three of us crack up, but it's that edgy, nervous kind of laughter rather than the "Haha, that was hilarious" kind. It dies out to an awkward silence, and I have no idea what to say.

Apparently, Levi does though. He takes Brooke's hand as we wander back into the house. He stops and asks, "Anyone up for another coffee…or a beer?" When he gets a "no thanks" from me and a shake of her head from Brooke, he directs her into the living room and sits at one end of the sofa, pulling her down next to him so she's in the middle. With a jut of his chin and the motion of his eyes, he directs me to sit on her other side. I do so slowly and gently as though I'm sitting on eggs. I'm a nervous wreck. *What is he up to*? That beer is sounding better and better because my mouth is dry. I try to look nonchalant, but Levi smirks at me and winks.

Without preamble, Levi begins, "Last night, Brooke told me her opinion and then pleasured me, and I was so overcome,

I passed out afterward. I think she needs a reward for being so patient with me because I haven't properly made love to her since before we were deployed. And, Skyler, I think you need special thanks for bringing us here to your home and making us fall in love with Honeybee Hollow and its residents. More than anything, I want to see the two people I care the most about in the whole world enjoy each other in a physical way. I'm getting turned on just thinking about it, and Brooke, your eyes are dilated as I mention this. So, Sky, please kiss Brooke. Kiss her like you mean it. You're both so perfect. I *need* to see you enjoying each other, and Brooke needs some loving. I've been a bad husband."

"You have not been a bad husband, Levi. I love you with all my heart. I…"

He interrupts her, "You've sure been using up a lot of batteries for someone whose husband does a great job of loving you."

Brooke gasps and looks down. I don't like the embarrassment on her face, so I tell her, "Hey, when a woman pleasures herself, it's hot. Don't be shy about it." Her eyes look deeply into mine, and suddenly I don't care if this is the worst idea I've ever had in my life. The tension is going to kill me if I don't taste that mouth I've lusted over forever. I lean closer to her.

Brooke doesn't pull away. Her mouth opens, and she licks her lips. I hear Levi growl, "Yesss, baby, do it."

I lose the rest of the distance between us and softly touch

my lips to hers. Instantly, a soft kiss isn't enough, so I increase the pressure, and I hear her whimper. But her whimper turns into a sigh. She lets go of Levi's hand and reaches for my thigh. She lays her hand on me, and it ignites something inside me. I scoot closer to her and try to figure out what to do with my hands.

Levi begins raising her shirt and says to her in a deep voice, "Yes, that's it. Kiss him like you kiss me. Show him what he means to us."

What do I mean to them? I wonder. Levi has a hand in her shirt, playing with her tits, and he leans in close so he can kiss her neck. I've never been so close to two people at once, and this is a strange sensation. But it's also a rush—I can't deny it. Levi's other hand reaches around behind Brooke and begins to stroke my face and play with my hair. *Holy cow*! I've never been touched in a gentle way like this by a dude. I…uh… like it.

Brooke seems to be relaxing. She starts kissing me back with as much enthusiasm as I'm putting into it. She welcomes my tongue into her mouth and duels with me with her tongue. She feels playful and passionate at the same time. Levi keeps whispering encouragement and tells us how sexy we are. I'm having a hard time believing this is happening, but I'm getting so aroused, it's uncomfortable, so I have to squirm around a little until my junk isn't choking in my jeans. Levi chuckles. He knows what's going on.

All at once, Brooke pulls away from me and turns to Levi

with a worried look. "Honey, are you sure this is alright?" she asks. "I know you encouraged it, but are you okay?"

"Never better, babe. I promise. I'm so hard right now I could pound nails with my dick. And I love seeing you all hot and turned on. Sky could make you really happy, I bet. He's so sexy, and he's crazy about you too."

This seems unreal. I'm glad Brooke slowed us down a little though. I want to jump her bones in the worst way, but I'm also worried about what Levi might feel if we were to actually do what he says he wants. But Brooke blows my mind when she tells Levi, "I told you I thought Skyler was in love with *you* though—not with me."

"Eh, we'll see. He looks pretty fond of you to me."

So the fact that I'm in love with him doesn't faze him in the least? Does he even care? I hope this isn't some weird game he's playing. He looks pretty damn serious though.

Levi reaches for Brooke's hand and places it right on his dick. "Feel this? I've had such a rough time with feeling anything for months, and now that I'm here with you and Skyler, I'm back to being me again. It's like I love you even more than ever, and Skyler, you're part of the whole picture now. I don't know if I'm making any sense, but when I saw how effortless Juni, Jack, and Asher's affection for one another is, I…feel…I feel like I need that too. What they have seems beautiful and right. I know I've always had strong feelings for you, Skyler, but it's only now that I also see it's more than us being best buddies. It's…everything."

I want to respond to this, I really do. Levi has opened up in a way that I admire like crazy. He's brave and deserves my truth. Unfortunately, as soon as I begin to try to unscramble my brain and get my thoughts in order, there's a knock on the front door. My immediate thought is that I'm glad someone wasn't trying to come in through the back where all the windows would have given them a clear view of our three-person pile-up on the couch. The knock sounds once more, and before I can stand up to go see who it is, the door opens, and a familiar—and unwelcome—squeaky voice calls out, "Skyler, honey? Are you home?" I ought to start locking the damn doors.

CHAPTER
Nineteen

WHAT THE ABSOLUTE FUCK? SOME CHICK JUST COMES waltzing into Skyler's house carrying a huge picnic basket and wearing the tiniest pair of red shorts I've ever seen. Sure, she's cute and has great legs, but…come on! Obvious much? Okay, maybe this is judgmental and hypercritical of me after wearing a thong around Skyler, but why is she here, and why does she think she can barge in like this?

"Cherry!" Skyler exclaims as he jumps up off the couch like his ass is on fire. "What are you doing here?" He does not sound pleased.

"Silly, I told you yesterday that we should get together,

and you agreed, so here I am." She sets down her basket and strikes a "tah-dah!" pose—just in case anyone missed her.

"What, are you nuts? I didn't agree to anything."

"Sure you did, honey. You clearly said, 'Uh huh!'"

I can't help snorting and telling her, "When a guy says, 'Uh huh,' you ought to know by now it means he isn't listening to you. Here's a tip…look at where his eyes are focused. If he's not looking at you and grunts, you're just part of the background noise."

This Cherry chick ignores me like I'm invisible, but her eyes go wide as she catches sight of Levi and exclaims, "Ooh! You're the 'Oh Say Can You See' guy from last night! You were really good! What are *you* doing here?" She seems to have developed a severe butt shimmy as she wiggles and giggles.

Skyler says a little too loudly, "Levi is *supposed* to be here, unlike you!"

As if she hadn't heard Skyler, she continues addressing Levi, "It was a really hard song, and it musta been extra, extra hard to sing it Acapulco!"

I start to laugh, but quickly cover it with a cough.

She pries her eyes off Levi long enough to glare at Skyler. "But honey, I *told* you I'd bring you a picnic. I thought we could have a romantic lunch out by the creek."

"I don't remember you saying anything of the sort. I never agreed to it, and I'm not your honey. I think you need to leave. We're busy."

Wow, she might be a tad—okay a lot—pushy, but that's harsh. I didn't know Skyler had it in him to be rude, especially when someone is delivering food—even though something in her basket smells burnt. I have to say my tummy is growling, even though I wasn't hungry until she showed up. It dawns on me that I've only had coffee and one little scone all day. I have every right to be hungry. Maybe even *hangry* by now with this charade going on.

"But I brought all of this fried chicken, potato salad, and a banana cream pie." I can't help whimpering as she whines this, even if something is burnt. Why does she have to mention all of this food? "I have wine too! And there's enough to feed an army! And you said…"

Skyler semi-bellows, "I didn't say anything!"

"Why are you in such a bad mood?" she asks him in a little girl voice that makes my head begin to ache. Maybe it's my advanced state of hangrytude.

That's when Levi looks at her with narrowed eyes and says, "I vaguely remember you from last night. You came up to us to talk, but weren't you with your husband? Or boyfriend? I remember now he wanted you to quit talking and go sit down with him."

"Oh, uh, we're not married."

"But he *is* your boyfriend," Levi persists.

"Uh…" she stalls. "Kinda, I guess."

Levi scoffs as Skyler says, "Yeah, just like I was 'kinda' your boyfriend when you cheated on me?" He definitely looks steamed now. "I distinctly remember you agreeing to go steady with me, and the next thing I knew I saw you with Marty Brubacher making out in his car in the parking lot at the Sock Hop, and your blouse was on the dashboard."

"Steady?" I ask Skyler with a tiny snort. "Who does that?"

He turns a grumpy face to me and says, "We were seventeen, Brooke."

"All the more reason you should be over it by now!" she pouts at him in that same cringy tone and stamps her foot.

Skyler fumes at her, "Once a cheater, always a cheater."

"Well, what were *you* doing at the Sock Hop without me then, huh?"

"We've been over and over this before, Cherry. Like I told you several years ago, I was picking up take-out for my family! We'd had a long day, and my mom didn't feel like cooking."

"Oh, yeah." She looks down at her feet. Cute sandals. I wonder if she got them here in town. "Well, you should be over that by now, Skyler," she repeats, only this time it's in a grumpy voice.

"So, what's *your current boyfriend* doing today?" he asks her.

"Oh, he's…uh…working…" she trails off as Skyler advances on her. He walks past her and opens the door.

Skyler's voice softens as he says, "Then take this picnic of yours to his workplace and surprise *him*. Be a decent human being to at least one man in your life. He seemed like a good guy."

"You don't want me?"

"Sorry, no. Not for years."

She points her nose in the air. "Well, okay then. If you change your mind, I can leave you my number."

"No thanks."

Cherry gives him one last sad-puppy-dog-eyes look and licks her lips. She juts out her tits that aren't nearly as impressive as her booty and switches her attention over to Levi. "What about you, handsome?"

Levi flinches and tells her, "Not now, not ever. I'm here with my wife, for one thing, and Skyler is my best friend for another. Catch a fucking clue, lady. It's time for you to go. And it's rude to walk into other people's houses."

"Well, at least my boyfriend isn't scared of a bunch of stupid balloons! You big sissy!" With a nasty laugh, she turns and flounces out of the house. Skyler follows her out and stands at the open door, watching to see if Little Miss Hotpants is really driving away.

I turn my attention to Levi who's gone a livid shade of red, and he's shaking. This isn't good. I wrap my arms around him and hold on tight.

There is the sound of tires spinning on the gravel drive, and Skyler finally comes back inside and locks the door. He looks furious.

I guess the mood has been ruined for now.

Skyler assures us, "Don't believe Cherry went to a lot of trouble to fix a picnic. She can't cook worth a damn. She's the only person I knew who failed home ec. three times. My strong guess is she went through the frozen food section of the Piggly Wiggly and got the chicken and the pie. Their deli does make a good potato salad, at least." He shrugs and shakes his head.

After some rather uninspired peanut butter sandwiches, apples, and potato chips for lunch, I get an idea that I hope will elevate the general atmosphere. "Hey, guys, I've never been fishing. Do you think you two could show me how it's done?"

They readily smile and agree. We spend the next few hours out at the creek. It's serene out there, so by the time we have enough fish for dinner, we're all relaxed again and cheered up. Thank you, Mother Nature.

When we get back to the house, Skyler sets us up to show me how to clean the fish (gross), and Levi heads in to call Skyler's therapist's office for an appointment. He joins us a few minutes later to finish the cleaning and says, "Somehow, just knowing I have an online chat set up with him in a couple days makes me feel better. Thanks, Sky."

The fish are delicious. I feel unusually accomplished by eating a dinner that I helped catch and clean. It's so different from shopping at the Piggly Wiggly.

After dinner, I ask Levi if he'd like to join me in the

shower, and his eyes light up. "Can Skyler come too?" he whispers to me.

A shiver goes through me as I look deep into my husband's eyes. He's so expectant and cheerful; I turn to Skyler, who's bent over as he loads the dishwasher, and I try for a nonchalant tone. "Hey, Skyler, Levi and I are going to take a shower, but Levi wants to know if you'll join us. What do you think?"

His head snaps up, and he stares at me a moment. Then he looks at Levi as he straightens his back.

CHAPTER
Twenty

Levi

Oh my God. This might be the moment of truth. Brooke looks calm and ready, and Skyler hasn't even blinked yet. He's just staring at me. He clears his throat and takes a deep breath before asking me, "Levi, are you absolutely sure you want to start this? It might change everything between us."

"I'm counting on it, Sky. I've felt dead inside for so long, and it was such a relief and a rush to see you kissing Brooke today. I just know that if you will do…well…*more* with her, I'm going to love it. And she needs it. Just look at this beautiful woman. She needs someone to fuck her…"

He interrupts my tirade to say, "But when Cherry was bugging you earlier today, I couldn't help but notice that you were adamant about not messing around because of your *wife*. You're clearly protective of your relationship, and I care too much for both of you to ruin it."

"I adore Brooke. You know that, but I've been useless to her. She's been good about not complaining, but I know she's been dying for some good loving. Please, Sky, do it for me and do it for Brooke. I want to be right there to see it up close. I know I'll be able to feel what you're doing. I *need* it as much as Brooke does. And I promise I won't care any less for either of you if...*when* this happens."

Brooke takes my hand and pulls me nearer to Skyler. She takes his hand too and says in that sexy voice of hers, "It's going to be okay, Skyler. Levi knows what he's talking about. We'll start slowly. That's why we thought we could try a shower together. We don't have to do anything heavy, but we can at least get used to each other...naked. If Levi says he needs this, I can't tell him no. I love him too much to deny him. And I know *you* care for him too much to deny him as well."

Skyler nods. He still doesn't look completely convinced, so we may have to work on him a bit more.

So this is how it starts. I can't even begin to express how much I love Brooke. I'm sure she's still a little worried, but she trusts me to be honest about what I want and need, and she trusts Skyler to love us both back.

Wordlessly, we head for the master suite and go into the bedroom that Brooke and I share. We all stand facing each other for a moment before I begin to help Brooke out of her clothes. As each piece of clothing falls to the floor, I watch as Skyler's eyes dilate with interest and his breathing accelerates. She's spectacular in all her naked glory, and I love to see the brave expression in her face that says, "This is me. I've worked hard on this body, so take it or leave it." Skyler's eyes lock on her smooth pussy, and he licks his lips. "Laser hair removal," she tells him.

"Thank you," he whispers reverently. "You're perfect."

Brooke and I step to Skyler and pull his t-shirt off over his head. She goes to work on his fly, and he can't stop staring at her the whole time. I think to myself, *Take it all in, buddy; she's amazing. Enjoy*!

Once his pants and briefs hit the floor and Brooke gets an eyeful of him, Skyler grins and assists Brooke in disrobing me. Unlike when undressing Skyler, she kisses each new exposed bit of my skin. I'm a little shy about the scarring and muscle damage, but neither of them takes any notice at all. Brooke's seen it all before—even when it was a lot worse than this—but not Skyler. I guess he has his own scars and isn't easily turned off by mine. He steps away and heads for the shower, giving us the full view of the terrible damage done to his shoulder, but I can't help staring at his ass as he saunters off. I never knew I'd be attracted to a man's butt, but his is firm and round with the same cute dimples as the ones Brooke has over hers. Brooke catches my eye and wiggles her eyebrows at me with a smirk. I can't help but laugh silently.

She caught me ogling and thinks it's sexy. Have I mentioned how crazy I am about this woman?

Skyler reaches in and fiddles with the knobs until he's satisfied. It's a nice, roomy shower with a generous bench seat inside, or I'd never have suggested this. Skyler and I are both large guys. Now I just have to be careful not to slip because I have no interest in taking my cane in for a wash.

As soon as I start to think about it, I feel a surge of panic. The fear of falling and damaging my weak hip even more haunts me. Brooke sweetly puts her arm around my waist as though she's being affectionate, but I know she's trying to help me balance. My heartbeat calms again. I kiss her neck and whisper in her ear, "Thanks, babe." She can take that any way she wants.

"Okay, come on in, it's all warmed up," Skyler tells us as he steps into the shower. Is his voice a little shaky, or does he just sound funny over the water? I'll take the second option. He can't be that nervous, can he?

But when we open the door and Brooke helps me over the threshold, I see immediately that Skyler is fully hard. Obviously, he's excited about whatever we're going to do, and he's not shy about letting us see him. I've seen his naked body before, but never in this state, and I must say, his boner is impressive. Brooke helps me take a seat, but when I start to lose my balance a little, Skyler rushes to help. As I plunk down onto the tile bench, I'm eye to eye with Skyler's junk. I swallow and try not to stare, but I can't deny the sight is doing things to me. I look up at him and can't help but wink. "Nice!" I tell Skyler with a cocked eyebrow and a jut of my chin. Skyler's expression is hard to read, but I'm going with the notion that he's pleased. "Why don't you and I work on Brooke and get her all soaped up and clean?" I ask him, and to Brooke, I say, "Move over between us so I can do your back while Sky gets acquainted with your front?"

"Happy to, handsome!" she responds and steps into position.

Skyler reaches around and grabs a bottle of body wash. He squirts a glob in my hand and one in his before setting it down next to me. Taking a deep breath, he begins coating Brooke's shoulders and arms with the gel and gets her all sudsy. I'm doing the same to her back, but I quickly drop down to her delectable ass and rub all over it.

Brooke makes some happy noises and then tells me, "Levi, give me a squirt too, I want to work on Skyler. I feel silly getting all the attention." I comply and squirt more gel into each of our hands.

"Don't be shy, Sky," I tell him. "Her tits are really sensitive."

Skyler locks eyes with me and then moves both hands to Brooke's breasts. I start to play with the crack of her ass at the same time he massages her tits. Brooke squirms a little and sucks in a breath. I can't see them, but from experience I can guess that her nipples are diamond-hard right now and begging to be sucked and tweaked. Skyler's gaze moves to her chest, and he grins. "So pretty," he says softly.

Her hands rove over his abdomen, and she makes appreciative humming sounds as she feels up his impressive six-pack. This is starting off great. Brooke widens her stance in a clear invitation to explore. Yes!

I'm playing with her hole with one hand and stroking her cheeks with the other, knowing how much Brooke enjoys ass play. I start to probe it a little. No fast moves when a butt is involved. I've learned that lesson. Timing is everything. I want to make her *need* the penetration. As I continue teasing and minuscule probing, I reach around and locate her clit. She's all slippery—just as I expected. I stroke her a few times, relishing the sound of her soft moans.

"Give me your hand, Sky. I want you to feel Brooke's pussy. She's so ready for you. Even with the water from the shower, she's all slick." I take his hand and place it between her legs. Then I remove mine, trusting he knows what to do now that he's there. I can tell by her movement and noises that he's playing her clit like an instrument. I knew it. This is perfect. "She likes a lot of pressure, so don't be too careful with her."

He smiles at me, and Brooke's voice is shaky as she says, "Oh, he's doing just fine. I'm…oh God…I'm going to come!" And she does. Wow. The man must have some hoo-ha magic in those hands of his. If I weren't so impressed, I might be jealous. Her stomach contracts, and she leans over as she spasms, gasping and moaning, "Skyler!"

I pull back and squirt a little more gel onto my hand, and as she spasms a second time, I slide my slick finger into her asshole. This sets off another contraction and a huge moan from her. "Levi! Oh, don't stop, please, you guys. This is… ohhh!"

"Can you put a finger in her, Sky? I want to see if we can feel each other inside her."

He does.

We can.

Wow.

"Oh my God, you guys!" she cries in a tone I've never heard from my wife before. We had a ridiculously good sex life before I was wounded, and I've felt horrible knowing I'd deprived her of it, but *this* is a new level. My heart is bursting with joy as I thrust in and out of her body, simultaneously stroking Skyler's finger inside her with nothing but a slippery, thin membrane separating us. I can just imagine what it would feel like if those digits were replaced by our dicks. I'm beginning to think maybe I could do it.

Skyler keeps playing with her clit with one hand and stroking in and out with the other, and Brooke keeps having spasms over and over until she finally says in a wobbly voice, "I don't think I can stand up anymore. Please. Enough."

"No. One more. I'm not done with you!" Skyler growls, and I'm a little shocked at his vehemence, but it turns me the fuck on too. I hadn't realized until now just how hard I am. It feels amazing, but I'm so swollen and stiff, I'm becoming uncomfortable. I eye her greedy asshole as it puckers with the next orgasm he wrings out of her and wonder…But I know I'd never be able to stand and fuck her in the shower. Too risky.

I kiss her butt cheek and ask, "Are you two ready to try more? Can we dry off and hit the bed, or was this enough for you?" I don't want to be too pushy.

Brooke looks over her shoulder at me and says, "We need to wash you too, my filthy husband."

Skyler hisses, and it's then I see that she has a good grip on his dick. She's stroking him up and down with both hands, and he's definitely enjoying the attention. *Atta girl, Brooke.*

I reluctantly let my hands fall away from her delicious body as she steps around to face me. "Why don't you lie back on the bench and get comfortable, Levi. I think Skyler and I can take care of you now." She looks at Sky who's eyeing me with what looks a little like hunger. My leaky boner is aching like a sonofabitch now. I need relief! He grabs the shower wand and sprays me down. The spray is hard and feels like needles on my ultrasensitive skin, but in a weirdly good way. When he directs it onto my groin, however, I cry out. He just grins and hands the shower gel to Brooke. He hangs the wand back up as she soaps me down, saying, "You too, Skyler. Help me clean him up."

It's an entirely new sensation to have four hands caressing my body, and I have to say I love every moment of it. After a bit, Brooke gets me to raise my knees and spread my legs. "Is your hip okay?" she asks, and I nod enthusiastically. I wouldn't stop this for anything. With a satisfied look, she directs Skyler, "I'm going to wash his balls and his crack, and you wash his dick. I need to see this." Well…who am I to say no? She's gone along with my plans to get Skyler to touch her, so I guess fair's fair. She gently soaps up my tender parts, and Skyler stares at me.

"Are you alright with me touching you?" he asks.

I nod again as Brooke tells us, "Just do it. You know you both want this. Don't try to pretend otherwise." She looks into my eyes and back at Skyler, saying, "Maybe you ought to kiss him first. After all, it's only polite." She snickers, and my stomach does a flip.

Slowly, Skyler lowers himself to his knees across from Brooke, and I realize this can't last too long. Their knees will give out on the hard tiles. Before I can even blink, his mouth is covering mine with a kiss that explodes my senses right out of the stratosphere. There is no hesitation. I get the impression he's done this hundreds of times in his own head already. I find I'm not shocked—I'm thrilled. His kiss tastes of desire and command. I've never thought about what it would be like to kiss a man, but his scruff gently abrades my skin and gives me an unaccustomed thrill while his tongue explores me like he's ready to plant a flag and stake his claim on new territory.

I want more, so I reach up and weave my hand into his hair, holding him in place. I try to shove my tongue into his mouth, but he's clearly setting the tone that he's in charge, and I'm at his mercy.

All too soon, he straightens up and leaves my mouth. But then an even greater euphoria barrels through me as he takes my ramrod dick in his hand and soaps it up. Up and down he strokes with his large, callused hands. He feels nothing like Brooke, but it's not better or worse; it's just a different sensation that takes nothing away from her style of loving me. My hips start to lift rhythmically of their own accord—adding some pain to my infinite pleasure—but it's beyond my ability to control the movement of my body as it synchronizes with his strokes. I can barely contain the delight firing through my body as Brooke's finger begins to probe me the way I did for her just moments ago. Deeper and deeper, she pushes her long finger into me until she finds that delicious spot. She begins to stroke my prostate as Skyler continues to pump me up and down. She stops momentarily, and I almost cry out, "No!" until I realize she's merely adding a second finger. She finds that spot again, and I don't think I'm going to last very long.

"Can you rinse him off, please, Skyler?"

He eyes her with a grin and says, "You bet!"

Again, the needle spray hits my ultrasensitive junk, and I cry out, "Aughh! Please!" I don't even know what I'm begging for, but I know I need relief in the worst way.

Sky replaces the shower wand and kneels back down. But Brooke is in his way this time because she just engulfed my entire dick down her throat. Her eyes catch Skyler's questioningly, and she slides her mouth off of me. "Come closer, Skyler," she tells him, and she kisses him. All this time, her hand is still busy with my prostate, and I'm losing my fucking mind. My two favorite people in all the world are leaning over me kissing each other like they've been doing it for years. I can't remember the last time I felt so happy. Brooke pulls back a little and looks down at my lonely, throbbing dick. Instead of swallowing it this time, she kisses along one side of it with her eyes on Sky the whole time. He takes a deep breath and acknowledges her silent command by leaning down and mirroring her actions on the other side of my dick! Skyler is kissing my boner! Jeeezus H. Christ! "Go ahead, Skyler, taste him," she prompts as she sits back a little.

Skyler looks into her eyes, then into mine with a silent question. I can't help but nod so fast I'm afraid my head will fall off. "Do it. *Please*," I croak.

And that is how it happens that Skyler Colfax, my best buddy in the world, gives me the first ever man-on-man blowjob of my life. Do I like it? *Fuck yes*! With Brooke's encouragement—telling him this is the sexiest thing she's ever seen—he sucks me down like a champ, and I'm ready to blow in seconds. I need to hang on though. I don't know if this is a one-time thing or something that will happen every day, but I'm not going to squander it. I squirm and moan, and that makes me feel Brooke's fingers inside of me even more. Sky can suck like nothing I've ever felt, and I realize it's a lost cause. I can't hold onto this. I cry out, "I'm coming!" Sky pulls back and thick ropes of cum shoot up into the air over and over as I holler a bunch of nonsense curse words. I paint my belly until there is nothing left in me. There is no embarrassment, just massive relief and excitement for what we've just done.

Panting, I ask, "Can you spray me down again, please? But watch the dick, I'm kinda sensitive right now." He grins and winks at me.

I think I'm falling in love. I admit I've always had a special attachment to Sky, but this new sensation transcends whatever I felt prior to today. Not only am I completely sated, I'm content as I look at my two beautiful lovers. It's like my heart has expanded to contain all the feelings I'm juggling inside.

Brooke pulls out and soaps up her hands while Skyler hoses me off with a much gentler spray setting this time. I tell them, "That was incredible. Thank you both!" My body is made of pudding right now, but I'm sure we need to see that Skyler has some relief too. I'm done with being in the water, so I suggest, "Can we get out of here, dry off, and take care of Skyler?"

They both grin at me. I guess that was the right thing to say.

Twenty-One

SKYLER

I DID NOT EXPECT THAT, AND I NEVER KNEW HOW MUCH I'D enjoy it. I hope Levi wasn't upset that I pulled off, but I wasn't quite ready to swallow cum the very first time I had a dick in my mouth. I mean, he *looked* happy enough. He has this goofy, dreamy look on his face that makes me laugh inside. Not that I think he's funny—it's more that I'm overjoyed and can't contain my feelings. It's like all of this good stuff is bubbling up in me and wants to come out. So I smile and look right into his eyes, hoping this conveys my happiness.

Brooke and I help Levi stand up, and she once again wraps her arm around him to help him navigate the wet tile safely. She whispers in his ear how much she loves him and kisses his neck. I find I'd like to do the same thing. Maybe even to both of them. It's too soon though. They would probably think I'm nuts declaring my love.

Once we're dried off, we make our way back into their bedroom. Both of the beds in the master suite rooms are wonderfully comfortable pillow-topped kings. I pull back the duvet and sit down. It's in my nature to tell them exactly what to do, but I wait for Levi to speak. I almost swallow my own damn tongue when he asks me, "What's your ultimate fantasy, Skyler? If you could do anything with Brooke right now, what would it be?"

A profound rush of desire pounds through my senses, and I have to swallow before I answer, "I'd fuck that amazing ass of hers." I look at Brooke—hoping like hell that didn't turn her off—and tell her, "You're so perfect, and I've been going crazy wanting your ass ever since the night in the hot tub when I saw you in that thong." I look at Levi and tell him, "I hope that doesn't piss you off."

Levi bursts into peals of laughter and pulls Brooke closer to his side. She has an enormous smile on her face. Finally, he calms down enough to say, "Brooke *loves* butt play. Doncha, babe?"

She squeezes her thighs together and says in a shivery voice, "God, yes. It's the best." She regards me with a sultry look and says, "I'll grab the lube if you grab a condom." I guess she came prepared if she brought lube, and I take this as a major positive sign. Was this wishful thinking or being ultra-prepared? I suppose it doesn't matter either way.

"I'm going to love this," Levi tells me gleefully as he plunks himself down on the bed. "We can both get her ready." He rubs his hands together.

I rush back through the bathroom and into my bedroom where I have to root around in a few drawers. *Where is it?* I finally locate a box and grab for it, hoping they aren't too ancient to use. Fuck! They're past the use-by date. Now what? I bring them back into their room anyway and tell them, "I have condoms, but they're expired."

"Haven't you needed any?" Levi asks with his brows furrowed. It's a reasonable question. "How long has it been?"

"Um…obviously a long, long time. Did you bring any, Levi?"

"Nope. It never crossed my mind," he answers. "We don't use 'em."

"Well then screw it," Brooke says. "If you haven't been messing around bareback with the local ladies, it's okay with me. It's up to you though whether you want to use one or not. You could always try one of the old ones and hope it doesn't fall apart. I don't know much about condom shelf life."

I think this might be killing the mood a little, and I need to get things back on track. "I'd love to go bare if you're alright with it."

Brooke gives me a lopsided grin and says in a sultry tone, "I love it when I can feel Levi's cum pour into me all hot and sticky. It's one of the sexiest things about anal. He swells up, and his thrusts get wild, and then *boom*!" She gives a little shudder. "Go for it. I'm sure we're all healthy, and I'm definitely not going to get pregnant that way."

I consider that and ask, "What do you use for birth control?"

"I have an IUD," she answers and then laughs. "They have a shelf life too, come to think of it. But I ought to be good."

"Ought to be?" I ask.

"Um, yeah, I'm pretty sure I'm okay, Skyler."

"So now that the business part of the meeting is concluded, let's get back to the fun," Levi tells us. "Brooke, bring that sassy bod of yours over here and lie down on your stomach."

"Oh boy!" she says with a laugh and climbs around Levi to lie down. Then she sticks her bottom up in the air and gives it a sexy wiggle. This woman is a walking wet dream.

"You are the luckiest bastard ever, Levi."

Brooke sits up and hugs him. "Marrying Levi was the best thing that ever happened to me." She kisses him, and that leads to a major make-out session. I'm just about to decide I'm a third wheel when she pats the bed next to her and unlocks her lips to tell me, "Sit here, Skyler." As soon as I do, she is kissing me the same way she did with Levi.

Levi lets out a low groan and says, "Yeah, babe. Make him want you." She keeps kissing and grabs for my dick. Yes! I like naked kissing the best. This is great.

Once I'm as stiff as a board again, I chance a peek at Levi

and see that he's almost as hard as I am. He really does get off seeing me with Brooke. He's stroking himself and smiling his head off. Finally, he tells her, "Okay, babe. Let's get you ready. Lie back down the way you were." He clicks open the top of the lube as Brooke positions herself in the middle of the bed. I climb around to the other side of her and wait for Levi to use some lube and pass it to me. Brooke has her legs wide open for us to have easy access.

Levi lubes up her pucker and starts rubbing around it. "Gotta be nice and relaxed, don't you, babe? Skyler's got a monster cock on him, so we want you to be extra loose." He kisses her cheek, and she makes a purring sound. He then starts to probe her little by little, barely making any headway at first. "Why don't you make some more magic with her clit, Sky? That will also relax her."

"Wait a sec, guys," Brooke says. "I want to see what's going on. Let me flip over."

Levi removes his hand, and Brooke rolls over to face us and quickly sticks a pillow under herself, so she's raised up a little. She spreads her legs, giving Levi access to her hole again, and he immediately resumes his probing.

My cock is dripping pre-cum, I'm so excited. This woman's body draws me like a magnet, and I can't help myself, so I lean over and lick all around her clit, eliciting a whole new set of appreciative noises from her. Levi ups his finger pressure, and I hear her gasp when he slides all the way in.

"Okay, Sky, I'm going to get a little more lube, and then you need to get your finger in here with mine," Levi tells me. My cock jolts with excitement, I'm so ready. I carefully rim her hole, gathering lube on my fingertip before I start to push my way in too. We both have large hands, and it must feel like a lot to Brooke. I don't hear any complaints though.

Slowly, slowly, I ease my index finger in alongside Levi. It's a rush. That's all I can say. Brooke's breathing accelerates, and I lean over again and suck her pretty little clit into my mouth. This is incredible! She almost screams with excitement, and we haven't even gotten to the main event yet.

"That's it, babe," Levi encourages her. "Give us another O!"

I guess she's taking him literally because I feel her muscles tighten up around our joined fingers and she cries out, "Ohhh, God!" She's bucking and squirming. I've never seen or done anything like this, and I love it! I suck harder on her clit.

"I'm putting in another finger, Brooke," Levi tells her, and I look up to see that she's nodding eagerly.

And in he goes. My finger is pretty squished in there, so I know she's going to feel outrageous around my cock.

Brooke continues to pant and squirm until I sit back up and say, "I need you now. If I don't get in there right away, I'm afraid I'm going to lose it all over the bed." I remove my hand and lie down next to Brooke. Then I lube myself up and say, "Stay facing Levi and lower yourself onto me.

That way he can see how you're doing, and you can control the speed." I have an ulterior motive, but we'll see how it goes.

Levi pulls his fingers out and helps Brooke move into position. He grabs my dick—which gives me an unexpected jolt of excitement—and helps her line up to it. "Oh, fuuuck…" I pant. "You're so hot and tight! This is fucking heaven!" She's slowly making her way down my shaft by small increments, and with each centimeter, it feels better and better. So right, and so naughty.

Levi has his eyes glued to the action, and he's clearly enjoying the view up close like this. Once he releases me— I'm sorry to see him go—he grabs his own boner with a death grip. He scoots even closer and kisses Brooke passionately before telling her, "You're doing great, babe. I love you so much."

After a couple of minutes of her careful descent, I'm finally all the way in, and I have to say, this is beyond amazing. Levi reaches for her clit and starts to make music with her body, and she begins to rise and fall over me. The enormity of what we're doing slams through me, and I moan with sublime pleasure.

"Levi?" I ask in a broken voice, "Is this what you wanted?"

"This is perfect. You're both perfect. It's everything and more."

"But do you want more?" I croak out. I can't even keep

my eyes open—the pleasure is so overwhelming. But I want him to participate, dammit!

"What do you mean?" he asks.

"Fuck her with me. Put your dick in her pussy and we'll do this together." I laugh. "Like the buddy system." I crack myself up.

"Wow, DP? A dream come true." Brooke breathes out on a sigh. "Come on, Levi. Let's do it. I need you too!" She leans back over my chest—exposing her front to him even more— and his eyes light up with the possibilities. I reach around and open her pussy wide for him to appreciate. I know it's pink and wet and gorgeous.

"I guess I can try." He lubes up his cock with a shaking hand and tries to position himself between our legs. He looks awkward, and I can imagine the pressure it's putting on his wounded hip as he says, "Don't be surprised if I can't complete the mission."

I hate hearing the nerves in his voice, so I make things easier for him. "Hold on a sec, Levi," I tell him. Then I say to Brooke, "Let's move over to the side of the bed so Levi can do this in an easier position. He can stand up." She immediately gets the picture and pulls off of me. I scoot over so my legs are off the edge of the bed, and she sits on my lap, sucking my dick right back into her body like I never left. It feels amazing, and I let out another long, satisfied groan.

Levi stares at us without blinking, and his breathing speeds up and deepens as he steps into position. I help him out by grabbing his dick to move things along. His cock goes from a semi to a rock-hard boner in my firm grip. I squeeze him even harder, and then…"Yes!" I cry in unison with Brooke. With my help, he's sliding in. "Levi, I can feel you. Oh God, this is incredible."

Levi's look of concentration is sweet. But it's sweeter still when he realizes he's all the way in and is lined up alongside me. His eyes pop, and he says with a hitch in his voice, "I did it, Brooke. I'm finally making love to you. Is it alright? Do you like this?" He pulls out a little and slides back in. I don't see any indication that he's in pain or—worse yet for his psyche—going soft. All is well so far.

"I love it, honey," Brooke says breathlessly. "And I love you so much. You guys are my heroes."

I swear Levi has tears in his eyes as he fucks his beautiful, sexy wife. I'm a little trapped under them, so I'm relying on his action to make this work. He seems transported as he pumps in and out. But I almost lose it when he asks, "Do you really love it, babe? Do you love having Skyler's dick buried in your ass while I pound your pussy? It feels amazing to me. I can feel him in there with me, and it's like nothing we've ever done before, This is…oh God, I could do this forever."

My heart skitters, and I'm speechless, so I start kissing Brooke's neck. I jam my hand in between them so I can continue to manipulate her clit. But this also means I'm touching Levi. He doesn't seem to mind and gives me a grin. "Oh, Sky…" he whispers softly. "You're the best."

The friction of Levi's action rubs against me beautifully, and Brooke's muscles contract and release, giving me incredible pleasure. This woman has definitely done her exercises. I'm getting closer and closer to the edge, and I think Levi is too.

"Can you come again, babe?" he asks her. "I'm about to blow! Please come for me and show me how much you love having two big dicks filling you up!"

Brooke begins to shudder and moan as Levi's face contorts, and it's obvious he's coming. He makes an ungodly growling cry as he pours his cum into Brooke. I'm spellbound watching him look so transported. It's agony and ecstasy as he shakes and moans. I frankly wanted this to last longer, but I'm so damn happy for Levi, I could cry. When he's all wrung out, he holds tight to Brooke and says, "We need to make Skyler come now." He slides his slick and sated dick out of her and steps back.

Levi leans in and laps at Brooke's pussy with his tongue like he's cleaning it. At the same time, he massages my thighs and then slides his hand up under my balls. This is such an incredibly novel experience, and the multiple sensations are about to drive me insane.

"Come on, babe, fuck that big cock of his. Drive Sky wild. I can see how much you love this." Brooke is pulsating around me and sliding up and down. Levi leans even lower and sucks one of my balls into his mouth, and that's it. I bellow out, "Ahhh! Yesss!" I'm transported by these two people. How come sex has never even come close to this before? I come and come and almost lose my breath from hollering so much.

"Skyler, you feel *so* good," Brooke tells me in a reverent tone. "You helped make Levi better, and you did just what I've dreamed of." She slips off of me, and we all settle on the bed with her between me and her satisfied husband. "This was amazing."

Not wanting to make a mess of the bed, however, I tell them, "I'll be right back." I sprint for the shower and wash quickly and carefully, then I get a couple of warm, wet washcloths that I bring back to them. They are in the throes of another major make-out session, but I start with Brooke's bottom and wash her off. Levi looks up, so I hand him the other cloth. Once we're all spiffed up again, I ditch the washcloths in the bathroom and stand there wondering what to do. Should I go back to my room and give them their space?

"Hey, Skyler?" Brooke calls to me. "You're coming back, aren't you?"

I guess that solves my dilemma. I saunter happily back into the bedroom saying, "I'm right here." I snuggle up to her on the side of the bed I'd vacated and pull the duvet over all of us. I am absolutely content, but I know we'll need to talk about what we've done.

There will be questions.

CHAPTER
Twenty~Two

I can't even begin to think about how happy and relieved I am right now. That was amazing sex. More divine than anything I've ever done with Levi, and we had some terrific sex before he was wounded. This was almost a spiritual experience it was so great. I felt my heart expanding to encompass Skyler as well as Levi. It was as if I was surrounded by love, and the love the two guys have for one another was also passing through me.

I am so happy for Levi. I know how awful he's been feeling, and this has to have been an enormous hurdle for him to finally overcome.

"That was incredible, you guys," I tell them.

"It was everything," Levi agrees and yawns contentedly.

"Best ever. Good night," Skyler adds, and we all drift off in a tangle of arms and legs.

I should feel crowded, but the sense of rightness fills me with so much joy, I drift off with what I'm sure is a goofy grin on my face.

An indeterminate length of time later, I realize that although Levi is still snuggled up to me, my other side is cool. Skyler either needed more space and moved way over, or he's gone. I don't give it a lot of thought before succumbing to sleep again.

But as the room fills with late morning light and I regain my wits, I turn around and see that Skyler has definitely gone somewhere else to sleep. This bums me out more than I would have expected. I hope he's not upset or nervous about what we did. If we could maintain this kind of relationship permanently, I wouldn't mind. This realization doesn't even shock me, and that in itself is a surprise. I want him to be part of us. Levi and I will have to talk when he wakes up. But now, I desperately need the bathroom and crave some coffee in the worst way.

I head to the bathroom, and when I'm done with the necessities and brushing my teeth, I peek into Skyler's room. I'm kind of shocked that he's not there, and his bed is made. Huh. That seems odd. I return to our bedroom quietly, not wanting to disturb Levi who's still softly snoring away. He's so beautiful and looks completely at peace. No nightmares have plagued him since we got here to Skyler's paradise in Honeybee Hollow. I quickly pull on a pair of shorts and a t-shirt and head barefooted for the kitchen.

Now it's getting to be even stranger. I felt certain Skyler would be sipping coffee and enjoying a pastry from Juni's bakery. He keeps a good supply of her confections in the freezer at all times. But the coffeemaker is cold and empty, and he's nowhere to be seen. I step outside to see if he's somewhere out back. Nope. Nothing. I even look in the garage, deciding he went to buy something different for breakfast—not that we needed anything—but his car and the truck are both parked in there.

I decide he must have gone for a walk, so I return to the kitchen and set about making coffee. He'll certainly show up soon. Won't he?

I've just finished an excellent bran muffin and I'm starting on my second cup of coffee when my handsome, barefoot, pajama-bottom-clad husband joins me looking mussed and rumpled, but thoroughly satisfied. His hair is sticking up in all directions, and it makes me smile. I do notice, however, that he's leaning on his cane a lot more than usual. "Mornin', babe," he says in a scratchy voice. "Where's our man?" He grabs a mug of coffee and eases himself gingerly into the chair across from me with a giant grin.

"I can't find him."

Levi's smile evaporates as he blinks and says, "What do you mean you can't find him?"

"He got out of bed sometime in the wee hours of the morning—I'm guessing around two or three maybe—and I've looked for him, but he's not around. He hasn't had breakfast, and the cars are still here, but he's not in bed or anywhere close by. I even wondered if he went fishing, so I checked, and the tackle is still here."

"Did you try calling him?"

"No. His phone was charging in his bedroom when I looked in there."

"Wow. That's odd and completely out of character for him. Did you try upstairs?"

"No. Why would he be up there?"

"I dunno." Levi scratched his chin. "But it's one more place to look before we panic."

"You think we have reason to panic?" Now I'm getting worried.

"Not yet, babe. He wouldn't get lost or anything if he went for a run or a hike. He'll be back. But he probably would have left a note and taken his phone…" Levi tries to look calm, but he's not fooling me. Then he brightens and adds, "Oh! Maybe he's up there changing bed linens after having my family visit."

"Good thinking! I'm going upstairs then. Have a scone or a muffin or something. The bran ones are yummy." I scoot off and make myself not take the stairs two at a time. Levi must be right. Only…I don't hear any movement, and he's been gone for an awfully long time to be making beds.

I've never bothered to come up here, so I have no idea what to expect. It's as silent as a tomb. There is a long hallway with several open doors. I take a look in each one and see that they're all nicely appointed bedrooms, and Skyler isn't in any of them. I'm getting pretty frustrated. At the end of the hall, there is an ell that leads to a closed door, so I decide to take a look. *Nothing to lose*, I tell myself. There's a crack of light beneath it. I open the door and realize it's a stairway to the attic. Up I go, and when I get to the top, my heart almost stops. *Oh my.*

The attic is huge, and I never realized from the outside of the house that it has two large skylights that let in wonderful natural light on the backside of the sloped roof. There are also three lovely dormer windows facing the front, making this the brightest, cheeriest attic I've ever seen. Between the windows are cabinets, cubbies, and shelves full of things I can't begin to take in. I see jars, cans, tubes, brushes, tools, and all sorts of art supplies. At the far end, there is a large utility sink and a kitchenette next to a door that leads to what looks like a bathroom. One could easily spend hours up here comfortably. But it's what is in the middle of the space that has my curiosity. There is a large tarp protecting the floor, and on it stands an easel. The space has a stool and a table holding a scatter of brushes in canisters, palette knives, and paints. I can't see what's on the canvas because it's facing away from me. Beyond the canvas and art supplies is a cot over by the wall where Skyler is sound asleep. He's bare-chested; the quilt that covers him has slipped down. Even with the windows open, it's warm up here, so that's understandable.

He looks delightfully peaceful, and I don't want to disturb him, but my curiosity gets the better of me, so I stride toward the easel to take a look. The wooden floor gives a loud creak at the same time as I take in the subject matter of the painting, and I gasp. The combined noises startle Skyler who sits up and croaks, "What? Who? Oh, Brooke, hi."

"Skyler, this is amazing! Did you do this last night?"

"Oh…um…yeah. I kind of passed out in your bed for a couple of hours, and then I was so fired up, I needed to get some of my feelings down on canvas. I couldn't help it."

I can't take my eyes off his work. It's Levi. Obviously, the painting isn't finished yet, but I can clearly see that Skyler is a huge talent.

"I'm calling it *Hero*," he tells me.

"That makes sense. You've captured his likeness and his attitude so incredibly well. I love this, Skyler!"

"Well, it's rough, but…"

"No! Not rough. It's expressive and bold. It's fantastic." My beloved Levi has a faraway look on his face and seems to be standing at attention. He's shirtless, wearing camo pants and dog tags. He's obviously a soldier, but also strong and committed to a cause. You can read it in his eyes. I finally tear my attention away from this beautiful piece and go to Skyler, who has now sat up on the edge of the cot and is wearing gym shorts. I sit down next to him and notice he has paint all over himself. His chest is a colorful mess of acrylic splatters, but there's a beauty to it.

"What a wonderful tribute to our man, Skyler. Thank you for painting it. How did you know you could do this? You were so worried before."

Skyler blushes and looks down. "I've thought a lot about the stories you hear of amputees relearning to do things with their mouths or their feet because they're so committed to making art, and I figured all I had to deal with was some lack of coordination and potential aches and pains. I still have both hands, so I was beginning to feel like a big baby about it."

"Oh, Skyler…"

He raises his gaze and looks directly into my eyes. "That's not all. Last night, what we experienced was beautiful. And perfect. And even if we never do it again, I'll always cherish the memory. I felt in some ways like I was creating something with my hands and my body that was like the feeling I get when I paint. It was liberating and exhilarating. I don't know if this makes any sense at all to anyone else. I woke up and realized that even if I can't control the brush exactly like I used to, I can still use my hands to make something beautiful —the same way I made you and Levi beautiful in your ecstasy. I just knew I could do this, and the image of Levi looking like he was willing to sacrifice everything to save the people he loves was stuck in my head. I was so full of ideas, I couldn't hold still, so I had to come up here. Stepping into the studio again was like coming home after being held captive. I let my fears fall away and just let myself go. I painted for hours until I couldn't keep my eyes open anymore. This bed is up here because I've always gotten lost in painting, and sometimes I forget to sleep and eat."

I take his hand, not caring that it's covered in dried splatters. "Are you ready to come downstairs and have some breakfast? Levi and I were worried when I couldn't find you anywhere. He sent me upstairs to investigate because I'd already exhausted everywhere else I could think of. I'm so relieved to have found you, but we're keeping Levi in suspense down there, and I don't want him to worry. Come have something to eat, and you can get back to your work after that. And Skyler? I am so proud of you. This is perfect. You're perfect." I lean over and kiss him. The kiss feels pretty perfect too, and I'm a little curious about why I feel not one single shred of guilt about doing it without Levi around. I pull back and say, "Come on. Let's tell our man what you've been up to."

"I like that, Brooke."

"What?"

"'Our man.' Like you'll share him with me, and he's mine too."

I smile at him. He has a sweet, vulnerable look on his face, so I say, "There was never a doubt. I know you love each other. Come on. You must be starving. It's almost noon." We stand and I take his hand again, saying, "Oh, and he also refers to you as 'our man.'"

We head down the two sets of stairs, and as we hit the ground floor, something occurs to me. "How does your shoulder feel after all of that work you did?"

He rolls it carefully and admits, "It hurts like a sonofabitch. I don't care though! I'll grab something for the pain after I eat breakfast."

We walk into the kitchen to a delighted Levi who lights up like a Christmas tree. "There you are! Where did you take off to?"

I can't help gushing, so I butt in before Skyler can get all modest. "Levi, you should see the studio Skyler has in the attic! It's wonderful, and he's been painting! His artwork is amazing." I don't want to tell him yet what Skyler is working on in case he wants to reveal it himself, but I also can't resist putting my arm around Skyler's waist and giving him a squeeze.

"That's fantastic! What are you painting?"

"Oh, I'm just playing around with…uh…technique so far. It's kind of a study. I'll show you after it's all finished. Right now, it's a rough work in progress."

Apparently, I was right not to spill the beans. He might be ready to paint, but not ready to talk about it much or show it off. I look him in the eye and give him a smile. He gives me a nearly imperceptible nod as if to say he's thankful. "Do you guys need more coffee?" I ask so I can give myself something to do. I grab the pot and start filling mugs. "Looks like we'll need some more." I understand the creative mind even though

I wasn't particularly blessed with one. Levi is also quite protective of his music until he's absolutely ready to share it.

Skyler nukes himself a couple of muffins and sits down next to Levi saying, "I'm going to call my physical therapist in a little while. I think I did a bit too much and need some relief. Would you like me to make you an appointment with him? He's a veteran, and he's terrific. The practice is right here in town next to the hospital."

"Oh, uh…sure, I guess. Can't hurt, right?"

Skyler chuckles. "Yeah, right. Sometimes it hurts plenty, but he never goes too far."

I grin at Levi and ask, "Now that Skyler is making beautiful art again, do you think you're ready to make some music? Apparently, you and I have been quite the inspiration. I can just imagine the kinds of songs you could write about us."

The guys give each other cheesy, lascivious looks and then crack up.

"Those potential songs may not be for everyone," Levi says with a snort. "But the idea is tempting. How do you like the name 'Bi-Bi, Baby?' Spelled with an *I*, of course. Or another possible hit…'Butt, I Love You.'"

"Uh…sure, honey." I hope he's joking.

Twenty-Three

SKYLER

AFTER SCARFING DOWN A MUFFIN, I LOOK DOWN AT MYSELF and realize what a mess I am. I'm also still exhausted, and I'm starting to get a headache. I didn't want to complain to Brooke, but I'd only been asleep for about an hour when she came in and woke me up.

"I'm going to go shower off my Technicolor body paint and crash for a few hours. If anyone would like to take a nap with me, the door is open, but I'm completely beat."

Brooke laughs and asks, "I'm good. Skyler. I slept like a baby. I'm going to go run a load or two of laundry. Would you like me to change the beds upstairs after having guests?"

"Oh, you don't need to do that. I gave Mrs. Henshaw a

couple of weeks off so she could go see her kids over the holiday, and I wasn't sure how long I was going to be gone, but she'll be back to work tomorrow."

"And she is…?"

"My housekeeper. She was helpful when I couldn't do much at all around here with my shoulder being a mess, but more recently, she's been complaining that she doesn't have enough to do. Don't offer to help her do any housework; she's easily offended. She's also pretty proud of her cooking; although, if you ask me, her results in the kitchen are horrible. I'd rather do the cooking myself at this point."

"Well, okay. I'll leave the beds to her. I guess I ought to get some work done for my company then. I also told them I was taking some personal time off, and it's probably been long enough."

"She'll do the laundry for you too, Brooke. If she doesn't have enough to do, she'll end up talking your ear off. Just relax and either get back to your regular job or find something fun to do. You could always go see Juni and pick up some more muffins and cinnamon rolls from her. Our freezer stash of bakery stuff is dwindling."

"Good idea. Maybe I'll go grab some pastries now before she sells out, and then I can get back to work when I come back. No sense rushing, right? Levi, would you like to go with me?"

Levi has slipped into one of his moody expressions, and that has me a little worried. He went from joking around to disturbed in no time. I wish I knew what triggered him. He looks at Brooke distractedly and finally says, "Uh…no. You go. I have some stuff I want to do here."

Brooke grabs her purse, kisses both of us, then sails out the door. As it shuts, I turn to look at Levi. I'm starting to feel like shit and need a migraine pill and a dark room in the worst way. I know better than to not get enough sleep and forget to eat and stay hydrated, but I can't always help myself. "Hey, buddy, you okay? You're looking a little off."

"Don't baby me, Skyler." Skyler, he calls me—not Sky. Did I do something? "Frankly, I'm starting to feel like a leech."

"What? Why?" I hope this isn't a long conversation because I'm starting to see black spots.

"You're doing great, Brooke is doing great. I'm not doing Jack Shit. I need a fucking job!"

"So find one. Work on your music, look online, ask around. I don't know what it is you want, but you're absolutely not a leech. You're here because I need you and you need me. It's simple. Stop feeling sorry for yourself." I can't help it—I rub my forehead and suddenly realize I'm about to barf, so I bolt into the bathroom off the kitchen. I hate these fucking migraines!

After losing my breakfast, I stumble back into the kitchen. It's so damn bright in here, it hurts! "Levi, would you grab me a Gatorade from the fridge, please? The bright light in there bothers me." He's staring at me like I have an extra head while I lean against the counter and shield my eyes.

"Sure, man." He limps across the room without his cane, and I realize I've asked him to do something I should have done myself. He opens the bottle and hands it to me, leaning against the counter next to me. We're quite a pair this morning…well, this midday. He asks, "What's going on? Are you sick? Bad muffin?"

I snort. "No. I let myself get dehydrated, and I haven't had enough food or sleep. That sometimes triggers a migraine. This one is bad, so I need to go take some medicine and lie down. I'm sorry."

"Nothing to feel sorry about. Can I bring you something to eat?"

"Not yet, although I'm going to need something in my belly pretty soon."

"Have you always had migraines, or…?"

"No. It's a relatively common side effect after what we went through, or so I'm told. My brain apparently got a little scrambled during the explosion."

"I see. I guess I'm lucky to have missed that one."

"That's looking on the bright side." I don't think I'd have been too happy if my dick stopped working, but I won't bring Levi down by mentioning his symptoms. "Thanks for grabbing the drink. I'm going to shower and sleep."

"Turkey or ham?" Levi asks.

"Huh?"

"I'll make you a sandwich, and you can eat it after you've showered. You probably want something in your stomach if you take any meds."

"Oh, yeah, right. Thanks, Levi. Either one." I chug half the bottle and feel my way down the hall with my eyes mostly closed, hoping for relief soon. I grab a pill, down the rest of the sports drink, and bolt for the shower. I don't even wait for the water to warm up, and honestly the chill feels good on my throbbing head.

CHAPTER
Twenty-Four

Levi

I slap together a quick sandwich, wrap it in a napkin in case he's in the shower a while, and then make my way to Skyler's room. He's just coming out of the bathroom when I get there. Most of the paint is gone, but there's still a smudge of blue across his belly that makes me smile as I hand him the sandwich. "Did you take your pill?"

"Yeah, as soon as I got in here. Thanks, man." He takes the sandwich and eats half of it in two giant bites. Then he sets the other half down and finishes drying off before he scarfs down the rest. I can't help but admire his naked body.

"Does massage ever help the headaches?"

Skyler squints at me and flops onto his bed—still naked. "You offering?"

"If you think it might help."

"The biggest help would be to close the drapes and make it as dark as possible in here. I really need to close my eyes, Levi. This is a bad one. But if you could give me a head massage, that might feel great."

I do what he asks and shut the drapes. It takes me a moment to adjust to the dark, but then I can see where he is and how to get to him without falling over the furniture and hurting myself.

It's good we don't have anything to get done today. My hip feels like it's on fire after fucking Brooke in a bit of an awkward position. I would do it again in a heartbeat though. Some things are so worth it.

"Okay, lie down however you're comfortable." Skyler stretches out on his uninjured side, and I climb onto the bed behind him. Fortunately, I can get comfortable next to him on my good side this way. I've never massaged anyone's head before, but I know mine is sensitive, so I start by gently running my fingers through his hair. It crosses my mind that this ought to seem weird, but it doesn't at all. His breathing goes from a little too fast to a smoother tempo as I switch to softly using my nails on his scalp. I scratch him rhythmically and notice how the muscles in his neck and shoulders relax.

"Feels good," he mumbles. "But I'm gonna try to sleep now. Stay?"

"Sure." I slide my hand out of his thick hair. I'm not exactly sure what to do with my hand, but he reaches around and pulls my arm around him. I have no choice but to be the big spoon this way. It's nice. Wow…things have certainly changed.

Skyler drifts off, and although I doubt that I can, I doze as well. After a couple of hours like this, though, I start to get antsy and disentangle myself from him. He moans a little when I pull away, and I can't help giving him a pat and whispering, "Stay asleep, Sky. You'll feel better soon." I hope he does.

I wander off in search of Brooke or my guitar. I need a distraction. She isn't in our bedroom, but my guitar is, so I grab it and head out. Playing outside might be a good idea in case I end up making too much noise for Skyler.

I find Brooke in the screened porch, scowling at her laptop. "Everything okay, babe?"

She sighs and says, "Yeah, it'll be fine. I shouldn't have left so much work undone though. A couple of the people in my department tried to fill in, and they messed up the code. Now I have extra work as well as makeup work. What have you been up to?"

"I tried to help Skyler get rid of his headache by giving him a scalp massage and ended up falling asleep with him. He's still out like a light, but I was done sleeping."

"Planning to make some beautiful music?"

Shrugging, I answer, "I don't know how beautiful it'll be,

but it might be fun to call that guy back at the bar and see about scheduling a gig there one of these nights."

She gives me her signature radiant smile and says, "Go for it!" Then she looks a lot more serious and adds, "You and I need to have a chat about what we plan to do. If we really are moving here, we'll need to go back and clear out our house and make some decisions. We sure don't want to pay an extra month's rent because we sat around and didn't do anything, but it's good we don't have a lease to worry about. We've been on vacation for a while and need to do some adulting." She smiles. "Play your music now, though, and I'll try to untangle some of this mess. Then we can talk about it after dinner if Skyler is feeling better."

Just as I reach for my guitar case, we hear a car drive up. We both turn to see a squarely built lady with salt and pepper hair somewhere in her late fifties stepping out and bustling up to the back door. She doesn't knock; she just reaches for the knob and huffs angrily when it doesn't turn.

"Can I help you?" I call out to her. Doesn't anyone ever knock? Is Skyler's house always open to just anybody?

She jumps and clutches her heart. Great. I've frightened her.

"Goodness gracious!" She pants. "You gave me such a start. Would you unlock this door? I can't imagine—"

"And you are…?"

"Oh, silly me," she simpers. "Sorry. I'm Marjorie Henshaw, Skyler's housekeeper. I was planning to show up tomorrow, but I was sitting around my little place with absolutely nothing to do, so I decided I would come back to work early. I hate having time on my hands. I've been gone so long, there must be laundry, shopping, cooking…whatever I can do around here. This is such a beautiful place, and Skyler is such a dear. I love being here, you know. And I'm quite good at my job. He's very happy to have me."

So much for privacy, and my ears are already tired. I head in and open the back door for her as she asks, "I can't imagine why on earth it was locked. No one in Honeybee Hollow bothers to lock their doors. Does Skyler know you're locking his door? It's just not done!" She immediately floods the room with brightness as she flips the switch for the kitchen lights. I don't have a headache, and it's a little too much even for me given that the room is already full of sunlight from the large windows.

"My mistake. It comes from my severe dislike of bad surprises, and we've recently had a walk-in who wasn't welcome." I seriously doubt no one locks their doors around here with the number of busybodies on the loose. It's probably more like Skyler doesn't trust her with a key and knows when she's coming. Although…he is a little lax about locking up.

She gives me a funny look as Brooke wanders into the kitchen and sticks out her hand. "Hi, Mrs. Henshaw, I'm Brooke Spencer. This is Levi."

Mrs. Henshaw stares briefly at Brooke's outstretched hand before giving it a perfunctory shake. She glances around and asks, "Where's my Skyler? You aren't here without him, are you?"

"He's kind of under the weather right now, so whatever you do, you don't want to be making too much noise," I tell her.

"Oh, my poor boy. In that case, I'll make him his favorite dinner—he just loves my cooking—and I'll tackle some laundry, but I'll leave the vacuuming for tomorrow. How long are you planning to stay, anyway? Skyler mentioned he might be having guests, but I thought you'd be gone by now. Aren't you about ready to head back to…uh…wherever?"

"We need to discuss our plans with Skyler, if you'll excuse us," Brooke tells her. "Um…actually, do you think you could just come back tomorrow instead? Skyler is feeling pretty awful, and I'm not sure he'll want much for dinner. If he does get hungry later, I'll be happy to fix him something. We have plenty of groceries."

"Well, I think I ought to check with my employer before I make any decisions like that…'"

"Ma'am," I interrupt. "No one was expecting you today. If you go home now, it won't make a bit of difference to Skyler, and you won't disturb him."

"Well! You're a little sure of yourself, mister. I've been taking care of him for a long time, and…"

"Mrs. Henshaw? What are you doing here?" Skyler croaks. He walks into the kitchen in nothing but boxers, looking mussed and wobbly. He's squinting and has his hand shielding his eyes, so I quickly reach to turn off the overhead lights. "Thanks, Levi," he says. "I need more Gatorade. Do you mind?"

"What you need is some of my chicken broth, young man, not that awful yellow stuff!" Mrs. Henshaw says too loudly. "You're obviously not taking good care of yourself, and you're running around practically naked in front of company. What would your parents think?" Skyler flinches at the volume.

I reach into the fridge and root around for another bottle. I offer it to Skyler, noticing that his hand is a little shaky. Poor guy.

Ignoring her comments about chicken broth and his lack of clothes, Skyler takes the Gatorade and twists off the lid. He chugs a few gulps and then looks at her with a pained expression. "Mrs. Henshaw, If you really need to accomplish something worthwhile, why don't you just go change the bed linens in all of the upstairs rooms? Forget the master suite for now. That's all I need for today. I'm going back to bed in a few minutes. Please don't bother my friends about *anything*, and the next time you insult me or one of them, you'll be looking for another job. They're going to be living here permanently. Consider Brooke and Levi your employers too from now on, and whatever they say goes for me." Apparently, he heard some of the conversation before he entered the kitchen, and well…wow. He has made a public declaration that we're here to stay. Honestly, there's nowhere I'd rather be. This place already feels like home.

Brooke adds, "We're covered for dinner tonight, thanks. Maybe another time you can fix Skyler's favorite for all of us. I'm sure he'd appreciate that." You can always count on Brooke to try to smooth things over in a tough situation. She probably developed that talent from being around me with my difficult moods. In any case, it makes me love her all the more.

Mrs. Henshaw ignores Brooke and says in a stilted voice, "Yes, Skyler." She heads for the stairs where she stops and turns back asking, "Are you having financial trouble and need paying roommates all of a sudden? Are you trying to cut my hours and pay me less because of that?"

"My personal life is none of your concern. You're on thin ice, Mrs. Henshaw." Skyler glares at her through his pained expression.

She sticks her nose in the air and huffs away, clomping up the stairs. Apparently, she doesn't do "quiet" very well.

Skyler sinks down onto one of the kitchen chairs as if this exchange cost him dearly. He looks miserable, so I step behind him and resume my scalp massage, hoping to give him some relief. He pushes against my fingers like a cat and makes a satisfied hum. Smiling at his appreciation, I can't help wondering at the housekeeper's familiarity in calling him by his first name, while he calls her Mrs. Henshaw. We haven't exactly gotten off on a good foot, so I hope it gets better…or he fires her. I wouldn't miss her.

"She seems a tad protective of you, Skyler," Brooke points out. "What's her deal?"

With his eyes closed he says, "Oh, that's so good, Levi. Thanks. When I first got back from Walter Reed, I stayed with my parents for a couple of weeks, and then my mom suggested I hire Mrs. Henshaw if I wanted to move back here. It seemed like a good idea for a while. But she's been getting on my nerves more and more. I was happy to tell her to take a couple of weeks off when I hoped you might come back with me. I thought I'd see how I did without her. Then I worried maybe you might think I was having you guys move in so Brooke would do all of the cooking and cleaning, and believe me, that *never* crossed my mind."

"You've easily done as much of the cooking as I have, if not more. I don't see why we can't all just share the housework. Do we really need a housekeeper? You could just get rid of her. Levi and I can help," Brooke says.

We hear a gasp from the doorway. Uh oh.

CHAPTER
Twenty~Five

BROOKE

WHY DIDN'T MRS. HENSHAW STAY UPSTAIRS WHERE SHE WAS asked to do her work? She's such a busybody, and she acts like she owns the place. I'm sorry she caught me suggesting that he can her though. I should have stayed out of it. I open my mouth to tell her I'm sorry when she screeches at me, "Who do you think you are telling Skyler what to do with his life?"

I blink in surprise and answer in a soft voice, "I'm someone who cares deeply for his well-being. Keep your voice down. He's in pain."

Skyler's hand goes over his eyes again; he was beginning to look relaxed there for a second. He says in a wobbly voice,

"What are you doing down here, Mrs. Henshaw? I asked you specifically to do your work on the second floor."

"Oh, so you all could plot against me and plan to 'get rid' of me? For your information, I came down to grab the laundry basket for all the sheets you want laundered. There's a lot of beds up there, you know."

Skyler lets out a big sigh and reaches to still Levi's hands and then wave him off. "Look, I know you haven't worked up there before, but there's a laundry chute right next to the linen closet in the hall. I distinctly remember showing it to you. Also, I never asked you to do any laundry today—only to change the bed linens." He rubs his eyes and adds, "I can't deal with any of this right now. I don't like the way you're speaking to me or my friends, and I wish you'd just go home. Now. We'll discuss your job tomorrow. Right now, I need to go back to bed." He stands and heads toward the hall.

"You better not try to skip out of paying me for today," she hisses at him as he passes.

"Listen, lady, you haven't done a damn bit of work, and you weren't asked to show up, so there's little chance you'll be compensated," Levi points out. "All you've done is complain since you barged in."

"Mind your own business," she snaps.

"One last time, Mrs. Henshaw, Levi and Brooke are also your employers from here on out," Skyler says. "Go home. In fact…don't come back. You're done here."

Bursting into deafening sobs, she flounces past us, heading

to the back door. She turns at the last minute and shouts, "You'll be sorry!"

ABOUT THREE HOURS LATER, SKYLER WANDERS ONTO THE porch where I'm trying desperately to get work done even though my concentration is shot for the day, and Levi is plunking away listlessly at his guitar without making any real progress either. Skyler looks better but still a bit shaky, and he's holding a bottle of water. His hair is wet like he's showered again, and this time he's wearing shorts and a t-shirt.

"Are you doing alright?" I ask. "Should I fix some dinner?"

"Oh, it's up to you. I'm starving though. My headache's gone. Maybe getting a pizza delivered would be faster than cooking." He has a hopeful look.

A short while later, we're happily munching on pizza out in the screened porch when another car drives up. This is beginning to feel like Grand Central Station. The car pulls to a stop, and Skyler's mother hops out. It's going on dusk, and the overhead light is on in the porch, so she sees us right away.

"Skyler, I need a word with you!" she says a bit shrilly. This doesn't sound good.

"Hi, Mom. Want a slice?" he asks as he unlatches the screen door and opens it for her. "It's still hot."

She's confused and doesn't answer. Looking at all three of

us in turn with a perplexed expression, she asks Skyler, "Why aren't you answering your phone?"

"Oh, sorry. I wasn't feeling well, and I had it turned off. Migraine. I guess I forgot to turn it back on once I felt better. What's up?" He politely pulls out a chair for her. She hesitates a moment and then sits.

"People have been coming into the garden center all afternoon reporting that you *threatened* Mrs. Henshaw, and she is too afraid to work here anymore. She also spread the news that you're flat broke, have a…ah…boyfriend who likes to play with your hair, and you wander around the house with no clothes on. So I ask again, what in the name of all that is holy is going on around here?"

Levi turns a livid shade of red, but Skyler shakes his head and goes pale. "That fucking bitch!" he whispers with enough venom to scare a cobra.

"Skyler!" his mom exclaims.

He skewers her with a look and says, "Mrs. Henshaw is an interfering, lying sack of shit, and she needed firing. She was not threatened with anything other than the loss of her job, but when she was asked to back off with her nasty comments, she persisted in insulting Brooke and Levi. I warned her, and she did it again, so I asked her to leave for good. She wasn't even supposed to be here today, but she forced her way in by being pushy and made everyone uncomfortable. As for having a boyfriend who plays with my hair, Levi was giving me a scalp massage because my head was in agony, and it was relaxing me—and it's probably why my headache went away so quickly this time. Furthermore, I was *not* running around naked." He stares at her a moment and adds, "But if I ever do feel like running around naked, it's my house and my business. I'd been asleep and didn't even know she was here when I came out to the kitchen in my underwear for a cold drink. If she got an eyeful, that's on her for being where she wasn't supposed to be."

"I'm sure she was just trying to help."

"She was butting in. I was thinking of firing her anyway, even before this."

"But she's a trusted member of the community, Skyler. She's worked for lots of people over the years without incident."

"Are you sure about that? Lots of people must have also let her go then. Why hasn't she worked for one family or one person for years and years? Probably because she's as obnoxious as all get-out."

Skyler's mother frowns and blows out a breath. I'm relieved to feel the tension dissipating. "Well, you may have a point, but I wouldn't know. I'm sorry if by recommending her I got you into something that didn't turn out well. I thought she was better than that, but I've never worked with her myself." His mom sighs. "She has certainly bent some ears around town about this today."

"Too bad she's better at shooting off her mouth than she is at anything else. She was helpful at first when I was trying to do everything with one arm, but I didn't like her cooking at all. It was just easier to put up with her until I had an excuse to let her have some time off. I'm sorry I put it off, now that Brooke and Levi were subjected to her."

"Alright, well, again I'm sorry. I don't really know what to do about the gossip. You know what this town is like. Somebody sneezes in church and suddenly you hear there's a shortage on tissues and cough medicine. But maybe it'll die down quickly."

Skyler snorts. "Yeah, right."

"I don't want to start a gossip war saying everything was her fault. It will just make you look petty. I would like to spread around a bit of truth though."

"Let her talk. I don't give a shit what anybody thinks of me. If they don't know me better than that, screw 'em."

"Well, you may be right, even if I'd like to hear less colorful language from you about it. At least when the next person tells me their version of her story, I can refute it instead of just acting surprised by it. Hopefully, folks will believe the truth. Now, I need to get home and feed your father. I have a meeting tonight after suppertime with the Sewing Bees. At least I can set those ladies straight when they bring it up, and I'm sure they will."

"Great," Skyler says in a flat voice.

I have to say something about this situation, so I tell his mom, "I'm afraid I was the one who used the words 'get rid of her,' but all I meant was to fire her. I wasn't suggesting violence, for heaven's sake—as if Skyler would rough up a woman! I think she came in on the end of a conversation and purposefully got the wrong idea, and now Skyler's bearing the brunt of it. It was certainly never my intention to frighten her. She was being nosy and rude, and I could see how badly she was bothering Skyler. You should know too that her parting words as she headed out were that Skyler would 'be sorry.' Or maybe she meant all three of us; she wasn't very clear. I think she planned to make life miserable around here. Also…I think she has a rather unnatural fixation on him. She called him 'her boy' and things like that. She seemed terribly jealous and wanted Levi and me to hit the road. That was obvious."

"Oh dear," Tracy Colfax sighs. "She does sound like she's gone a bit off her rocker." She looks around at us with a much warmer expression than she had when she arrived and says, "I'm glad to see that you're well, Skyler. I was worried when I couldn't get in touch with you." She looks at Levi who still hasn't said a word. "If a scalp massage works for his awful headaches, thank you for trying it." She looks back at Skyler and asks, "One last question. Why would she be telling people that you're broke? That one doesn't make any sense unless you've had a sudden investment failure, and how would she know about it if you did?"

Sighing, Skyler explains, "She wanted to be paid for today, and Levi pointed out that she wasn't scheduled to work, and she hadn't done a single thing except show up unannounced. She didn't like that and thought she could bully me into paying her. It was just one more example of her being nuttier than a squirrel's turd."

Shaking her head at her son, Tracy Colfax gets to her feet and says, "You and your colorful language. I'm sorry to have brought you more to worry about." She raises her hand to wave her fingers at us. "Y'all have a good night." She walks to her car and takes off.

Skyler doesn't look too good again, so I ask, "Will you be okay?"

He pauses before he reaches across to both of us with his hands, indicating to us both to take one. We do, and he answers, "I'll be great as long as I know you're both serious about moving in. Settle your affairs in Hopkinsville and stay with me. Please?"

Levi and I regard each other, and he looks so hopeful and happy. It's a look I haven't seen enough of lately, so I answer Skyler, "We'd love to." Looking back at Levi, I say, "How do you want to get us moved, honey? Shall we all go back? Just you and me? Do you trust me to go back and do it on my own? I could hire someone if I decide I need help, but we don't have a lot of stuff. And I don't mind saying I won't miss that house or living near the base."

"That's too much to ask you to do…" Levi begins.

"I honestly don't mind. You can get started here with Skyler's PT guy and the PTSD counselor, and you can start exploring what it is you want to do either with your music or a different job, and I'll take care of it. You know I've never minded driving. I'll just listen to a couple of racy e-books and maybe get some inspiration for when I get back." I wink, and we all laugh at that. "And honestly, the small bit of furniture that's ours and not the landlord's isn't worth moving, so I can just get rid of it all. I might be able to fit everything into the car if I'm by myself. It would just be our clothes and personal stuff. It was a good idea when we got rid of the second car, so we don't have to worry about getting that here."

We discuss all of the details as the light fades completely to night and the sky fills with stars. The guys get into a friendly argument about paying rent. Skyler doesn't want any, and Levi says we refuse to be freeloaders, so we all agree on contributing to a household account that will be used for expenses like taxes, utilities, household repairs, and whatnot. I'm the only one who has set work hours, but even those are flexible, so we also commit to sharing and dividing duties as much as we possibly can. Levi says he's willing to handle all of the bill paying if Skyler and I will handle the grocery shopping. We know we'll all have to make adjustments as we go.

And then the elephant comes walking into the room and sits on the table right in our faces as it laughs at us. The elephant in the room is, of course, sex, and our relationship to one another.

Skyler didn't want to have a beer or anything alcoholic after his headache today and taking medication, so we all had sodas with the pizza. We're stone-cold sober, and that's probably the best way to handle this conversation.

"Do we need to define anything?" I ask. "Can't we just see how things go?"

Skyler looks worried and says, "I need more structure than that, Brooke. The last thing I want to do is interfere with your marriage. I want to be completely honest by saying if you guys want to live here with me like roommates, I can be happy with that—meaning the way we did when you first arrived, and we stay in separate bedrooms…"

Levi snorts and interrupts, "You mean with you sneaking peeks at us and whacking off afterward?"

"Levi!" I scold, but Skyler laughs.

"Yeah, probably that. What I was going to say was that if you want to continue to explore a physical relationship, all the better. I want to be clear that I have no expectations about that and respect your marriage one hundred percent."

Levi loses his grin and looks first at me and then at Skyler. "I can't predict the future, obviously, but I think we need to explore what we've begun. I have never felt so good as when we were all three together. It was a high like never before, and you both know I really needed it." He looks closely at my expression then and explains, "I don't mean to belittle our sex life from before, Brooke. It was amazing. You're amazing, and I love you deeply and forever. But part of what I love about you is your openness. I hope you're still willing to include Sky in our bed. Thinking about what he and I can do for you together turns me on like…well…wow."

I can't suppress a small shiver when I think of the possibilities this offers. "I love the idea," I tell him softly. "You've known Skyler for several years now, and I see how much you mean to each other. Your connection doesn't worry or threaten me in the least; I frankly think it's hot. While I can't say I'm in love with Skyler in such a short amount of time, I can visualize that happening." I turn to Skyler and ask, "Are you at all worried about blowback from the community if and when they figure it out? Would you like us to be discreet? You're the one who grew up here; you know the attitudes of the residents way better than Levi and I do."

"I'm sure the reactions will be a mixed bag, but there isn't a lot we can do about that. You heard how Mrs. Henshaw reacted to Levi giving me a scalp massage, and she weaponized her attitude to get a rise out of her cronies. That's a small town for you. Some people will feel—or simply act— scandalized by us if they become aware, and others will celebrate our commitment and our happiness—if we decide commitment is the way we're headed. I think we just need to mind our own business and be ourselves. I have no room in my life for prejudice or bigotry, so I won't change to avoid it. It all boils down to this: it's no one's fucking concern who we choose to sleep with."

"Agreed. Well said," Levi says somberly. "But it may not always be easy. If you look at Juni, Asher, and Jack—they are all newcomers to the town. You're not. They might have different expectations placed on them by the community because of that. Some of the locals may even feel a certain—

for lack of a better word—*responsibility* for your actions because they've seen you grow up. The old 'it takes a village' thing. You're theirs."

Skyler laughs and says, "Well, anyone who thinks they have a right to an opinion ought to be told that I was swayed by more newcomers. Honeybee Hollow is obviously turning into a den of iniquity due to an influx of missionaries for sexual deviance."

"Aww…but 'missionary' is such a mundane way to do it," I scoff and then crack up. "We need to be the spice police!"

Levi stands and scoots his chair next to me. He sits and gives me a hot, probing kiss that makes my toes curl, and as he slides his hand under my shirt and up to my boob, he pulls back and says, "Then we'd better start practicing."

"Skyler's had a hard day." I tell Levi. "I think we need to take extra care of him and make him feel incredible."

CHAPTER

Twenty~Six

Boing! (That's the sound I hear in my head when my giant stiffy makes an instantaneous appearance). *Holy cow. She wants them both to take care of me? What does that even mean? Whatever it is, it's bound to be good.* I leap up from the table like my ass is on fire and whisk the pizza remains into the kitchen. "Come on!" I call to them, but I hear them snickering. *Why are they taking so long to make it to the bedroom? Oh yeah, Levi doesn't walk quickly yet.* I dash into the bathroom and brush my teeth and take care of business before they arrive. They're sitting on the bed having a quiet conversation when I meet them in their bedroom, and they both look at me with eager expressions.

"I locked the doors," Levi assures me with a half smile, and I nod because clearly, I need to remember to do that more often. Then he tells me, "I asked you what your fantasy was last night, and you told us you wanted Brooke's ass. Excellent choice, in my opinion. So just now, I asked Brooke her fantasy, and can you guess what she wants?"

I look at him then look at her. She looks pleased with herself. I don't have a clue. "Uh…no."

Levi winks and gives me a big smile.

"Skyler, honey…I think it would be amazing to see Levi make love to you." Brooke begins in a voice that's almost a purr. "Levi has fucked my ass many times, and he's great at it. But I've heard that it's even more pleasurable for a man to be on the receiving end of that. Would you like to have him do it to you? Are you ready for it?"

"We're not trying to pressure you," Levi says seriously as my breathing speeds up.

Is he for real? I close my eyes for a second, and before I can answer, Brooke adds, "But I want you to be making love to me at the same time."

Oh wow. That means I'll be the meat in the sandwich—the cream filling in the cookie the…fuck me! Well…literally this time. I clear my throat and croak, "God yes. Let's do it. Sounds good." My heart starts to race, and my eyes are riveted on her as Brooke begins to take off her clothes piece by piece. This is what she meant by taking care of me. I think I might be falling in love with her right here, right now. Not only is she gorgeous—she has the *best* ideas.

Levi also begins taking off his clothes, and I'm still staring at the two of them like a starstruck fool when Levi says, "Sky? I can't do anything for you with your pants on."

"Right. Um…okay." *Whoosh*, off go the shirt, shorts, and boxers, and I'm standing there with my eager boner practically pointing at the ceiling. Levi smirks a little, and Brooke licks her lips. She's naked now and looks me up and down with those incredible eyes of hers. She seems to see right into my soul, noticing my desire as well as my worries, so she smiles sweetly.

"I think you're going to love this, Sky honey. Come closer." Oh, I like it when she calls me that too. It's more intimate and personal than my full name, and no one but the two of them ever do it.

I step toward them, and while Levi finishes getting undressed, she reaches for me and strokes my cock. Her hands are warm and silky and—"Holy fuck!" I cry as she engulfs my dick right up to the hilt in her hot mouth. Levi stands and puts his hand up to my face, turning it toward him. He leans in and kisses me deeply, and I feel myself nearly coming in Brooke's mouth. I have to pull back. "Wait!" I cry. "It's too much. Slow down."

"If you come, we'll wait, and you can just come again," Levi assures me as he reaches around and strokes my butt. "Don't worry."

Brooke grabs my erection by the base with an iron grip, and while it feels great, it does slow down the inevitable. She definitely knows what she's doing. She eases up a little on the suction so I can catch my breath.

Levi kisses me again, sucking my tongue into his mouth and making a pleased sound as he strokes up and down in the crack of my butt. After shoving his tongue back into my mouth again, he pulls away and says, "'Scuse me, I need the lube." One of them has already placed the bottle on the bedside table so it's readily handy. Someone thought ahead.

While he squirts a generous amount of lube into his hand, Brooke scoots back and grabs a pillow that she positions under her hips. Smiling, she spreads her legs, and I stare at her, mesmerized, as she strokes her pussy. It's already glistening, pink and slippery—so ready for me to dive into. But I wait. This is no time to be greedy. I lean over and kiss Brooke the way Levi kissed me. Deeply. It turns out I love kissing her.

Levi urges my feet apart with his foot, and as soon as I'm bent over kissing his wife, he begins to lubricate around my hole. I jump at the first sensation of cold lube, but he strokes me and kisses my back. I warm to his ministrations quickly.

I kiss my way down Brooke's body, paying close attention to her beautiful tits. Her nipples are responsive, and she shivers when I suck first one then the other into my mouth. I don't even know what to concentrate on when I have those beauties in front of me and Levi fingering my rear. I gasp when his finger pushes inside me for the first time. I've done this to women, obviously including Brooke, but it is a new sensation entirely being on the receiving end.

I love it so far, so I'm trying to stay calm about what's coming. *I trust Levi*, I keep telling myself.

I back up a little so I can kiss my way down to that delicious cunt of hers. I lick all around it and slide my finger inside her as I find her clit and lick it with a firm tongue. Her response is magnificent and immediate as she cries, "Yes! More!" So I suck her clit into my mouth and go crazy with my tongue. My finger slides in and out of her, and I lick that nub for all I'm worth until Brooke hollers, "Yes! God yes!" and she shudders with what looks to me to be a satisfying orgasm.

"You're beautiful, babe," Levi tells her with reverence. "Can Sky fuck you now? He's so ready." I guess I am. I'm positively dripping pre-cum.

"Yes, please!" she says with a sparkling smile. "Make love to me, Sky."

I start to position myself, but Levi's hand joins mine on my dick. I guess he wants to guide me into her. This thought makes me even harder, if that's possible. I slide in and the feel of her is ambrosia. She's slick and tight. Hot as Hades. I hold myself still for a moment, just relishing this, when suddenly, I feel Levi shove what must be two fingers into my backside, and I start to shake. This is it. He's about to fuck me. I'm going to be fucked by my best friend. And I…love the idea. I tighten and release my muscles as if giving him a signal to go ahead, and I hear Levi chuckle.

"Alright, buddy, here I come." He slips his fingers out, and I immediately miss the pressure while he quickly lubes his dick.

He's doing a masterful job of staying hard tonight. I want to congratulate him, but that might not go over well, so I just say, "Now, Levi. I need your dick. Plow my ass while I fuck your wife!"

And with a firm grasp on my hips, in he goes, inch by inch. It's a strange feeling—not like his fingers because while it's bigger, it's also smoother and…well…just plain hotter. I'm so overcome with delicious sensations I don't know what to feel. Nothing…I mean *nothing* has ever come close to this. No wonder women like DP. I gasp for air because I forgot to breathe for a moment. I had to close my eyes, but when I finally do open them, I see Brooke looking up at my face with tenderness.

"You okay?" Levi asks. I nod as I realize I may have even blanked out for a second there. I remember that while I'm inside Brooke, the polite thing to do is to move in and out, so I attempt to do so, only to discover that Levi has me sort of pinned in place. "We'll get moving, Sky. Don't worry. I just wanted to make sure nothing was hurting you."

"Hurting? You've got to be kidding me," I say with a laugh. "This is fantastic!"

"Well alright then." He squeezes my hips and slides back, allowing me some room to move out of Brooke's pussy a bit.

Then he shoves back in, pushing me deeper, and Brooke lets out a deep moan.

"Oh, yeah," she whispers. "More, please. You know how I like it fast and hard, Levi. Give it to me, baby. Shove Skyler in so hard we'll both feel it tomorrow. Make him fill me up with his hot cum."

Ack! He does just that. Instead of pain, it causes an amazing chain reaction of exploding sensations. I can't get enough, so I cry, "Yes!" He hits my prostate at the same time as Brooke's muscles squeeze me. Ye gods, this is incredible.

"You guys are so hot together. You're making me crazy!" she exclaims. "Look at you loving on each other. Doesn't Levi's dick feel amazing, Sky? He's so big, and he fills you up so well. Have you ever felt anything like it? I loved it when you two were rubbing together inside of me, and I want more of that, but I love this, too! Come on, Levi, fuck us harder!"

And he does. I didn't know he could go any harder or faster than he was, but he's a living jackhammer in my body, and he's kissing my neck at the same time. Hard and soft, heat and desire. Why doesn't everyone do this? Why haven't we been doing it before now? Okay, I know the answer to that, but I'm sure going to make up for lost time if it's up to me. This is everything I ever imagined and more.

Wham, wham, wham, I pound into Brooke as Levi hammers me. Harder, faster, over and over until I can't take it anymore. "Coming!" I holler.

"Yes!" Brooke cries and convulses with spasms. "Ohmygod!"

"Almost there," Levi says through gritted teeth. And a few seconds later, I feel hot spurts fill me up as he pours himself into me. This is the strangest—and best—feeling ever. I'm still squirting my load into Levi's wife, who is shaking with her massive orgasm, while he ejaculates hot cum into my body.

What a rush. I want to do this forever.

Twenty~Seven

BROOKE

LAST NIGHT WAS ONE FOR THE BOOKS. TODAY, HOWEVER, I wake up with a mild case of cramps and decide this might be the best time to head back to Hopkinsville and pack up our stuff. No sense putting a damper on our budding sexual extravaganza by bowing out due to lady issues. I pop a couple Advil, sit down to breakfast, and let the guys know I'm heading to the house today.

"It shouldn't take more than a few days. If I have any questions about something you might want to keep, I'll call you and discuss it before getting rid of it," I assure Levi over breakfast. "And if you know of any items you're afraid I might overlook, make me a list, okay?" Levi nods with a mouthful of muffin, so I continue. "While I'm gone, the two of you might want to explore your new—let's call it 'awareness' of each other." I wiggle my eyebrows at them and get nervous laughter back. I hope I'm not pushing them.

Levi shoots a questioning look at Skyler, who grins back and says, "I never thought I had a queer bone in my body, but apparently, I was wrong. I don't know if it's just you, Levi, or whether I was brought up in a bubble where I never questioned my sexuality because I played football like a 'real man' and then became a soldier." He snorts. "Being able to experience things with both of you is beyond anything I ever imagined. We can *try* it with just the two of us, but I wonder if it will seem like the major ingredient is missing without Brooke."

"I understand what you're saying, but we'll also never know unless we try. I get it though. I swore I wasn't queer, but…" He shrugs at Skyler and looks at me as he takes my hand. "If at all possible, I love you more today, babe, than I did even just a couple of days ago. Your openness to exploring and your acceptance of Skyler—who is vitally important to me—goes beyond what I could ever imagine in a wife."

"I know what you mean," Skyler adds. "I've been so worried about fucking up your relationship, but I see that maybe I'm making it even stronger. When you weren't communicating with me, I felt horrible. I was missing something crucial, and that made me feel incomplete. But with Brooke *too*, it's like all the stars are aligned or some poetic crap." We all laugh at him. "Hey, I'm not the songwriter here. I may paint a picture about it, but poetic words are Levi's business, right, buddy?"

"You do just fine," Levi tells him with a fond look on his handsome face. "But a song might be a great idea."

"Okay, well, then let's just admit it," I tell them.

"What?" Levi asks.

"That we have something special and beautiful, and we're *all* falling in love."

They look momentarily surprised and then turn to each other.

"Probably," Skyler says.

"Could be," Levi says at the same time, and they both laugh. "I think I'll work on that song today after our beautiful Brooke heads out."

"And I think I'll do some sketching down here instead of way upstairs away from you," Skyler tells Levi.

"You don't want to paint today?" Levi asks.

"I do, but I also want your company, so I won't hole myself up there alone. I'll wait until you're busy with something or you can make it up the stairs comfortably. There are good acoustics in the studio; I know because I play music a lot when I paint. Keep that in mind for inspiration to get stronger."

"That reminds me, I have an appointment tomorrow with your PT guy."

"Yeah, he booked us back-to-back, so we can drive over together."

"Perfect," I tell them. I have a feeling things are going to go well for the three of us. Who'd have expected anything like this when I fell in love with Levi?

I don't need to pack much because I left clothes and whatnot at home, so less than an hour later, I'm on the road back to Hopkinsville. I downloaded a couple of ménage books to listen to on the road, just in case they give me some inspiration. One is by a favorite author of mine—Willa Camden. Rumor has it she doesn't write about ménage anymore because she married two guys and doesn't want people speculating that her bedroom scenes are autobiographical. The three of them are quite open about their polyamorous marriage, though, and I think that's amazing. The other book is by a famous author named Dolly Gunn. Her life is much more of a mystery. I can never find out anything about her. Too bad. I'd love to tell her how great her stories are, but I guess leaving five stars and a great review will have to suffice. Anyway, I look forward to their takes on threesomes.

I just have to remember to pay attention to the road while I'm driving and not get carried away by the stories.

A couple of rest stops—one for lunch—and a few hours later, I pull into our driveway. Somehow, the little house we shared looks a lot smaller and shabbier than I remember. The neighbor kid who was supposed to water the flowers I planted has neglected them. They're drooping and brown. Pathetic.

And just as I get out of the car, a helicopter flies over the house making a racket that makes me cringe. I'm sure we're making the right decision to move away.

The first thing I do when I get inside is check in at work and make sure I'm not leaving them in the lurch. Everything seems under control—amazing—so I ask to take another week off to move. After a lot of grumbling, my boss gives in. He knows what a hard worker I am, and I've been working a lot since the first week we arrived in Honeybee Hollow. I promise to tackle anything he throws at me as soon as this week is over.

The next thing I do is call the landlord and let him know we'll be out completely by the end of the month. Once again, I'm happy not to have a lease. I start packing and amassing stuff that will either be donated or tossed out.

FOR THE NEXT FOUR DAYS, I PACK, DISCARD, AND CLEAN MY way through the house. I've made lots of arrangements for changing our address and ending services like gas and electric. It's boring as all get out, so I continue to listen to audiobooks, and *whooee* am I ever getting an education!

I'm glad Levi didn't push to come help me do this, thinking he'd be the gentleman. He'd also have gotten worn out and would have been in a lot more pain than he'd have admitted to. I know him.

I catch up with a few friends and go out for drinks a couple of times, but I find I'm missing the guys terribly. At least I'm not worried about their lives, so missing them knowing they are safe and together is way easier to handle than when they were deployed. Still, I want to speed up this process and get back to Honeybee Hollow and my men. I check in with them each night before bed, and Levi and I have texted quite a bit about things to keep and things to ditch.

The guys have been somewhat silent on what they're doing together—if anything. I don't want to push or butt in, so I just ask generally how they're doing. They've both been to their appointments, and they've been painting and singing, so that's great. Levi is excited about a meeting he has with Buford Wallace, the bar owner who wants him to perform. Apparently, Buford has some musicians lined up for a gig this week and wants Levi to come in and hear them and then talk to them after the show. They're losing their singer because the guy's wife is getting transferred out of state, and Buford immediately thought of Levi for them. Things just might be happening for him in a positive way if he likes them and they like him.

Everything has been fairly calm, so I never, ever expected to get the phone call from Levi that prompted me to throw everything into the car, leave the keys on the kitchen table, and hightail it back to the Hollow as fast as I could. At least I was done sorting stuff. Maybe the house wasn't spotless when I left it, but this will have to do. Besides, I left it in better shape than when we originally moved in. I hadn't yet found a new home for a couple pieces of furniture of ours, so I left them there for the next tenants.

I'm a nervous wreck as I drive and have to tell myself repeatedly not to speed. Levi's tense words repeat in my head over and over, "Come home, Brooke. I need you. Skyler's been arrested!"

CHAPTER
Twenty~Eight

As soon as Brooke left the house, I felt the lack of her energy. Levi seemed to be doing fine emotionally, but there was a missing spark. Honestly, this didn't surprise me. She is a force of nature, and without her, we're just a couple of dudes. Sure, we're crazy about each other, but just as I suspected, we need Brooke to make this a complete relationship. Levi has been affectionate; I couldn't fault him there. But I'm sure that wherever we fit on the LGBTQ+ spectrum, it's not as purely homosexual men. We must be bi or pan or whatever defines men who are into each other but also need our woman to flourish.

We exchanged a few friendly kisses and some naked night-time snuggling for the first couple of days of Brooke's trip. It definitely feels good sleeping with Levi, and I love his big warm presence in the bed. But I didn't feel any huge desire to fuck or be fucked by him. Don't get me wrong—I loved what we did with Brooke, and getting my ass plowed by Levi was amazing, but I was also balls-deep in his gorgeous wife's pussy at the time.

Okay, I'll admit to jacking off in the shower, but it was only to get rid of morning wood. And sure, I thought about the two of them when I was doing it, but I didn't have to rub one out just because of Levi.

But on the third day, I was feeling more of a need. Maybe it's because that morning he woke up squashed against me with a huge boner poking my butt. I rolled over to face him, and he kissed me like he meant it this time. He grasped our dicks and began rubbing up and down on both of them together. It felt so good I had to let out a long moan. This was way better than doing it myself in the shower. I clasped his hand, and together we jacked us off simultaneously while rubbing our boners against each other. I'd never felt anything like it, and before long, we were both spilling all over ourselves, making a big, sticky mess. When we were finished, we both burst out laughing.

"We need to change the sheets," he told me.

"Totally worth it. Where'd you learn to do that?" I asked.

"I never learned it anywhere. I think it was just instinct." He gave me a goofy grin. "I liked it a lot."

So now, on day four of our bachelor life together, we're becoming a little more adventurous. And by that, I mean we're sucking each other off in the classic sixty-nine position. I wonder what Brooke would think of this. Knowing her, I bet she'd love seeing us do it.

On the fifth day of Brooke's absence, we both slept late because Levi had an appointment last night with Buford Wallace at his bar. I thought he was just going to meet some musicians and talk about maybe working with them, but when he finally wandered in at three in the morning, he told me he'd listened to them play, and when the bar closed, he jammed with them until they were too tired to play anymore. He hadn't been drinking, but he was high on the excitement of a new adventure. It was great to see him like that. He's agreed to play a bunch of gigs with them. I'm sorry I didn't go with him, but I didn't think it was going to be anything other than talking.

I used my solo hours productively, however. I painted up in the studio until I could barely lift a brush. My shoulder is burning this morning, so a good BJ sounded way better than using my right hand and arm to do anything strenuous. It turns out I'm pretty good at giving left-handed blowies. Anyway, I thought we needed to celebrate. So here we are sucking the daylights out of each other, and man is it feeling good. We blow our loads at almost the same time, and this time I'm not afraid to swallow his cum. It tastes…eh…okay. But I know he likes that I'm doing it because he's doing the same for me, and I feel this great sense of belonging to him when he does it. My God, I love this man.

We spend a few minutes relaxing, and he laughs softly. "Much neater this way, and we don't have more laundry to do."

I snort back at him. "Yeah." We're a couple of romantic beasts with each other, obviously.

I know we need showers, but the need for coffee and food outweighs that issue, so I grab the shorts I was wearing last night off the floor and toss them on, saying, "I'll meet you in the kitchen. My stomach is starting to eat itself, and I don't want another headache. I'll start the coffee." I should have set up the coffee pot last night, but I was too engrossed in my painting. "I don't know about you, but I'm still exhausted." Levi chuckles and nods at me.

Levi must have taken a quick shower because he shows up with dripping hair and wearing nothing but a pair of low-slung jeans. He's beautiful, and I relish the sight of him. I get the urge to lick him, but I have to eat. Food.

We're on our second cup of joe and almost finished with our eggs, bacon, and cinnamon rolls when we hear a knock on the door.

"What a nice change from people barging in. I'll get it," Levi says. "Finish your breakfast." He limps away—but just a little—with no cane, and I realize how much better he's moving after only one visit to my PT guy. The exercises he's been doing seem to help a lot too, or maybe it's also partly due to his positive outlook on life now. I hope so.

I hear a deep, familiar voice ask for me. Levi sounds puzzled as he says, "Uh, sure. Come on in. You can have some coffee with us. He's in the kitchen."

Heavy booted footsteps follow Levi's nearly silent bare-foot ones into the room, and I'm as shocked as shit to see Deputy Sheriff Blake Ogden's gloomy expression as they join me. He's worked in the Hollow now for about three or four years, as I recall. He's a nice guy, and I've only had friendly interactions with him. We've even had a beer or two together.

When Levi goes to grab a mug, Blake tells him, "No thanks. I'm here on official business."

Huh?

"Mr. Colfax, may I ask your whereabouts last night between the hours of ten and one?"

I blink at him in confusion and answer, "I was here at home, Blake. What's going on?" Why isn't he calling me Skyler like he always has in the past?

"Is there anyone who can vouch for that?"

Levi speaks up. "I know he was here."

"Were you here too, Mr....?"

"This is my buddy Sergeant Levi Spencer," I tell him. Maybe using his military title will sound more official or some shit. Blake is former military himself.

Blake narrows his eyes at Levi and says, "Weren't you the anthem singer at the Fourth of July party?"

"Yes, sir. And no, I wasn't here with Skyler all evening because I had a late-night meeting to go to, but I know he was here when I left and here when I got back. I took his car, so…"

"Are you in the habit of meeting people in the middle of the night?" He eyes Levi suspiciously, and I don't like it a bit.

Levi lets out a frustrated breath. "I'm a singer—as you know—and musician, and the meeting was with Buford Wallace at The Hive. I had to wait for the show to end to talk to the musicians there. I assure you, I was not up to something shady. You can ask Buford, and he'll tell you I was there on business."

"Do you have any other means of transportation besides your car, Mr. Colfax?"

"Well, I do have a business truck from our family garden center that I keep here. But stop calling me that."

Ignoring my suggestion to lighten up, he asks, "And did you drive it to leave the house last night?"

"No, of course not."

He looks at Levi again and reiterates, "So you were here before ten and after one, but you cannot swear to Mr. Colfax's whereabouts during those hours. Is that correct?"

"Yes, but he wouldn't lie about it. He was upstairs working in his studio the whole time I was gone."

"Sergeant Spencer, please do not leave town. We will be contacting you again for more information after I verify what you've told me about your whereabouts. Mr. Colfax, I'm going to have to ask you to come with me. You're under arrest for the assault of Marjorie Henshaw. She named you as her attacker." He proceeds to recite to me my Miranda rights. This is fucking unreal!

I jump up and grab my hair. "What? What do you mean I'm under arrest? I haven't seen Mrs. Henshaw in days, and why would I want to hurt her? This is a huge mistake!"

"Sir, what are those stains on your shorts?"

I look down and see some rusty splashes on my shorts. I didn't even realize I'd made a mess on them. "I was painting! Those are paint! You can't arrest me for *painting*!"

"I'm sorry, Mr. Colfax, I see now that the stains are paint, but you're going to have to come with me anyway."

"What? Blake, come on, man! You *know* me. I'm not in the habit of going around hurting people or breaking the law in any way!"

Finally, he looks contrite and answers, "Yeah, I know. But I am under a strict directive from Sheriff Hansen to bring you in. I wish I didn't have to, but orders are orders."

"Isn't he some kind of distant cousin to Mrs. Henshaw or something?" I ask.

"I believe that may be true."

Trying to exhale some of my mounting stress, I ask, "Can I at least take a shower and put on some clean clothes?"

"Sorry, no. Your friend here can go get you a shirt and a pair of shoes, and that's it. You'll have to stay here with me. According to Sheriff Hansen, I'm not supposed to let you out of my sight."

Levi scoots out of the room, and while he's gone, I ask shakily, "I'm really sorry she's hurt. How badly injured is she?"

"It appears someone was quite angry with her and beat her rather severely. But at least she made it to her neighbor's house for help when the attacker left."

"Oh jeez. I think I'm going to be sick." Yep, I was right. I bolt to the kitchen sink where I lose my breakfast. I rinse out the sink and my mouth and turn around. "How could you possibly think I'd have anything to do with that?"

"Honestly? I don't. But word around town is that she's been complaining about how you threatened her and refused to pay her for working here. She reported to several people that you were belligerent and scared her. I guess that information reached Sheriff Hansen, and he wanted a quick resolution, so I was sent to pick you up."

"That's ridiculous. Levi and his wife were both here and can vouch for what was really said when I asked her to leave. I don't owe her a dime. And I sure as hell never touched her!"

Levi reappears and hands me a clean t-shirt and a pair of sneakers. His face is pale, and his eyes are huge.

"Please put on the rest of your clothes, Sk…Mr. Colfax."

I want to brush my teeth, but I doubt that's going to happen, so I pull on the shirt and sit down to tie my shoes. Levi looks as shocked as I feel. Who would hurt an old lady? And how bad did the gossip get for the sheriff to think it was me? I stand up, and Blake cuffs me. *He cuffs me*! I've never felt so mortified in my life. At least he put the handcuffs on in front of my body instead of behind my back when I showed him that my arm doesn't move in that direction very well yet. He saw my damaged shoulder while my shirt was off, so he didn't object. That was decent of him, at least.

"Levi, please call my dad." I rattle off the number to him as he punches it into his phone. I'm glad he has it handy. "He'll know a lawyer, I hope."

Twenty~Nine

Levi

I can't believe any of this. I'm utterly speechless as I see Skyler being driven away in the deputy's vehicle, and in cuffs, no less. We're trained soldiers, and we're used to combat situations—and sadly Skyler and I have had to take some lives. But it's a hideous feeling even when the person who is maimed or dies is your mortal enemy who wanted to kill you first. It's the kind of memory you bury in the deepest, darkest recesses of your brain and hopefully never revisit again.

But Skyler being vindictive enough to beat up a gossipy old shrew? Never. She may have been obnoxious, but no one deserves to be thrashed for that. There must be a terrible person at large in this town. Is Honeybee Hollow deceptively tranquil but actually harboring a madman? As I was leaving to get Skyler some clothes, I overheard the deputy say Mrs. Henshaw was in a bad way. I know Sky wouldn't have wished that on anyone.

Still…I hate that I'm even thinking this. I did call Skyler from the bar when I knew I'd be extra late coming home, and he didn't answer me. So I sent a text to let him know. I didn't even remember it when I got here because I was so excited about how well it had gone with the band. Maybe he was in the bathroom or had his music up too loud and missed the call. I don't know…*No*! He couldn't have left and hurt an old lady. It's just not in his nature. I banish any doubt right then and there. He would never!

I do as Skyler asked and immediately call Mike Colfax. With a shaking voice, I try to the best of my ability to explain what happened, and I ask if he can get Skyler a lawyer. His father is justifiably outraged and swears he'll take care of things. "Skyler should have sued that old biddy for slander when she first started spreading those awful rumors about him," he grumbles into the phone.

"Yes, sir," I reply, but I know Skyler would never have sued her. He expected her story to blow over.

Obviously not paying much attention to me, he continues, "And Sheriff Hansen isn't much better for believing that crap about my son. He has so little to do, he's probably overly excited about having a crime to handle before he retires. I'll make that call right now, Levi. Thanks for alerting me. Take care, son. We'll get this fixed."

Then I call the one person I need now as much as air to breathe—Brooke. I can barely choke out the words, "Come home, Brooke. I need you. Skyler's been arrested!"

Naturally, Brooke is flabbergasted with my news, so I try to make the situation sound better by explaining that Skyler's dad is getting a lawyer, and hopefully, he can get him out quickly on bail. I'm sadly ill-informed about people getting arrested for assault—or pretty much for anything. All I know is that I'm spiraling, and unless I can get a grip soon, I won't be any good to myself or anyone else. I'm scared and angry and feel like dogshit. What started out a great day has devolved into crap.

I decide to clean up the kitchen and discover by the smell that someone was sick in the sink. Poor Skyler. He tried to clean it up, but he missed a bit. At least this gives me something to do. I don't know how long it will take Brooke to get here, and I don't know if I can do anything for Skyler if I go sit in the sheriff's office and try to argue his case. I don't want to make anything worse. I just fucking don't know what to do.

My dilemma is somewhat handled when, about twenty-five minutes after Deputy Ogden hauled Skyler away, some other officers show up with a warrant to search the house. Nothing will come of me being anything other than a hundred percent cooperative, so I let them in and resolve to answer any questions they may have. They don't have many. I also have no idea what they're looking for.

They search all over the ground floor, including the unmade bed that we vacated not too long ago. I'm sorry I hadn't thought to straighten up because I don't like the smirks I get when they realize there is just one messed-up bed that clearly accommodated two people. Closed-minded assholes. When they see women's clothing in the closet, they probably decide one of us is a cross-dresser to boot. I don't bother to comment when they squint at me.

They tromp around upstairs a while, and I don't want to risk making my hip hurt more, so I don't follow them. When they come right back down quickly, I tell them, "You missed the important part. Skyler was upstairs painting for hours last night on the third floor in his studio. My hunch is strong that you'll find both a semi-dry painting and some color splotches that match the stains on his shorts he left here wearing." And I can't help but add sarcastically, "You're welcome."

They stomp away, clomping up the stairs to the attic. I still can't imagine what they think they'll find unless something was stolen from Mrs. Henshaw when she was beaten. I wonder too what might prompt someone to break in and fight with her. I have so many questions. I don't even know if it was a break-in.

Once they finally leave—telling me not to skip town—I proceed to start cleaning up the bedroom and try not to get too upset. It's not working. I have too much anger and too much quiet. But then Sky's dad calls to tell me they have a bail hearing set for an hour from now. "Want me to pick you up, son?"

"Yes, sir. I'll be ready right away," I tell him. Skyler needs to see that I support him.

WHAT A FUCKING NIGHTMARE. SKYLER AND I FINALLY GET home around the same time Brooke shows up. He's met with his lawyer—a guy named Hamilton—and posted bail to the tune of $5,000. I think that's the maximum they could ask for, so of course they gave him that. It turns out that in Kentucky, the sentence for assault is ten to twenty years with a $10,000 fine!

Skyler's lawyer, however, has taken photos of Skyler's hands, showing that there is no bruising or damaged skin that would be consistent with a severe beating as described by Mrs. Henshaw. We haven't seen her to determine for ourselves what kind of shape she's in, but his lawyer asked for a complete account of her injuries, including photographs. The whole thing seems like someone is trying to frame Skyler for something he couldn't have possibly done—even if he didn't answer my call. I'm keeping silent about that. They don't need any more fuel for their ridiculous charges.

Skyler has been morose ever since I first saw him in the courthouse. Getting out of cuffs didn't even do much to raise his spirits, and he was pretty silent on the way home. Now that we're here with Brooke, I thought he might cheer up a little, but all he said was, "I'm going to go take a shower."

"I'm sure Skyler's starving by now, babe. We should make some supper," I say to Brooke. "I can probably grill something if you want to put a salad together."

When Skyler returns to the kitchen with wet hair and fresh clothes, we're both in the throes of cooking. "Thanks, guys. I could go for a beer. Anyone else want one?" he asks.

Brooke smiles and suggests, "Here, have some cheese and crackers before you drink on an empty stomach." She pushes a tray toward him on the counter. I love that she's taking care of him. "You know, Skyler, we believe you," she tells him and walks around the counter to wrap her arms around him in a warm embrace. My heart gives a little jolt…and so does something in my pants. What is it about seeing the two of them together that gets me so worked up? He buries his face in her neck and breathes in the sweet smell of her. Like a moth to a flame, I scoot over and join the group hug, wrapping my arms around both of them. I can feel Skyler giving a big sigh, and his muscles relax a bit.

"After we eat, I think we need to…you know…" I suggest. I don't know what to call it. Fucking? Making love? Having extracurricular activities? "Cheer up with some fun in the bedroom."

Brooke makes up my mind when she says, "Yes, I desperately need to make love to both of you. I missed you so much while I was gone. I want to show you how badly."

"Works for me," Skyler says with a groan.

"You need to eat first," Brooke says with finality as she hands him a cheese-topped cracker. "And I have a special idea for later."

"Yes ma'am." He winks at her, and arousal zips through me like a lightning rod. At least he seems to be relaxing.

Thirty

BROOKE

I KNOW NONE OF WHAT HAPPENED IS MY FAULT, BUT I FEEL guilty for leaving my guys anyway. It took no time at all for everything to go to pot. Except for walking a little better, Levi looks terrible—he's a nervous wreck again.

Skyler isn't doing much better. He has a haunted expression in his eyes that I'd love to kiss away. He should have little reason to be scared because he hasn't done anything wrong, but mistakes can be made, and he might be worried about a wrongful conviction. I don't know anything about how they deal with crime in this town, but I assume there isn't much of it, which means it's hard to know how the townspeople will react. I'm so mad at that Henshaw woman for blaming Skyler and for casting doubt on him in the first place. No one deserves a beating, but it's hard to drum up a lot of sympathy for her considering her cruel gossipmongering.

I try to keep the mood light while we have our meal, but Skyler is still awfully quiet. I tell them about how I managed to clear the house of the things we owned but wouldn't need and how the landlord said he had a waiting list for people wanting to rent the place. Levi shows a little interest in my stories, but not much. He only perks up when I ask him about his meeting with the musicians.

"We're going to start playing together on Wednesday nights at the bar, and I'll have to have some rehearsals with them, of course. If things go well, Buford says he might add Saturdays to our schedule, and we'll start looking for gigs around Kentucky and Virginia. I don't want to be away a lot, though, and I told them I'm more interested in songwriting and singing locally. They were cool with that. We'll just see how things develop. It's going to be fun to pursue this."

"I'm proud of you, buddy," Skyler tells him as he rubs Levi's back. But he doesn't offer any more than that. I know his head must be spinning with his own troubles.

"So!" I say with enthusiasm. "Are you guys ready for something fun and extra hot? I did some research during my trip, and I have something amazing in mind for us."

"What is it?" Levi asks.

"Don't worry, you'll see. I'll lead you both through this,

and we should all love it. Just keep an open mind and stay relaxed." I hope this is the right time; we need to lighten the mood around here.

"This doesn't require any restraints, does it?" Skyler asks with narrowed eyes. I get the feeling he didn't appreciate the handcuffs and would not find them sexy.

"Absolutely not. This is all about mutual satisfaction and demonstrating our affection for each other." They seem to be relaxing a little, so I say, "It's best if we try this in the bedroom, and we'll need plenty of lube. Ready?"

"Lead the way," Levi says.

"Yeah, all the better for enjoying the sight of that ass of yours as you walk down the hall ahead of us," Skyler says with a snicker.

I give an extra swing to my steps as I guide them into the bedroom. I know my butt is cute, but it's not the focal point of this sexual romp we'll be having. I'll let them enjoy it while they can anyway. As we trail down the hall, I pull my top off over my head and glance over my shoulder to see that the guys are following my unspoken suggestion. Good boys. I give them a wink and undo the zipper of my jeans as we hit the bedroom. I kick off my sandals and slide off the pants so I'm down to sexy lingerie. I turn to face them and feel a warmth spread through me when I see their appreciative stares at my body.

"Okay, guys, lose the rest of your clothes and then I want

Levi to lie down in the middle of the bed. Get comfortable. Skyler, where's the lube?"

Skyler grabs a generously sized bottle out of the bedside table and places it next to the alarm clock. I close the drapes, and Levi turns on a lamp. "Good thinking, Levi," I tell him. "You'll both want to see this as we each do our part."

I whip off the undies, climb onto the bed next to Levi, and kiss him. My hands wander all over his beautiful body, taking in his toned abs and his strong arms. I lower my hand and circle his cock. It's getting there, but it's not hard enough yet, so I beckon Skyler over, "Help me with some of your magic here, please." I indicate Levi's semi. Skyler scoots next to Levi and kisses his chest, then slides down my husband's body to use his mouth on Levi's dick. I love this. These men are so amazingly masculine and yet not afraid to appreciate each other's body this way. Levi groans into my mouth while I kiss him and Skyler sucks on him, playing with his balls and his taint at the same time.

Then I turn my attention to Skyler's dick and take him into my mouth. Immediately, both men groan.

There it is. Levi loves seeing me with Skyler, so he's now fully at attention and flexing his hips as Skyler pumps up and down on him. "Don't get carried away yet, guys. We have lots more to do," I tell them. I release Skyler's cock, kiss him, and climb over Levi in the classic reverse cowgirl position, looking toward Levi's feet. "Hold him steady, Sky. I'm going to slide down onto him. Can you play with my clit at the same time with your other hand?"

"Sure."

Levi grasps my hips and pushes his way into me as I slide down onto him. He feels so wonderful, and I'm so wet for this, there's no need for lube…yet. I don't want to dwell on how much I missed this, but that long dry spell was hard to take.

Skyler's eyes are riveted to the place where Levi and I are connected, and he's grinning. He leans in and licks my clit and then swirls his tongue around the base of Levi's erection. He alternates licking us for a while as Levi hisses and groans with pleasure. I can feel Levi's hands go up to my breasts, and he fondles them a while, caressing and plucking at my sensitive nipples. Each time he does it, a zing goes through me, straight to my core.

Skyler eventually focuses on my clit long enough to bring me to a magnificent orgasm that goes crashing through me like a tidal wave. I pant my way through it and relax a moment before asking Skyler, "Okay, now grab the lube and then give me your dick. I need to suck you some more and make sure you're as hard as steel."

"Yes, ma'am," he says with a silly salute.

With the lube in his hand, Skyler gets up on his knees in front of me and presents his lovely hard cock. It's already like steel, but I don't want to miss an opportunity to turn him on even more, so I grasp him and swallow him as deeply as I can go.

"Holy fuck!" he shouts as Levi chuckles. I gag a tiny bit, and my eyes begin to water.

Once I know he's about to burst, I pull back with a pop and drop him from my mouth. I take the lube from him and slather him up. He has a quizzical look on his face, so I explain, "You're going to put this monster inside my pussy alongside Levi."

"No way!" he says breathlessly. "How's that supposed to fit?"

"Don't worry. My body is pliable, and it'll accommodate you. Just start with a finger in there and then add another. Once that feels okay, you can slip your dick in instead."

"My wife certainly has some interesting ideas," Levi says with a strangled laugh as Skyler takes me up on my instructions. "Wow! Sky, do that again with your finger. That feels amazing!"

Skyler's finger rubs up and down inside me, caressing Levi's dick at the same time. It's a tight fit, but I'm so freaking turned on, it's incredible. I'm still ultrasensitive from my recent orgasm, and I can tell it won't take much to take me over the top again. Skyler pulls his finger out and goes back in again with two this time. It's amazing! I feel such fullness and an almost burning stretch. Pleasure is hitting me in places I never knew I had. I can't help groaning.

"Are you okay, Brooke?" Skyler asks softly.

Levi chuckles. He knows all too well that I'll never back down from something like this.

"I'm so ready for you, Skyler. Use your gorgeous dick to make love to both of us." I'm breathing hard, and my heart is pounding. I regret not being able to see Levi's face right now, but he's like a titanium rod inside me. He's loving this as much as I am. I know he's getting off on something new.

Skyler slips his fingers out, squirts an extra dollop of lube on himself, and straddles Levi's legs to get into position. The head of his dick is broader than his fingers, so it's going to take some effort on our parts to accomplish this, but I make myself relax as much as I possibly can. And there it goes. Just a little at a time, and I can't deny there's some pain. But I honestly love the burn. It's intense, though, so I open my mouth and breathe deeply in and out, concentrating on getting air into my lungs while Skyler concentrates on getting himself into my body. Finally, with what feels like something that should have made an audible pop, his dickhead completely breaches my entrance, and he's sliding in next to Levi.

"Ohmygod, you're in!" I cry.

"Yes!" Levi hollers.

"Oh, holy fucking fuck!" Skyler bellows. "I've never imagined anything like this!"

I hear the snap of the lube lid opening, and suddenly there is the added excitement of Levi's finger slipping into my ass. Talk about total immersion in sensation. This is even more than I'd bargained for. Skyler starts to pump in and out of me, rubbing up and down against Levi. Levi's body shudders, and he's sliding his finger in and out of me from behind. I quake

with an orgasm that threatens to make me black out. This is…
well…there are no superlatives strong enough to describe it.
Skyler swallows my cries with a breathtaking kiss as I attempt
not to bite his tongue while I spasm and shake with ecstasy.

Levi is hollering up a storm behind me, telling Skyler,
"Harder! Don't stop! I love this! I love you both so much I
could die of it," and so on until he grits his teeth and makes a
noise that I swear sounds like a bull elephant.

Skyler's arms go around me, and he chokes out, "Levi,
your hot cum feels so good coating me *inside* of Brooke. I
think I've found my happy place," he laughs. After a few more
pumps, he's the last to come with a giant victory cry. He
throws his head back and closes his eyes, and the look on his
face is one of sheer delight. We all savor this moment until
their dicks begin to deflate, and I feel the hot ooze of their
combined releases seeping out of me. Levi removes his finger
from my backside and pulls me down to him so he can kiss my
neck.

Love shines out of me in all directions.

This was even better than how it sounded in the Dolly
Gunn book I listened to. I'm so glad I asked my men to go
along with my plan.

I don't want to stress Levi's hip, so I position myself
beside him while Skyler moves to the other side. We probably
look like a contented pride of lions with stuffed bellies right
now. Lazy and drunk with satiety. Only it's not our stomachs
that are full—it's our hearts. Nothing has ever felt this good.

"Brooke, honey?" Skyler asks.

"Hmm?"

"You sure do know how to take a shit day and turn it around. If I haven't told you and Levi enough times that I love you yet, then shame on me."

"Aw, Sky. You say the sweetest things. I love you both too," I say softly. I'm about to fall asleep.

"Me too," Levi mumbles. "Love you…"

It's about fifteen minutes before we stir from this position. The fact that we're all sticky with cum and lube hasn't bothered anyone yet, but I finally suggest a shower.

"Sounds good, and then how about a soak in the hot tub?" Skyler offers. We agree that would be a relaxing end to a day fraught with all kinds of emotion. I just hope no one shows up out of the blue. This privacy is nice.

We quickly shower and head outside wrapped in our towels, keeping the outside lights off. Skyler heads to the kitchen for some bottles of water while Levi turns on the hot tub jets. I light some citronella candles, and then he and I climb into the tub. Ahh…feels great. I don't know if the candles really work the way they're supposed to, but the flickering light creates a pleasant atmosphere, at least.

Levi has a quizzical look on his face, so I ask, "Is something wrong?"

"Not really. I'm just curious about something I meant to ask Sky about and haven't remembered until now. I'm sure there must be a logical answer."

The back door opens, and Skyler is all smiles as he approaches the tub with our waters in his hands just as Levi, who is facing away from the door, says, "I called Sky last night to tell him I'd be back later than I expected, and he never picked up or answered my text message. That seemed weird."

My eyes immediately go to Skyler and see his jaw drop.

Uh oh.

CHAPTER
Thirty~One

I can't fucking believe it. Levi...my best friend in the entire world—someone I love to death—actually doubts my whereabouts last night? How could he?

"So *you* think I'm guilty too?" I swear to God, I feel like crying. This *hurts*. I smack the bottles down and turn to go back into the house. I have to get away from him, but dammit, this is my house. Before I grab the doorknob, I whip around and say, "Maybe it's time for you to leave. I sure as fuck don't need any more doubters around me."

Levi looks shocked, but I don't give him a chance to say anything. I stomp back inside, rush down the hall, grab a pair of shorts, and thunder upstairs to my studio, taking the steps two at a time. My sanctuary ought to provide some comfort, but it doesn't. Once I hit the attic level, I'm way too upset and out of breath to paint, but I also can't stick around and listen to how *he* doesn't trust me. I'm too worked up to do anything except pace around.

But…he called me? I wonder why I didn't know that. I reach into my shorts pocket to check my phone and realize it's not there. Then I wonder when the last time I saw it was. I scan around the room and see it sitting next to the sink. Oh yeah. The darn battery ran out of juice again, and I'd meant to take it down to the bedroom to plug it in last night. But it was so late by the time I quit painting, I forgot about my phone, and all I did was clean up and head downstairs. Then Levi showed up and we had our fun. Damn. I can't even power it up to see any missed calls or texts. I need a charger up here too, I guess.

As I stand there contemplating what to do since I just impulsively gave Levi his walking papers—and possibly too swiftly—I hear a noise coming from the stairway. Frowning, I turn toward the door, and in shuffles Levi. He's beet red and limping worse than I've ever seen. This gives me a serious pang in my heart. I can't believe he forced himself to climb all the way up to the third floor when stairs are so horrible for him. While I appreciate the effort, and I hate seeing him in pain, I'm still furious with him. And I'm hurt.

I glare daggers at him as he takes a deep breath. He's still only wrapped in his towel, so apparently it was more important to see me than it was to get dressed. Huh.

"Sky," he says softly through his labored breathing. His beautiful brown eyes are filled with so much sadness, it *almost* breaks my heart. Not quite though. I do acknowledge that he must be in considerable pain after climbing up here, but I'm not ready to forgive.

"Save it. I can't listen to one more person tell me how I did something awful—least of all you!"

"I *can't* save it. You need to understand that I was not doubting *you* for one minute. I was just curious about why you didn't answer my call, that's all." His eyes bore into mine intensely. "When I got home, you never mentioned anything about it. Why? It's a simple question. Were you too busy painting something wonderful or…stuck in the bathroom?"

"I never knew you called. Dead battery. I think I need a new phone; this one isn't holding a charge very well anymore. But you must have doubted my whereabouts to even bring it up, Levi, and that kills me."

"I swear I never doubted you. I just remembered about the call and happened to mention it to Brooke. According to her, you heard part of that question but not the part where I said it wasn't any big deal—just something I was curious about. I meant no accusation at all."

"Oh."

"You were pretty swift to tell me to hit the road though. Are you having second thoughts about Brooke and me moving in permanently? Are you not ready for us? I thought you loved us, and it was your idea to bring us here in the first place. But if you truly want us gone, we'll find somewhere else to live."

Levi has a miserable, pinched look to his face and is having trouble standing up straight, so I tell him, "I think you ought to sit down and rest your hip. You look bad."

"Yeah, my hip hurts, but not as much as your rejection." That hits me like a fastball to the solar plexus. It nearly shatters me.

"I can relate to that. The idea that you were throwing me under the bus pains me like hell. I guess it hurts the worst coming from someone I love and assumed trusts me."

"I do trust you," Levi says with a grimace as he lowers himself onto the cot that I keep up here for emergency naps. Relief fills his face as soon as he alleviates the pressure of standing from his hip. He's gonna feel the hike up here for days to come, I bet.

I stare at him, and suddenly I can't stand it any longer. I take a deep breath and flop down next to him. "Levi, I'm sorry. This whole getting arrested thing has messed with my brain. I know you love me, and I certainly love you and Brooke. I want you here, and it was wrong of me to jump to conclusions about what you said. Can I get you a pain pill?"

"I'll get one later, thanks. I apologize too. I shouldn't have even brought up the phone call. It was just a throwaway thought that popped into my head, and I can see how you could have misinterpreted my intentions. Are we good? I sure don't want to move out, especially after the amazing things we did after dinner. That kind of lovemaking was transcendental." He lifts his hand and strokes my arm, then grasps my hand and holds on tight.

I squeeze his hand and ask, "Why didn't Brooke help you up the stairs?" I hope she isn't doubting my innocence too.

Levi gives me a rueful look. "She told me I needed to clean up my own mess, so I left her in the hot tub. She's pretty exhausted from packing and driving all day and then arriving in the middle of our emotional chaos. She said she had faith that we'd figure out our differences."

"She's a wise woman then. Are you ready to go back down and join her, or do you need a moment?"

"Emotionally, I want to go back down so all three of us are together, but physically, I need a break from the stairs."

"Okay. Then lie back and relax with me, and we'll head down when you're ready." I put my arms around Levi, and we both collapse onto the pillow together. It feels so good to spoon him and keep him in my arms. I hated being mad at him. I nuzzle his neck and whisper, "I'll try to do better. I was a jerk."

"You'll have to speak up, Sky. You know...my hearing problem?"

"Yeah, right. You heard me."

"Yeah, I did. I was a jerk too."

"I was a bigger one," I insist.

"Alright, you win."

Once we finally begin the laborious trip back down with me supporting a lot of Levi's weight, I lead him into the bathroom to grab a pain pill. It's then that we discover Brooke, who has already turned off the hot tub, locked up the house, and gone to bed.

"Are you guys both good again?" she asks groggily as she sits up in the spot in the big bed I've been claiming as my own for the past few days. It's wonderfully obvious that Brooke has decided to sleep in the nude.

"Yes," we both say.

"Have you kissed and made up?"

"Not yet," Levi tells her. He turns to me and grabs my face. He lays one on me that I feel all the way to my toes.

"That's better," she says. "Now come to bed. I have more ideas for tomorrow, and we all need our rest. One particular part of *me* needs lots of rest," she says with a soft laugh and snuggles back down under the blanket.

How did we all get to be so lucky? In the midst of a horrible day, we have Brooke and her love to shield us like a colorful, safe umbrella in a crazy shitstorm.

I stand there for a moment pondering what to do when Levi whispers in my ear, "Just climb into the middle. I'm sure

Brooke would love it if you spooned her, and I need to hold you."

Okay then. I will wallow in their affection tonight after the shit show earlier today. I smile, whip off my shorts, and before I crawl under the covers, I plug in my phone. Once in bed, the amount of warm, naked skin on both sides of me is like a dream. It only takes a moment before we're all sound asleep.

CHAPTER

Thirty-Two

Levi

Unsurprisingly, we all wake up famished in the morning. "Let's go start breakfast," I suggest as Skyler takes his turn in the bathroom. "Sky can find us when he comes out."

We pull on some clothes and head for the kitchen. Brooke decides to make pancakes and tells me to take care of the bacon and coffee. Sounds good, but I'm going to throw in some scrambled eggs too. I'm starving.

As we're about to sit down to eat, there's a loud knock at the door, and all three of us groan. Skyler drags himself off to answer it. We hear him say, "Hey, Blake. Are you here to arrest me again? If so, you better come on inside, I don't want the embarrassment of getting cuffed again in case anyone sees us out here."

Skyler returns with Deputy Sheriff Blake Ogden who looks contrite as he says, "No one can even see your house, Skyler. It's too far back from the road."

"You never know who's going to show up around here lately though. Coffee? You don't look like you're on official business today since you're out of uniform,"

"Oh, uh, yeah, please. I'd love a cup. Cream if you have it. It's my day off."

"We don't have any donuts, but Brooke made a big stack of pancakes if you're interested," Skyler offers.

"Ha ha. Everything sure looks good, and I'd be a fool to turn it down. Thanks. Look, Skyler, I came to apologize again. I know you're an upstanding guy, and you'd never hurt a lady. I had to come get you yesterday because it was my job, and sometimes my job sucks, especially with my arrest-happy boss. I can't wait for that old fart to retire. He watches too many cop shows and believes we have a crime spree in Honeybee Hollow if he sees a piece of litter in the road."

When we chuckle, Blake shakes his head, "I'm not joking. When we're in our patrol vehicles, we're supposed to keep an eye out for litterbug criminals. So when Mrs. Henshaw accused you, it got him so excited he about had a heart attack."

"I get it," I tell him as Levi and Brooke set down platters

of food in front of us, and she grabs another place setting for Blake. Finally, she sits down with us and holds out her hand.

"Hi. We haven't met. I'm Brooke Spencer, Levi's wife. We live here now too."

"Pleased to meet you, ma'am. Welcome to Honeybee Hollow."

"Thanks. It's Brooke. Not ma'am. And there's lots more batter if we need more pancakes, so don't be shy."

"Yeah, okay. Brooke. Sorry. Thanks for breakfast." He turns to Skyler and says, "So, besides apologizing, I wanted to come by and give you some information about a private investigator you might want to have your lawyer contact. He's like a PI ninja, and he gets amazing results. This case smells like bad fish, so if you want to get to the bottom of things, Doug Freeman is your guy. He's had some terrific results in cases all through Kentucky I can't talk about, and one of them was so sensitive, he left the country with his family for a few years. I have my suspicions about what the threat against him was, but now that the person I suspect was his tormentor has passed away, I guess he felt safe returning home again. Here's his card." He produces a business card and passes it to Skyler. All it has on it is a name and phone number.

"I appreciate that, Blake. Thanks. Now, let's not talk about this crap anymore and just enjoy breakfast."

"I'm all for that," I agree.

"Dig in, guys," Brooke says with a sweet smile.

"You have no idea how nice it is to have a home-cooked

meal for once. I'm a hopeless cook, and I'm getting tired of cold cereal and take-out burgers. This is a real treat."

"So, I take it you're single, deputy?" Brooke asks.

"When I'm out of uniform, it's Blake, ma'…uh, Brooke," he says with a laugh. "Yes, unfortunately, I find myself unhappily single these days."

"What a shame," she says with a sad smile, and I wonder if my wife is planning some matchmaking or just making conversation. Anyway, he seems like a decent guy, but I have no idea what Brooke could do about his single status. She doesn't know many people here yet, and she certainly doesn't need any more men in her life. I laugh at the thought. Someone told me once that a happily involved woman wants everyone around her to be all hitched up. Maybe she just needs a new hobby. We'll see.

"So, you guys are Army buddies, I assume? Are you planning to buy or build a house here?" he asks me.

"Uh…yes, we are and no." I'm not sure what to say, and somehow, I feel that Skyler ought to answer this kind of question since he's the one who's from this town, but maybe I'm just a chicken. We need to discuss what we plan to tell people.

But Skyler looks me in the eye and then looks at Blake and answers for us, "Brooke and Levi are going to be living here with me. Permanently, I hope." He looks at Brooke, who smiles and winks at him, so he continues, "We are in a three-way relationship. We *all* love each other."

Blake, to his great credit, barely blinks, although he clears his throat after taking a swallow of coffee. Maybe it was too hot. "Oh! Like your new neighbors who are building nearby?"

"If you mean Jack, Asher, and Juni, yes. Very much like them," Skyler explains.

"Hmm. Must be something in the water around here." Blake smiles and says, "I wish you all luck. I can't see it for myself because I'm a jealous bastard, but if it works for you, that's great."

"Well…you're the first to know," Brooke adds. "It's still somewhat new for all three of us. The guys were friends for quite a while before I married Levi. Are you by any chance also a military man? You seem to have that kind of bearing."

"Yes. I needed a way to pay for college because I wanted to study police science, so right out of high school, I joined the Marines. It was an interesting experience."

"I bet," she says. "Have you ever been married?"

"Brooke!" I exclaim, "What's with the probing questions?"

"It's fine," Blake assures me. "I was engaged a couple of years ago, but it wasn't meant to be. Since then, I've been as single as a monk."

"Aww. Too bad," she tells him.

"Maybe it's for the best. I've been told I'm not all that easy to live with."

I think about all the complaining Kate did about me as a kid and laugh to myself. "I used to hear that too until Brooke civilized me," I offer. "My big sister used to say I was impossible every chance she could get."

"Well, you grew out of it," Brooke says and plants a kiss on my cheek. "Now look at you all domesticated." Skyler snickers at me.

The rest of the breakfast conversation consists of small talk about local entertainment, fishing, and music. Blake does seem like a nice guy, and I can't hold anything against him for doing his job. It was thoughtful of him to come apologize and try to help Skyler by letting him know about the private investigator.

Before he leaves, Blake promises to come to the gig I have scheduled next week at The Hive, and he makes sure we all have his private number in case we need anything or just want to shoot the breeze. I get the sense he might be a little lonely, so maybe Brooke's matchmaking idea has possibilities. Eh… not my problem.

I need to call the guys about rehearsing. That thought gets me going. I have so much to look forward to all of a sudden, but it makes me feel worse for Skyler because he has to look forward to slogging through a bunch of ridiculous legal issues.

About an hour after the deputy leaves, there is *another* knock on the door. This time Brooke answers it to find a nervous young man standing there with a packet in his hands. "I need to speak to Skyler Colfax, ma'am. Is he available?"

She looks at me questioningly, and I tell her, "He just went upstairs to paint for a while."

"Just a minute. I'll have to go up and get him," she tells the guy. I have a bad feeling about this, but she politely asks him to step inside so she can close the door.

A couple minutes later, she comes back with Sky who already has a bright streak of blue paint that goes across his cheek and into his hair. He looks frustrated. "Can I help you?" he asks.

"Skyler Colfax?"

"That's me."

"This is for you." The guy hands him the envelope and scurries out the door without another word.

Skyler sighs unhappily like he knows this is bad news, but he opens the envelope anyway. With a troubled expression, he tells us, "Just to make things an even bigger pain in the ass, Mrs. Henshaw is suing me for personal damages in civil court. She's arbitrarily decided that I'd be good for a cool million dollars. What a miserable bitch."

All we can do is surround him in a warm hug. "It'll turn out okay, Sky," Brooke tells him. "You'll be fine. There's no way she'll win any of this nonsense or they will convict you. *No way.*"

CHAPTER
Thirty~Three

BROOKE

ONE THING I CAN SAY FOR CERTAIN ABOUT HONEYBEE Hollow is the town sure has some great looking men. Skyler, Asher, Jack, and now Deputy Blake. *Wow*. My gorgeous Levi fits right in with these hotties. Despite being older, even Buford Wallace is an exceptionally handsome guy if you're into silver foxes.

Anyway, the town's eye candy aside, over the next few weeks, Levi and I settle into our new life as permanent Honeybee Hollow residents. He rehearses a few times a week whenever his new alternative country band can get together, and they play a fantastic combination of country, rock, and pop at The Hive on Wednesday and Saturday nights. Now that they have Levi as their new singer, they changed the band's name to Wildflower Whiskey. Their ridiculously handsome drummer they call Banger—and it gives me the giggles each time I hear it—has been in contact with a place up in Lexington where they might perform now and then. That would be terrific because it would give Levi an extra excuse to see his sister and her family. He's excited about the music and performing regularly. He's also been writing songs again, so I'm thrilled about that. They plan to play one of them next week at The Hive to see how people react to it. He's shopping around for an agent, so he seems committed to his music. This is as happy as I've ever seen Levi, and it warms my heart.

He's kept up his appointments regularly with both the PTSD counseling and the physical therapy, and I'd say he and Skyler are both looking a lot healthier despite the worry of Skyler's upcoming trial…well, now it's unfortunately *trials*, plural. I still can't believe any of this crap is happening to our sweet man.

My job is going okay. I have enough work to keep me interested and busy, but not so much that I feel as if I'm missing out on anything with Levi and Skyler. The pay is great, so I'm not about to give it up anyway.

Skyler hired the PI, Doug Freeman, but he hasn't had much contact with him yet. No doubt the guy is out privately investigating or whatever. I hope he turns out to be helpful.

He also meets with his lawyer pretty often, and he doesn't want to talk about it much. Levi and I ask if he's doing alright after a meeting and leave it up to him whether or not we are going to discuss anything. He doesn't seem happy though, and that has me a little worried. I hope he's not keeping it all inside, so he doesn't worry Levi too much. I've asked him if having us here is what he wants, and he assures me he never wants that to change, so it's not our unusual relationship that has him down. He's no doubt just worried about the lawsuits.

Last week, he came clean to his parents about what the three of us are doing and how he sees Levi and me in his life. I can't say they were exactly thrilled to discover their son was "suddenly bisexual" and part of a threesome. They were cordial enough about it; no one yelled or disowned him, fortunately. But I can't say they opened their arms to Levi and me like we were immediately part of the family either.

"Are you sure this is a good time to make such a big change in your lifestyle with your current legal problems?" his dad asked.

"Yes. It's the best time. I need their love and support now more than ever," Skyler answered. "Levi and Brooke are wonderful."

"Are you going to have children?" was one of the first questions his mom asked.

"Hopefully, God willing," Skyler answered. Fortunately, we'd discussed it a couple of days before that and decided we weren't in a big hurry for me to conceive, but the idea sounded wonderful to all of us. We need to have another conversation about me getting rid of my IUD and when, but that's our business—not anyone else's. I'd like to feel totally solid in this arrangement before we make any plans—not that I doubt anyone's love.

And I recognize that if there is even a remote possibility Skyler could be convicted, making a big change like getting pregnant might be an awful lot of emotion to handle at once. We need to concentrate on each other for a while, at least. We're not just playing around; this relationship is the real deal for all of us.

After the second week of trying not to worry about Skyler's often gloomy attitude, something came to light without him needing to say anything. He offered to accompany me to the Piggly Wiggly because we were terribly low on staple groceries, and he knew I'd have a lot to load into the car. He justified himself by saying, "I haven't lifted any weights today yet, so this will be my workout."

I readily agreed—happy to have his company—but when we got to the market, I noticed a lot of shoppers giving him the side-eye or turning around quickly so as not to pass him in the aisle. There were whispers and out-and-out hostile stares. My heart hurt for him, but I was also apparently guilty by association because very few people returned my polite smile.

However, when we made our way to the cashier, she was kind enough to proclaim in a loud voice, "Skyler Colfax! It's so good to see you. You're looking great. Listen, I know you're too nice a guy for any of those horrible claims that crazy old bat is making against you to be true. So you just keep your head up and know that me and my Bible study group are all prayin' for you!"

Skyler blushed when she came around the counter, wrapped him in a hug, and patted his back. "Thanks, Maybelle. That means a lot," he said in a choked voice.

I wish I could say she cheered him up for a while, but too many other folks were suspicious of him, and it broke my heart to see it. I can just imagine how he felt.

Skyler retreated to the creek with a fishing pole when we got back and told Levi, "I think I need to be alone for a little while," before he left. Levi nodded his understanding, and later Skyler returned with no fish.

Despite the gloom, my two men are incredible. The devotion and care they demonstrate within our relationship is beyond amazing. I feel cherished by them, and I see the way they love each other, and it melts my heart. It's sometimes just little things like a casual touch or a kind word in the middle of normal life. They look out for each other and for me like it's their purpose in life. I hope I'm doing as well with them as they are with all of us.

Oh, and the physical aspect of our loving! I knew Levi and I had something special when we married, but adding Skyler to the mix blows my mind. Our "two-in-one" lovemaking is a favorite for all of us because of the incredible closeness and intimacy it creates, but we also experiment with all sorts of configurations and positions. Some are better than others. You sure can't trust online porn for any great ideas because most of what you see is something a director sets up for good camera angles rather than reality. And books glorify everything for the purpose of storytelling. We've figured out that we need to try things for ourselves and be honest with one another as to whether it did anything for us or not. Thankfully, we're almost always on the same page.

Almost as much as our "two-in-one," I love getting fucked by Skyler while Levi takes his ass, and Levi loves to fuck me while Skyler plows my ass, but Levi's decided he's not that crazy about bottoming for Skyler. I wonder if it's because Skyler's dick is such a monster. Levi doesn't mind being played with back there, and he responds well to finger pressure on his prostate, but…well, it's up to him what he likes and doesn't like. At least he tried it before making up his mind. Skyler is happy with anything and everything, so we make it all work.

One thing we discussed the other day was what happens when one of us is out of town for business or whatever. Levi spoke up and told us, "If I'm, say, gigging up in Lexington and you guys decide to stay here, it's fine with me if you have sex. You know I love to see you two together. It actually makes me happy. But, Brooke, I know you have to make a trip out to San Francisco soon to have a meeting at your company, so how do you feel about Skyler and me together?"

"I was fine with it when I went back to pack up our stuff to move out. And you can always have phone sex with me so I can watch." I wiggled my eyebrows to illustrate my enthusiasm, and they laughed. I sobered and said, "I'll be lonely without you, so I hope I don't have to stay for more than a couple of days."

"We know," Skyler said and squeezed my hand. "And if I go anywhere—like prison for ten to twenty years—I can hardly complain about you two being together, seeing as how you're the married couple here. I would miss you both terribly, but I wouldn't feel bad about you loving each other. How could I?"

Skyler's comment was meant in jest (I hope) because there is no way anyone could convict him, so I'm not taking it completely seriously. Is that what they call gallows humor? I still can't help saying, "You know you're not going to jail, Skyler." Dear God, I hope I'm right. But something else bothers me just a little. I turn to Levi and say, "Honey, you seemed nervous about Skyler and me leaving you for one another when he first came to see us in Hopkinsville. I don't mean to be second-guessing you, but are you a hundred percent sure you're over that?"

"Water under the bridge, babe. I know I freaked out, but now that we all have each other, I feel different about every-thing—way happier and more relaxed. I've talked to my thera-pist about it, and I'm good, I promise."

So this is how we are. We're respectful of each other's feelings and careful with what we say.

Juni was right. It's amazing.

Thirty-Four

SKYLER

I DON'T KNOW WHAT I'D DO NOW IF I DIDN'T HAVE LEVI AND Brooke—probably lose my mind. It's not just the sex we have —often and enthusiastically—it's the closeness we share and the unspoken understanding they offer when all this crap gets me down. The other thing that's keeping me from losing it completely is my painting. It's even helping me strengthen my arm and use my hand better.

Levi has made it his purpose in life to make it up the stairs once a day to keep me company in the studio, and he plays and sings the most beautiful songs. It makes me love him more and more each day—especially when I see what a toll the trip up there takes on him. On days I have an inkling he's not going to be able to make it too well, I suggest painting outside might be fun. That usually happens after he's stayed up late singing with Wildflower Whiskey, and he looks tired.

And speaking of his playing with his new group, the only time I've been able to work on the painting of him is when he's rehearsing or gigging with them. The rest of the time, I've had to keep it stored away so he doesn't see it. I love the way it's turning out, and it's almost done. I need to figure out the best time to show it to him.

That raspy, emotional voice of Levi's is amazing. And he's written a couple of songs that he's perfecting before trying them out on the public. He was worried that I'd find his practicing annoying until I assured him he can't make a bad sound with either his voice or his guitar, and if he needs to repeat the same line over fifty times to get it just right, I'll enjoy it fifty times.

Brooke has been trying to find ways to cheer me up. Today she asked, "How would you like to have Jack, Asher, and Juni over for dinner soon?" My first instinct was to say no—I wasn't ready for more people to deal with. But when I saw the hopeful look in Brooke's eyes, I decided differently.

"Sure. Ask them to come over, and we'll have a barbecue." *Maybe it'll be fun*, I tell myself. After all, they're great company and understand us in ways many folks never will.

Two days later, they show up with several desserts—courtesy of Juni's bakery—a lovely flowering plant that Asher tells us we can use many ways in cooking, and a case of beer. The plant makes more sense to Brooke than to Levi and me, although I've seen them in my parents' garden center, I think. She seems fascinated by it when Asher tells her it's a native plant. We like the beer a lot though. The three of them are good people and good friends.

"We're going to be moving into the house soon," Jack announces as he pops open six beer bottles. "Next week, in fact."

This leads to a long conversation about moving and decorating a new place, and the ladies seem anxious to do more shopping together. I'm glad Brooke and Juni have hit it off so well.

The conversation also leads to a discussion of puppies. They want to get at least one dog—possibly two—as soon as they're settled. I see how Brooke lights up about this, and I made a mental note to talk to Levi about it privately. I think it would be a wonderful surprise, and I know she has a birthday coming up.

We end up having a delicious meal and a terrific time getting to know them all better. It's well past midnight when everyone starts to yawn.

After they leave, we all fall into bed and have a slow, gentle session of lovemaking unlike our usual frantic, hot pursuit of pleasure. Experiencing our favorite position—the one Brooke calls "two-in-one"—with my lovers, I truly feel surrounded by not just passion but soul-baring affection. We're quieter than usual until Levi says reverently, "Our love is like those gorgeous fireworks on the Fourth of July. It almost explodes out of us in colors and shapes as if it's too big to contain."

I'd bet anything he's going to write a song about big, bright love.

"Oh, Levi," Brooke purrs as she kisses his neck and squeezes us both with her inner muscles, making us groan with ecstasy. Soon we're all succumbing to our individual climaxes, and I see colors behind my eyelids, just as Levi predicted. It's beyond incredible. We drift off to sleep in each other's arms.

It feels like only minutes later when my phone goes off. Oh crud. I'm not ready to face anything yet, but Levi reaches for it, unplugs it, and hands it to me. "Mornin'," he rasps. "Good luck. Maybe it's good news." Judging by the light filtering in around the drapes, it's a lot later in the day than I'd have guessed.

I grumble something at Levi even I can't understand as I look at the caller ID. It's Hamilton, my lawyer. I clear my throat and croak, "Hello?"

CHAPTER
Thirty-Five

Levi

It's interesting to watch Skyler's facial expressions as he listens to the caller. He's wary, then happy, and finally pissed off in less than a minute.

"Okay. Well at least some of that is good news. Thank you," he says. "Now what am I supposed to do?"

They have a conversation back and forth for a while, and I finally have to get out of bed because it's morning, and I need to pee. So I don't hear all of it. Brooke also follows right behind me into the bathroom and takes her turn. She looks sleep-mussed and beautiful. I love this woman so ferociously. When she finishes, I set down my toothbrush and rinse out my mouth before capturing her in a full-body embrace, kissing the daylights out of her. I want her to know how much I appreciate and adore her.

We're in the middle of a great make-out session when Skyler barges in. "I thought that guy would never shut up! What is it with lawyers loving to hear themselves talk?" he crabs as he shuts the door to the toilet area.

Brooke snickers, and I can't help laughing too as we head down the hall.

Finally, Skyler shows up in the kitchen and makes straight for the coffee. He has a funny expression on his face, so I ask, "Well? What did he say?"

Skyler plunks himself down at the table. "Good news and not-so-good news." He swallows some coffee as we stare at him curiously. "The good part is that the criminal charges were dropped when my lawyer presented the photos he took of my hands to the prosecutor. He also finally has Mrs. Henshaw's medical report. My hands aren't bruised or cut up in any way that would indicate I'd slugged anyone. Any evidence they had against me was as insubstantial as smoke."

"That's great news!" I say as Brooke flings her arms around him smiling her head off.

"Furthermore, her medical report included a twisted ankle and skinned knees as well as deep bruising that would indicate the possibility of falling down some stairs as well as being hit —she claims I slugged her, but she never mentioned falling. I guess I'm lucky she didn't accuse me of shoving her down the stairs." He still doesn't look happy enough for this news, and I wonder why. "The prosecutor agreed to drop the case when he heard all of this. I guess he figured it was a waste of his time to pursue something so ridiculous."

"Wonderful!" Brooke exclaims and kisses the top of his head.

"But…" Skyler takes a deep breath. "According to my loquacious lawyer, Mrs. Henshaw is still insisting that I forced my way into her house and beat her up no matter what anyone says, and she is still going to pursue the civil lawsuit against me for a million dollars. He thinks she hopes her hungry shark of a lawyer can persuade a jury that this big, mean bully—me —took terrible, cruel advantage of her and ruined her life. She claims she can't work anymore, and I owe her for that."

"Because her pain and suffering and lost potential wages are worth *that* much? Is she still hospitalized?" I have to ask.

"No! She never was. She showed up at the ER and they stuck some bandages on her and sent her home with the instructions to take some Advil *if* she needed it."

"How did your lawyer get that information?" Brooke asks. "Isn't it private because of HIPAA?"

Skyler snorts. "Nothing is private in Honeybee Hollow, as you may have noticed. My lawyer's wife is a nurse at the hospital. But he subpoenaed the records anyway and finally got the official report. There is no doubt that something happened to her, but it sure as hell had nothing to do with me. This makes me curious as to why she's not looking for another possible attacker."

Brooke looks like a light just went on when she asks, "Do you think the old fraud might actually have thrown herself down her own stairs to make it look like she was attacked?"

"No clue." Skyler looks at me. "What do you think?"

"She could have killed herself doing that, so I'm not sure she would have done it on purpose, but maybe she tripped and then decided it was a lucky accident."

"Ugh," Skyler moans. "That sounds like something she'd do."

"Are you going to countersue for slander?" I ask.

"No. I only want my legal expenses covered, so I'm countersuing for that. I don't need to try to make money from her craziness. The less I have to think about her, the better. Also, I should mention that as soon as the prosecutor dropped the charges, my lawyer immediately filed a motion with the judge asking that the civil case be dropped for lack of evidence. The judge isn't as reasonable as the prosecutor, obviously. He denied the motion, so the civil trial will go on as planned."

"Sorry, man." I tell him. "That sucks."

"I'm beginning to wonder whether Sheriff Hansen and the judge are poker buddies or something." Skyler jokes, but he sounds defeated. "Maybe they're looking for some entertainment."

This begins a series of depositions and discussions with Mr. Talkative, Esq. Skyler is right. Hamilton loves the sound of his own voice, but I get the feeling he's competent. Mrs. Henshaw's lawyer, on the other hand, is a poorly dressed slob who comes across like a guy who bought his law degree from someone in a dark alley. Not that it means anything, but he has a protruding belly that usually has bits of food stuck to it, and his beard is just as unkempt. He's pretty off-putting. I wonder if he's the only shyster around who would agree to take her case.

Thirty-Six

SKYLER

TODAY'S THE DAY MY TRIAL BEGINS, AND I'M ABOUT TO BARF. Levi and Brooke have been incredibly supportive, but I know they're nearly as worried as I am. I hope it doesn't drag on forever because all of us have put our lives on hold for too long already. It's taken months of preparation. My lawyer even asked if I wanted to bargain her down and offer her fifty thousand bucks to see if that would make her go away. I won't do it though. I don't owe that awful woman a penny, and I'm ready for the world—or at least Honeybee Hollow—to see that I'm in the right.

Jury selection was interesting. They couldn't find anyone who wasn't at least remotely acquainted with one or the other of us. So, among others, we ended up with my second-grade teacher, a friend of my mom's from her Sewing Bees club, and a neighbor who lives across the street and down two houses from Mrs. Henshaw. The plaintiff's lawyer excused three people Mrs. Henshaw worked for. They swore their connection to her would not sway their thinking, but he was bright enough to see through that—or at least to be worried about it.

The trial begins with Schroeder, the plaintiff's lawyer, making his impassioned opening statement about how I ruthlessly mistreated a poor, innocent woman and not only cheated her out of her rightfully earned wages but also caused her such physical harm and mental distress that she could barely manage her own affairs, much less earn a living. I supposedly threatened her and then forced my way into her house, terrifying her and beating her nearly to death in a fit of rage. What an absolute crock of shit. I fight to keep from rolling my eyes since Hamilton cautioned me against it. I keep a straight face and sit up tall.

Hamilton makes his opening statement, regaling my service to my country as a brave soldier in Afghanistan where I was seriously injured in the line of duty. He tells how I have always been a model citizen in Honeybee Hollow and loyal to my country and how I have always had the respect of my peers. Then he switches gears and talks about how Mrs. Henshaw has a history of greed and dishonesty. Her lawyer objects, and the judge tells the jury to disregard that statement. Hamilton apologizes and says, "Evidence will clearly show that Mrs. Henshaw has no reason to hold my client responsible for her injuries and for her self-imposed unemployment. We will demonstrate how this case is a frivolous lawsuit."

And so it begins.

The shyster Schroeder parades a series of people onto the stand asking them about their association to Mrs. Henshaw. Each one says she worked for them in the past. Each one swears she did her job satisfactorily, but no one is asked why she doesn't still work for them. My lawyer's cross examination doesn't amount to much until he gets to the fifth one.

He asks, "Why did you eventually terminate her employment?"

The witness clears his throat. He shifts in his seat. When he finally answers, it's truly magical. "My son kept complaining that his piggy bank was getting raided, so we put a hidden camera on it. We have video of Mrs. Henshaw stealing from a ten-year-old."

There are audible gasps all around the room, and her lawyer jumps to his feet crying, "Objection! My client isn't on trial here!"

"Your honor, I am simply establishing the possibility that Mrs. Henshaw stretches the truth now and then."

The judge stares at Hamilton for a moment and finally huffs, "I'll allow it. Overruled." He doesn't look too happy, but I steal a glance at the jury, and they all seem to be glaring at Marjorie Henshaw.

Several witnesses are brought up to the stand for no

apparent purpose that I can tell. They only seem to be there to testify that Mrs. Henshaw is a lovely person. My attorney has no questions for any of them.

Finally, Schroeder puts his client on the stand. She uses a walker to get there and makes a big show of how difficult it is for her to move around. It appears as if she is in terrible pain.

The first thing her lawyer does is post a life-sized photograph of Mrs. Henshaw with terrible bruising on her face. Her left eye is swollen shut and her chin is bleeding. There are several gasps from people around the courtroom, including some of the jurors. He leaves the photo there for everyone to look at as he proceeds with his interrogation.

"Mrs. Henshaw, will you tell us what happened on July the sixth when you went to work at Mr. Colfax's home?"

In a shaky voice, she begins a blathering pack of lies about how she showed up early to make sure I had enough to eat after she'd been out of town for a few days and was worried about my well-being. "He always loves my cooking so much, and I was afraid he was eating too many nasty TV dinners or pizza. I wanted to make sure he was alright. He had company, and one of them—the man—seemed to be very fresh with him. I didn't like it a bit because Skyler didn't seem to be at all well. I tried to get some work done, but the two guests were terribly rude to me, and Skyler didn't understand that I was looking out for him when he threatened me. It scared me so much, I left without getting paid."

"I see. So you were frightened for your safety on that date?"

"Terrified." She says this with a wobbly chin as she dabs at her eye, but there isn't any evidence of moisture.

"And would you tell us what happened on the night you were attacked?"

"Objection!" my lawyer cries. "There is no proof of an attack from anyone, least of all my client."

"Sustained. Please try again, Mr. Schroeder." Wow, the judge is starting to sound a little brighter.

"Mrs. Henshaw, please explain to us the series of events that led to your appearance in the emergency room."

"I was watching the eleven o'clock news when Skyler barged in, hollering at me. I swear he seemed drunk or high or something, and he accused me of all kinds of terrible things. He said I'd stolen from him and spread lies about him, and he was going to show me! When I stood up to tell him to get out of my house, he grabbed me and socked me as hard as he could in the face. Then he threw me against the fireplace where I hit the brick hearth. It hurt so bad, I couldn't even breathe." Big crocodile tears finally drip unchecked down her cheeks, and I half wonder if someone did attack her. I just know it wasn't me.

"Then what happened?"

"He swore at me in the foulest manner, using words that I won't repeat, and then he left."

"And what did you do?"

"I dragged myself to my neighbor's house, and she took me to the hospital."

"Thank you, Mrs. Henshaw. I have no more questions for you at this time."

She starts to get up, but my lawyer approaches her and says, "Not so fast, ma'am. It's my turn." She glares at him. "Mrs. Henshaw, who was with you in your home the night you claim you were attacked?"

"No one…except when Skyler was there."

"Then why didn't you call your neighbor instead of making the painful trip over to her house on foot if you were so seriously injured?"

Mrs. Henshaw stares blankly for a moment. Her mouth opens and closes two times before she finally says, "I…I guess I didn't think of it. I was scared and I wanted to get out of my house."

"You're sure you weren't afraid of someone who was still in your house?"

"Uh…n-no."

"You know that perjury is a crime, don't you?"

"Um. What's that?"

"Lying, Mrs. Henshaw. When you lie under oath in court, you can go to jail or pay a hefty fine." Her face turns red, but she doesn't say anything. "Alright, so you claim you were alone, and you had a burst of energy that propelled you to your neighbor's house despite your multiple injuries." She opens her mouth to speak, but he keeps going. "You said that Mr.

Colfax grabbed you and slugged you. Do you remember which hand he struck you with?"

"Well, obviously it was his right hand. He's right-handed, and I got a black eye on the left side of my face. He grabbed me with his left. I remember it distinctly. I wish I could forget the horrible look on his f—"

"Please just stick to answering my questions, ma'am."

"Oh. Okay. But—"

He interrupts her quickly, "When you were hired to work for Mr. Colfax, you were made aware, were you not, that he was seriously injured in Afghanistan and that injury has left him with only partial strength in his right arm and hand?"

"Well, I…uh…."

"Can you explain how someone so grievously injured while heroically serving our country could do the things you claim he did to you?"

"Objection!" Schroeder bellows. "My client isn't a physician!"

"Sustained," says the judge in a bored voice. "Please stick to the facts, Mr. Hamilton, and don't ask the plaintiff to make assumptions."

"Sorry, your honor." He looks at Mrs. Henshaw closely and asks, "When he allegedly forced his way into your house, was Mr. Colfax wearing a pair of gloves or was he barehanded?"

"Oh, um…he wasn't wearing anything." People in the

courtroom start to laugh, and she raises her voice to add, "On his *hands*, not the rest of him."

"I see, and while you were in his employ, what kinds of things was Mr. Colfax having you do around his house because he couldn't?"

"Oh, laundry, vacuuming, changing bed linens, taking out the trash, reaching for things he couldn't get to. That kind of thing…besides cooking, of course."

"So you contend that someone who can't toss laundry into a washing machine or pick up a wastebasket was able to beat you to a pulp?"

"He was lots better! Just look at him! He's a big, strong man!"

"You were on vacation for several days before the day Mr. Colfax fired you, were you not?"

"Yes."

"So you really had no idea how he was doing, did you?"

"I have eyes!"

"What did he do on July the sixth that made you think he was fully recovered? You said yourself just a moment ago that he didn't look at all well. Shall I have your statement read back to you?"

"No. He looked terrible. He just looked *strong* and terrible."

"Did you see him actually use his right hand or arm for anything before he fired you?'

"He was drinking from a bottle."

"An alcoholic bottle?"

"No. It was one of those awful yellow sports drinks."

"One of the quart bottles or the smaller kind?"

"It was a smaller one," she says in a wobbly voice.

"Anything else? Possibly more strenuous than lifting a ten-ounce drink all the way to his mouth?"

She squints her eyes and looks deflated. "No."

"Thank you, Mrs. Henshaw. I have no more questions for you at this time, but we may have to talk again later."

She begins the slow process once again of climbing out of her seat and, with the help of her lawyer, shuffling back to the plaintiff's chair. I wonder how much of this is an act.

Then it's my turn on the stand. After establishing that she did work for me, Schroeder asks, "Did Mrs. Henshaw come to work for you on the sixth of July?"

"No. She came to my house that day."

He has a perplexed look when he asks, "So you contend that she came for a social visit?"

"No. She tried to come to work, but she wasn't supposed to be there." I remember back to something I've heard—that lawyers shouldn't ask questions unless they know they're going to like the answer. I try not to smirk.

"Were you upset with her?"

Now I see why he's asking. "Somewhat. I was upset that she was bothering us when she wasn't supposed to be there."

"So you took it out on her and refused to pay her for her

time, even though she was there out of the goodness of her heart?"

"She never got around to doing any work, and I didn't take anything out on her. I merely told her to stop saying rude things to my guests, or I'd fire her."

"So you threatened her?"

"I did not threaten *her*. I threatened to *fire* her. And for a good reason."

"So you admit you were angry, and you threatened her. No further questions."

As the plaintiff's lawyer returns to his seat beside Mrs. Henshaw, my lawyer steps up to the plate. "Skyler, what kind of work did Mrs. Henshaw do for you?" he asks.

"When I first moved home, I couldn't do very much because my right arm was in a sling from my injury in Afghanistan. She provided housekeeping services and did some cooking for me until I could do things better myself. It was always going to be a temporary position."

"And were you satisfied with her work?"

"Yes and no. She kept the house looking good, but she's an atrocious cook."

Mrs. Henshaw lets out a huge gasp. She looks ready to pop. Several muffled laughs echo through the courtroom.

"Did you eat her cooking?"

"I tried for a while, but she wouldn't pay attention to my instructions and kept fixing these awful vegetarian dishes full of lima beans, kale, or brussels sprouts, no matter what I said. I'm normally not picky, but she kept insisting on putting mushrooms in everything, and that was the one thing I told her I'd never eat. So I finally just waited for her to leave and ordered take-out meals to be delivered from Sock Hop and stuff like that. I actually asked her finally to stop cooking, so she brought food she'd made from home."

"So she was kind enough to provide food for you?"

"If you can call that a kindness. I threw the food away because no one in their right mind would want it. I guess she thought I was eating it because I returned her empty dishes all the time."

"Alright, well, I guess it's fine that everyone has different tastes in food. Were you happy with the housework she did for you?"

"She did alright."

"But you say the position was meant to be temporary. You planned to terminate the job all along, isn't that right?"

"Yes."

"So tell us once more what prompted you to terminate her job on a day when she showed up uninvited at your home."

"I didn't expect her that day. I had guests, and she was rude to them. She kept butting into our conversation and trying to push everyone around like it was her house and she made the rules. I wasn't feeling well because I had a migraine, so I told her it was time for her to leave permanently. That was it. I never said anything threatening to her other than she was about to be fired if she didn't leave my friends and me alone. She wouldn't stop, so…that was it."

My lawyer takes a pause, looking pensive, and then asks, "Can you tell us what happened later that evening?"

"Yes, my mother stopped by and asked me why Mrs. Henshaw was going around town telling people that I was a terrible, scary dude who'd threatened her life, I ran around half-naked in front of her, and I'm having financial trouble." I leave out the part about Levi being my boyfriend.

"Is any of that true?"

"Well…sort of true." There is a lot of murmuring in the courtroom that prompts the judge to ask for order.

"Which part is true, Skyler?"

"I was sleeping when she first arrived, and I didn't know she was there. Since I was suffering from a migraine and feeling dehydrated, I came out to the kitchen to grab a Gatorade from the refrigerator. I was only wearing boxer briefs. I was shocked to find her in my house. I'd never been undressed around her. I would never have done that had I known she was there."

And that's about all the time we have for the first day. So much of what happened was just time-wasting on the plaintiff's part. I'm anxious for this fiasco to be over, but Hamilton tells me as we head out, "I think it's going well, so get a good night's sleep and be ready for some interesting testimony tomorrow. You'll be fine."

I wish I had his confidence. I'm still getting a lot of funny looks from people. Some look suspicious and others look like they feel sorry for me. I think.

Thirty~Seven

Brooke

I'M SO RELIEVED THIS TRIAL IS FINALLY GOING ON. SKYLER has been a nervous wreck. Jack tried to come over about a week ago to speak to him again about doing a show in his gallery, and Skyler couldn't even think about it. He said he needed to paint to relieve stress right now but couldn't concentrate on business just yet. Being a good friend, Jack told him he understood, and he'd try again later when things settled down.

Also, when my birthday happened last month, they had a cake for me, but both Skyler and Levi told me they had something really special planned for me, but they decided we all needed to wait until after the trial for it. They figured we weren't yet in a good enough head space for it. I have no idea what they meant, but they were so sincere, I told them it was fine. Levi promised, "When we do it, you'll love it, babe. We promise." They took care of me like I was their queen in bed that night, so I certainly had no complaints.

Now we're into the second day of the trial, and it's Skyler's lawyer's turn to provide his defense. The first thing he does is put a detective on the stand who was sent by the sheriff's office to look for evidence in Mrs. Henshaw's house. The findings were fascinating. There were traces of her blood, but not only on the fireplace as she'd claimed. They were also at the foot of the stairs on her carpet. I'd feel a lot sorrier for her for being injured like that if she weren't trying to use Skyler as her meal ticket for the rest of her life.

Mr. Schroeder's only question to the detective is, "Is it possible Mrs. Henshaw bled on her carpet near her stairs after being thrown against the fireplace bricks?"

He answers, "It's possible, but the stains appeared to be ground into the carpet as if she'd fallen there or been pushed rather than just dripping blood while she was walking around."

Schroeder looks disgusted with that answer and dismisses the detective from the stand.

The next witness is Deputy Blake Ogden, looking even grumpier than usual. That man would be a heartbreaker if he'd ever manage to crack a smile.

Mr. Hamilton doesn't have much to ask, but he does pose the question, "Were you the officer who arrested Mr. Colfax?"

"Yes, sir."

"And did you place handcuffs on him?"

"Yes, sir."

"I suppose it's safe to say you got a good look at Mr. Colfax's hands. Do you remember seeing any signs of cuts, bruises, or blood on them that would be consistent with hitting someone really hard barehanded?"

"No, sir. His hands were in fine shape except for a few splotches of paint."

"Are you sure the splotches were paint and not blood?"

"They were blue, sir."

"Thank you. That's all, Deputy."

Schroeder has no questions for him, so Blake gets up and hightails it out of the courtroom.

The third witness is Doug Freeman, the private investigator that Deputy Blake recommended. He provides video that was time-stamped a month ago. It shows Mrs. Henshaw in her backyard mowing her lawn and hanging clothes to dry on a clothesline. She did not appear to be favoring any part of her body and certainly wasn't using a walker. Some of the clothes are obviously a large man's shirts and pants. He also shows photos of a large man going in and out of her house at various intervals. Furthermore, Freeman has copies of receipts Mrs. Henshaw paid to the local handyman for repairing a broken banister in her house.

When asked if he can identify the man in the photos, Mr. Freeman says, "Yes, sir. His name is Monty Henshaw, the ex-husband of Marjorie Henshaw. They were divorced nine years ago." He produces documents to support all of that.

The plaintiff's attorney has no questions. I doubt he could think of anything to refute Doug Freeman's testimony.

The next witness Hamilton calls is Mrs. Henshaw's next-door neighbor. She testifies that on the night she took Marjorie to the ER, she heard lots of screaming and yelling coming from the Henshaw house. When Marjorie ran to her door, she never mentioned Skyler by name, only said that she had been hurt and needed to get out of the house. When asked if she merely assumed the attacker was Skyler Colfax, her answer is, "Well, Marjorie did say he'd threatened her, but there was another possibility. I didn't ask because it wasn't my business."

"And who was that possibility, ma'am?" Hamilton asks politely.

"Her ex-husband. I saw him there earlier that day. He's a mean brute of a man."

Mrs. Henshaw's face goes red, and she scowls at her neighbor.

As the testimony continues, we discover it was the neighbor's idea to take her to the hospital because Marjorie was beaten up and bloody. She also says that when the hospital released her after a few hours, they went back to the neighbor's house for the rest of the night, not to Marjorie's.

When Mr. Schroeder has his turn with the neighbor, he asks, "Who do you *really* think beat Mrs. Henshaw? It must have been Mr. Colfax, right?" Immediately, Mr. Hamilton objects, and the judge agrees that it is not the witness's place to make assumptions. Schroeder has no further questions, and Mrs. Henshaw glares at him.

But the absolute best part of the defense testimony comes from Skyler's physical therapist. He testifies that even now, over a year since his injury happened in Afghanistan, Skyler cannot make a firm enough fist to do the kind of damage that Marjorie Henshaw received to her body. Skyler's shoulder was smashed, and he therefore doesn't have the strength to wield such a blow either. He says Skyler does daily exercises to get his strength and flexibility back, but the damage to his shoulder and arm were so extensive, it's going to take a long time for him to fully recover—if he ever actually does.

Throughout this testimony, we're treated to X-rays and photographs of Skyler's horrible injuries. The PT guy explains each one in detail. He says the only way Skyler could have bruised Mrs. Henshaw as badly as she claimed would have been by using a weapon like a bat.

Mrs. Henshaw had testified that Skyler had grabbed her and used his fist to hit her. There was never any mention of a weapon.

At this point, the judge says we're going to take a lunch recess. Schroeder looks miffed, but Hamilton looks pleased. I notice that Mrs. Henshaw sneers at Skyler, and he ignores her.

Levi, Skyler, and I head out to find some lunch. Levi and I are expecting to give our sworn testimonies as to what happened on the day when Skyler fired Mrs. Henshaw, so no one has much of an appetite. We end up in Juni's bakery for a bagel and coffee.

The sight of Juni cheers us up. She knows what we're going through and tries to distract us with enthusiastic stories about what it's like building and moving into their dream house.

As soon as we return to our seats in the courtroom, the judge reenters and we all rise. I wonder idly if it makes judges feel all-powerful when people have to stand up for their arrival. He has a disgruntled look on his face when he addresses Skyler's lawyer. "Please call your next witness, Mr. Hamilton."

At this point, I'm asked to give my account of what happened the day Mrs. Henshaw came to the house. I corroborate what Skyler said earlier, and the judge looks as bored as can be with me. Schroeder tries to get me to say that Skyler threatened Mrs. Henshaw, but I tell him Skyler did nothing to threaten her physically, and he was feeling so sick that he wasn't much of a threat to anyone at the time. But the big jerk tells me to stop making assumptions about Skyler's health. I try to add that he took medication for a migraine in front of me, but he shuts me down there too.

The worst part comes later when Levi is called to the stand, even though Mr. Hamilton does his best to characterize

Levi as a brave soldier who served his country with the best of intentions. Levi tells Mr. Hamilton he was with Skyler the night of Mrs. Henshaw's alleged attack. He swears that Skyler was home when he left to go to The Hive, and home when he got back.

Sadly, Schroeder looks at Levi like he's a tasty snack when he asks, "So you were gone to a *bar* that serves alcoholic beverages for a few *hours*, leaving Mr. Colfax plenty of time to leave and attack Mrs. Henshaw before you returned to his house. Is that correct?"

Hamilton objects, and his objection is sustained, but we know this is possibly damning for Skyler, no matter what. It sounds bad all the way around. Levi tries to interject that he was there on music business and not for drinks, but he doesn't get the chance to explain.

"How would you characterize Mr. Colfax's well-being the next day?" Schroeder asks.

"He was in good spirits but tired," Levi answers. "His arm and hand were really sore from paint—"

Schroeder interrupts Levi loudly and asks, "Could he have been tired because he'd beaten up an innocent woman the night before, and that was why his arm and hand were sore?"

Hamilton jumps to his feet and hollers, "Objection!" at that question. Again, his objection is sustained.

Schroeder thanks Levi and says, "No further questions."

After that little fiasco, the judge tells us all we're done for the day, but he looks sternly at the members of the jury and admonishes them, "Ladies and gentlemen, you've heard this before, but I caution you all again—do not discuss this case with anyone while the trial remains active. Thank you. Now everyone please go get some rest."

We do our best to keep Skyler's spirits up that night, but the stress has us all down. The whole mess is such a colossal waste of time, money, and effort, and it's agonizing for Skyler to have his good name dragged through the mud by that horrible woman and her creepy lawyer.

Thirty-Eight

Levi

The next morning, we all get up and dress in near silence. I have no idea what to say. After coffee and some of Juni's muffins, we head downtown to the courthouse.

Mr. Hamilton presents a few witnesses who speak about Skyler's character. He has some great supporters in this town, and it has to make him feel better to hear they declare with confidence what a good guy he is, but the judge maintains his stoic face through each of the testimonies. I try to look at the jury now and then, but most of them are also pretty blank expression-wise. I don't know what to think.

Schroeder doesn't have any questions for these folks, and

the judge finally asks Hamilton if this parade of fans is necessary. I can't help but think that's pretty rude of him.

"Your honor, I'm just establishing that Mr. Colfax has people who trust him and know he's an honest man. But I only have one last witness."

The next witness is a nervous woman in her fifties or sixties. She apparently hired Mrs. Henshaw when she was recovering from surgery and could barely get out of bed for a week.

"How did you happen to hire her?" he asks.

"I'm a widow, and my children are grown and have moved out of state, so Mrs. Henshaw was recommended by a neighbor before I went in for surgery."

"And how did you feel about the work she did for you?"

"She seemed to be doing alright. She showed up on time. I wasn't very interested in eating at first, so I didn't pay much attention to the food she offered me, but after I started to feel a bit better, I was miserable with the diet she tried to feed me. She refused to pay attention to my needs, so I didn't eat much. But it wasn't until after she was gone that I discovered certain items were missing from the house."

"What kind of items?"

"My son's coin collection and a few things from my daughter's room that she left behind when she moved out. That kind of thing."

"Did you confront Mrs. Henshaw about these items?"

"I tried to, but she would never answer my phone calls,

and frankly, I was still too weak to bother with much. I finally just gave up."

Schroeder has no questions for her.

The judge grumbles something unintelligible and calls for a recess before the lawyers give their closing arguments. He must have gotten up on the wrong side of the bed.

Fifteen minutes later, it's Schroeder's turn to give his final words to the jury to try to convince them to find for Mrs. Henshaw's claims. He again puts up a greatly enlarged photo showing her injured face and asks the jury members to take a good, long look at it. After carrying on for fifteen minutes, he ends with, "This strapping young man, a trained combat fighter who has undoubtedly killed his share of people, unleashed his temper on a defenseless woman, and this was the violent result. I implore you all to find in her favor."

I want to barf. I'm seething inside with so much rage, I could scream. How can he say such things about Skyler? I have to grab Brooke's hand so I don't jump out of my skin, and I can tell she's trembling. She must feel as awful as I do. But I have to say that even the judge gave Schroeder the stink eye when he mentioned Skyler killing people.

When it's Mr. Hamilton's turn, he says, "Ladies and gentlemen of the jury, I'll keep this short and sweet. Mr. Colfax simply could not have delivered the kind of damage to the plaintiff that she claims. He's just not physically able. Mr. Colfax has nerve damage and destroyed muscles in his shoulder that you've seen—thanks to the expert testimony from his physical therapist. Furthermore, he is an upstanding member of society, a war hero, and suffers from frequent debilitating migraines that make him averse to conflict. We have heard testimony that Mrs. Henshaw, on the other hand, has stolen from her clients *and their children,* and we have seen video proof that she is currently completely able to fend for herself without using that walker she flaunts. It's a prop. It's a ruse. We don't know what really happened that night because she's clearly lying about it in an attempt to get rich from Mr. Colfax. Do not let that happen. Skyler Colfax is the innocent victim here, not Mrs. Henshaw. Thank you for your time and attention. I trust you will do the right thing."

And that's it for the day in court. It's up to the jury at this point, so we head for home.

♡♡♡

WE HAVE JUST ENOUGH TIME TO GET OUT OF OUR "COURT clothes" and listlessly pick at the sandwiches Brooke makes for lunch when Skyler gets a phone call from Hamilton.

Amazingly, the jury has already made their decision. "Isn't this awfully fast? Do you think this is good or bad?" he asks and listens to the reply from his lawyer. "I see. Okay. We'll be back as soon as we can get there. Thanks."

We all scramble back into our dress clothes and head to the car. "I'll be happy to drive," Brooke tells us.

"Uh, sure," Skyler answers absently. I sit in the back with

him and clasp his hand all the way to town. His hand is clammy, but I don't care. Then he looks at me and says, "Usually, a quick verdict is bad for the defendant."

I open my mouth to speak, but I have nothing to say, so I squeeze his hand instead.

Brooke, however, declares, "No fucking way," and that's the end of that conversation.

Skyler calls his mom and dad to tell them we're heading in, and they say they'll meet us.

THE AIR IN THE COURTROOM IS SOMBER. I HAVE TO LOOSEN MY tie because I suddenly can't breathe. I can just imagine how Skyler is doing sitting in the defendant's chair in front of us. Brooke scoots closer to me, and I drape my arm around her shoulders. I wish I could do the same for Sky.

Finally, the jury files in, and I can't gauge their expressions at all. I glance at Mrs. Henshaw and see that she's looking smug. I'd love to give her a piece of my mind. Or kick her. Okay…not really. She's pathetic.

All too soon, we're standing up for the judge again, and he takes no time asking if the jury has their verdict. The foreman rises—a youngish guy whose face is vaguely familiar. I've probably seen him around town, or maybe he's been in to hear us play at The Hive. I space out a second as it dawns on me that he's been in the audience several times when suddenly I realize he's saying loudly and clearly, "In the first suit brought by Mrs. Henshaw, we find in favor of the defendant, Mr. Colfax. He owes her no damages. And in the countersuit, we find for Mr. Colfax also. He sued for legal fees, but because of the slander to his good name, we award $10,000 damages above and beyond whatever his legal fees are."

There are gasps and cheers all through the courtroom, so the judge smacks his gavel and asks for decorum. He looks at Mrs. Henshaw with a stern face and says, "I recommend to the plaintiff that you not spread any more falsehoods about the defendant who has proven himself to be an upstanding soldier during wartime and a fine citizen of Honeybee Hollow. He had every right to sue you for slander, and yet he did not, so I commend the jury's decision. Clean up your act, Mrs. Henshaw. It's clear that someone—perhaps your ex-husband —got into an altercation with you, and I am sorry for your pain. But that does not give you the right to sue an innocent man for a ridiculous amount of damages and drag his good name through the mud just because he was a convenient target. This is not a get-rich-quick solution to your problems. I hope to never see you in my courtroom again." He looks toward the jury box and says, "Members of the jury, thank you for your time, you are all free to go."

The people in the audience all clap, and the judge tells them again to knock it off and be quiet. Mrs. Henshaw jumps up and yells at her lawyer, "You lousy, worthless piece of scum. You're about as dim as a burnt-out lightbulb! Now what am I supposed to do? That bastard Monty threatened to *kill* me if I didn't win this!" Then she storms out, forgetting her walker.

Levi and I are all over Skyler with hugs, and his mom and dad are there with huge, relieved smiles.

Mike Colfax invites everyone out to dinner, including Mr. Hamilton and his wife and our physical therapist. He wanted to invite Doug Freeman, but the private investigator has already vanished. Hamilton declines because he and his wife have plans already, and the PT guy says he's been moving his appointments to the evening so he could testify and hear the outcome. So it's just us with the parents.

We have a fantastic dinner at the Honeybee Hollow Inn. Word must have traveled through town quickly because several people come up to congratulate Skyler at the Inn and along Main Street, and they assure him they never doubted him. I hope that's true, but I'm not completely convinced after the sneers at the Piggly Wiggly. Skyler is gracious to each of them, nevertheless, and shakes a lot of hands. I hope his hand doesn't hurt after tonight.

The celebration is nice, but the three of us are itching to get home, get comfortable, and get busy…in bed. The heated looks we all give each other are burning me up.

Thirty~Nine

SKYLER

OH. MY. GOD. IT'S OVER!

I feel like I can finally take a deep breath. What a colossal waste of time that experience was. Levi and Brooke have been so great through it all. I know I've been a moody bastard now and then when the stress got me down. I need to step it up and let them know just what their love and support mean to me.

As soon as we get home, however, Brooke sails into the house and says breezily, "How would you guys like to have a scary movie marathon night? I can pop some popcorn and make hot chocolate. Or I can bake brownies, and we can have them with ice cream…"

We both gape at her like she just grew an extra head. *What?*

"Hah! Gotcha!" she giggles. "You should see the looks on your faces. Let's go to bed. Now!" She zips down the hall with us in hot pursuit, all three of us pulling off articles of clothing along the way. Since Levi and I are in suits, undressing is a bigger pain in the ass than it is when we wear shorts and t-shirts.

Brooke is the first one out of her clothes and grabs the lube while Levi and I hang up our suits. Soon, we're all piled on the bed kissing and stroking anything that's handy. "I think," she says breathlessly, "we need to focus our attention on Skyler tonight. He has something big to celebrate."

I get a different idea though, and before Levi can answer, I say, "Can you guys wait a bit for the fun to begin? I have something I want to show you, and this seems like the best time to do it." They look at me questioningly, so I add, "I promise I'll be right back." I streak out of the room and head up to my studio. I'm out of breath once I get there, but I'm so excited, I barely even care. In less than two minutes, I'm back again in the master bedroom with them. I can barely catch my breath when I find them making out on the bed. *I guess they didn't miss me too badly*, I think as I chuckle inwardly. They look so beautiful together, it makes me hard, despite the sudden rush of second thoughts washing over me. I clear my throat.

They pull themselves apart, and Brooke gets a knowing look when she sees what I have in my hands.

"Ooh, it's finished?" she asks. "Levi! Wait till you see this!"

Levi looks curious, but he's still stroking Brooke's body. He can obviously see it's a painting; I hope he loves it. Brooke only saw it in the beginning stages, and it's changed quite a bit since then.

"Levi," I tell him, "I did this for you. It's the best way other than just loving you that I can express what you mean to me. You're my hero, and if I'd never met you, there's no way I'd be this happy. You exploded into my life, and you bring me incredible joy. When you insisted that Brooke could be an equal part of my life with you, I was blown away. I think what the three of us have is perfect and special, and probably better than anything I deserve. And maybe after I show this to you, we can finally give Brooke her birthday present. What do you think?"

"I think that's a great idea," he tells me. Brooke looks baffled but happy. Everyone loves a good gift.

"Ready?" I ask as I switch on the overhead light for optimum illumination.

"Show me already!" he laughs.

I flip the painting of him around and hold it up so it rests on the bed. Brooke gasps, and Levi stares at it bug-eyed. "*Wow*. That's how you see me?"

I grin as Brooke begins to carry on. "He's captured your

bravery and patriotism so well. You can also tell, looking at that painting, that Levi has an enormous capacity for love. It's absolute genius." She looks at Levi and says, "You could use this for an album cover one day."

"I'd be honored if you did, Levi."

"I've never been so impressed with a painting in my life, Skyler. Thank you from the bottom of my heart. I love how you incorporated the fireworks in the background and made me look military and brave but also approachable at the same time. It's just amazing, and I'm incredibly flattered."

"May I have my gift now too?" Brooke asks, looking all excited as she almost jumps out of her skin.

Levi laughs, making a crack about her being greedy, and I take the painting into the other bedroom so we don't knock it over before it's hung. I return with a gaily wrapped package in my hands. It's large and flat, and Brooke reacts to its weight as I hand it to her.

"Hmm. Heavy. Feels like a book…" she muses.

I sit down on the other side of her opposite Levi and tell her, "We want you to look through this and choose what you want."

She gives us a quizzical look and then rips off the paper. As soon as it registers what we're giving her, she squeals. "A dog? I can choose any dog? Oh, I can't wait to read through it. Thank you, guys!" She opens the book and flips through some pages exclaiming over and over at the wonderful photography of all the different breeds. Every section explains the specific breed's characteristics, personalities, special requirements, sociability, and on and on. It was a great find. Sure, we could have used the internet for dog shopping, but the book itself is kind of a piece of art. It was worth it, too, to see her excitement.

"We also printed up a list of AKC breeders of note in case you want to call around and see who has puppies or visit the dogs to see which ones you like. Levi and I have our favorites, but the choice is all yours. We can also talk to Dr. Lassiter—the local vet—to see what he knows about puppies around here. Their family has always had lots of dogs."

"Do you know any breeds that are particularly good with children?" she asks.

"Several of them are," I tell her. "My parents' three labs are great with them, for instance."

"Okay…well…" Suddenly Brooke is blushing. "Since we're all giving gifts, I guess I have a big one for both of you too."

"You guess?" Levi says with a soft laugh. "What is it?"

"Um…a baby."

"What?" Levi cries.

At the same time, I grab Brooke and squeeze her, asking, "When did you find out and what happened to having an IUD?" I can't stop smiling and laughing.

"Well, I know we thought we should wait a while, but I haven't had a period since I went to Hopkinsville, and when that finally dawned on me, I made an appointment with an

OB/GYN. She confirmed the pregnancy and immediately removed my IUD a few days ago. I just wanted the trial to be over before I told you two because there was so much stress around here. I guess the length of time I'd had my IUD sort of slipped my mind. So…you're both happy?"

"Thrilled!" I tell her.

"Ecstatic!" Levi crows. "So that day you were supposedly working over at Juni's bakery, you were really seeing the doctor?"

"Yes," she says in a small voice. "I didn't want to tell anyone ahead of time in case it wasn't true."

"Thoughtful. I love it. And I love you," he says and gives her such a passionate kiss, I'm ready to explode just watching them.

I take the book from Brooke's hands and set it aside. The time for puppies and babies can wait. We have what feels like all the time in the world. For now, we need to concentrate on one another. With murmured declarations of love, we all fall against each other. There is so much glorious naked flesh to enjoy. Brooke and Levi maneuver me into the middle, and I find myself balls-deep in Brooke with Levi deep inside me. They shower me with kisses, only letting up to kiss each other deeply. I'm caressed and pummeled, soft and hard, slow and fast. Brooke squeezes the daylights out of me while Levi grinds against my sensitive prostate, and I know I won't be able to hold on long. There is too much love, too much emotion and relief surrounding us, and I'm going to detonate with it.

Levi, however, beats me to the punch and shouts, "I'm coming!" and groans out how much he loves us, filling me with hot cum.

I am right behind, bellowing my release to the heavens. I swear I pour a quart of hot jizz into Brooke's body, laughing and hollering, "This is the best day of my life!"

Brooke still hasn't come yet, so I pull out and position her in the bed, zeroing in on her clit with my mouth. Levi jams two fingers into her and pumps her pussy while I grind my mouth over her and then suck on her clit like a vacuum. She literally screams. *I guess we did it right*, I think smugly to myself and just about die when Levi pulls his cum-coated fingers out of her and licks them clean.

"You both taste delicious together," he claims with a wink. Then he tells us, "I have one more gift, but you'll have to wait. I can't give it to you yet, but soon, I promise."

"What more can there be?" Brooke asks breathlessly.

"You'll just have to wait and see," he says with a twinkle in his eye.

After cleaning up, we all fall asleep wrapped around one another. I truly have never known such contentment.

CHAPTER
Forty

I'VE TAKEN MY GUITAR OUT TO THE CREEK SEVERAL TIMES IN the past few days so I can sing and play by myself. The acoustics aren't great, but it's nice and private. Brooke and Sky have been too busy to notice, and that's just fine with me. Brooke has been engrossed in catching up on a new project for her job that she let slide a little during the trial, and Skyler is wrapped up in putting finishing touches on his paintings.

He finally had a discussion with Jack and agreed he's ready to do a one-man show at Imagine. I'm so proud of Sky. The painting he did of me is going to be used for the publicity for the event—even though he stressed to Jack that it wasn't for sale like all of the other paintings. Jack was so moved by it he didn't care. He said he would display it in the gallery for everyone to enjoy, but it will have a red "sold" dot by the title.

Tonight, we're all heading over to The Hive, and for once, I'm not too proud to say I'm a little nervous. All of our friends and Skyler's parents will be there because Brooke bugged everyone until they promised to show up. She even told Deputy Blake to bring a date, and he gave her the stink eye.

"I'll be there if I can, but I'm not dating anyone," he grumbled at her.

"That needs to change, you old curmudgeon!" she said as she poked him gently in the chest. You should have seen his face. I don't think he's used to women like my…our…Brooke. Right after that, she called Juni, and the two of them decided to put their heads together and find that man a woman. I'm staying out of that project—as far away as I can get.

After a light dinner, we head over to the bar. Brooke proudly declares she is our designated driver for the next several months and plans to drink nada coladas because "Fruit is good for you!" We both kiss her. I swear she's already starting to glow.

The Hive fills up to bursting, and I'm delighted to see so many familiar faces in the crowd. The first set goes extremely well as we play some covers of popular songs interspersed with originals. Our drummer Banger is also a songwriter, and he's not only awesome, he's terribly popular with the ladies—especially when he rips off his shirt mid-set when he gets too hot. He always flings it out into the crowd, causing a minor ruckus each time. The crowd loves our originals, so we're on fire tonight.

Before we end the set, however, the other guys leave the dais, and I stay there by myself. I move a stool front and center, and I'm spotlighted on an otherwise darkened stage—just me, the mic, and my guitar.

"Thanks, everyone, for coming out tonight. I have a special new song I want to sing for you that the guys in the band haven't even heard yet." I pause as I smile and shrug a little bit. "I didn't want to bug 'em with it." There is some polite laughter around the room. I'm sure people are starting to think I might be a little nuts. "Seriously, this is a very personal song. It's about the past year of my life and how I almost didn't make it this far. But I did, and I'm here because of the love of two very special people. I call this song 'My Water and Air,' and it's my way of saying thank you." I quickly doublecheck the tuning of my guitar and then open with a riff.

I take a deep breath and start to sing…

You call me your hero.
I don't know—maybe it's so.
There was never a doubt.
I would not last without
My beautiful, golden Sky.

Our world exploded that day

When plans went astray.
The heavens were tattered
Our bodies were shattered.
But oh, how you mattered,
My hero, my golden Sky.

Because of your love
When hate crashed from above,
We're here, while friends fell.
Home to love, but not well,
I'm sorry to tell,
To a fresh glimpse of hell.
Demons plague us still.
Maybe always will.
My brilliant, talented Sky.

You've saved me twice over
I'm not the hero here.
We both owe so much to
Our sparkling lady who
When times were black
Loved us through hell and back.

Dazzling Brooke and glorious Sky,
I'll need you and love you till the day that I die.
Why do I deserve you?
Do I even deserve two?

Was it always God's plan
When I was a broken man?
Others sadly died,
But our love magnified.
You're how I survive,
My sparkling Brooke and golden Sky.
My perfect pair.
My water and air.

By the time I'm done—with my voice cracking—I swear the entire audience is in tears along with me. The final note fades to a moment of complete silence…and then the crowd is on their feet, cheering and stomping. Wiping my eyes with the back of my hand, I take a few polite bows and then exit the darkened stage. I barely make it off the steps before I collide with Brooke and Skyler, who swamp me with hugs and kisses. Apparently, our relationship is public knowledge now.

Fine by me.

Epilogue

SKYLER

A year later

It honestly doesn't give me much satisfaction to say that Marjorie Henshaw got what she deserved because she is clearly a troubled woman. She had to sell her house to pay for everything the jury awarded. Her creepy ex-husband disappeared into thin air after she admitted to the sheriff that Monty Henshaw was the one who beat her up and threatened her into making false claims about me. She was so embarrassed about the lawsuit, she tried to leave town and move in with her married daughter, but apparently her daughter and son-in-law wouldn't take her in. Word around town—spread by her daughter's local friends—is that her family claims they don't want their kids to grow up in the toxic atmosphere that woman creates, and they don't like that things of value routinely go missing whenever she visits. I don't know if it's true or hearsay that the only job she could get is as a cook in the women's prison in Pewee Valley. If so, that's adding insult to injury for the inmates. I'm just glad she's not part of the Honeybee Hollow community any longer.

On a much happier note, my gallery exhibition at Imagine was fantastic. It felt like most of the town showed up for the opening gala, and *all* of the paintings sold during the month they were exhibited. I have lots of orders for new ones, and Jack was so thrilled he wants to do another one-man show once I have enough inventory again. It might be a while, but it feels wonderful to be painting like this. I still have to rest my arm and hand when I go overboard with inspiration (icing it helps), but I see gradual improvement there all the time. I'm happy people respond favorably to my freer, looser style of painting. I rely more on the use of color than I used to now that my strokes are more expressive and less intricate. Anyway, it's the best I can do, and I'm learning to love it.

I never did go back to the garden center to work, but my parents are happy with that. They have wanted me to concentrate on my art for a long time because they understand how much it fulfills something in me.

Levi is doing great. He still has his moments of moodiness and depression because he can't completely shake the guilt he carries about our buddies who died. But we both continue with therapy, and it helps. Perhaps time will heal his psyche even more.

And yes, I still get those damn migraines now and then—mostly when I don't get enough sleep. I try to be careful.

Levi's music has gotten serious attention, and he writes all the time. Brooke and I have talked to him about auditioning for *The Voice*, but he says he could never be away from us that long if he did well enough to go the distance. He's satisfied to sing locally and sell his songs to famous singers, which brings in some nice royalty income. He rarely has to resort to using his cane to get around and doesn't even have much of a limp unless he's completely exhausted.

Exhaustion, however, is a common theme in our household now that we have baby Samuel Colfax Spencer, named after Samuel Adams—the founding father, not the beer. We liked the name, but Brooke joked she hoped he wouldn't become a revolutionary at too young of an age. Anyway, we looked through names of American patriots—not the football team—and that one kept popping out at us as something we'd like to say all the time. Sam. Sammy. Samuel. Our son.

In case you're wondering, he has dark hair and brown eyes and looks like a baby version of Levi. Cool, huh? I couldn't be happier for Levi, considering the doubts he carried for so long. The look of love on Levi's face when he first held Sammy is an indelible image in my brain. The warmth in his eyes could have melted a glacier.

My parents are over-the-moon excited to have a grandson,

so I guess it's safe to say they have finally accepted our three-some as a permanent thing. This lucky kid is going to have three sets of grandparents, and all of them have been for a visit over the past few weeks. Levi's sister Kate also brought her family down from Lexington, and Lulu gave Sam her stamp of approval by saying he was "cute." She wanted to know if he'd grow up faster than her little brother, though, because she wanted someone to play with. Kate reminded Lulu of her responsibility to be a good big sister and said that included being a good big cousin too—and it was important to be patient.

As expected, Brooke is a wonderful mother and generally wears Sammy in a sling where he has unimpeded access to those delicious tits of hers. Lucky little guy. She's on extended parental leave right now, but I think she's feeling ready to get back to work soon. No matter what, at least one of us will always be around for anything Sam needs. We have a freezer full of Mom's milk in case he's hungry while Brooke is on a conference call. Levi and I also try to do the middle of the night feeding and changing so Brooke can sleep.

It's no surprise that Sammy loves it when Levi sings to him. He can sing to me anytime. Sometimes I get up with him just so I can watch them together and hear that amazing man croon lullabies to our son.

We tried to figure out the best way to make us all equal partners in our relationship, so we made sure our emergency, insurance, and medical paperwork includes each of our names.

I also had my lawyer put my property into all three of our names.

A few days after he was born, I became Sam's godfather. The hospital refused to put both Levi's and my name on his birth certificate at the same time, although Brooke raised quite a stink about it. They said I needed to either be the biological parent with DNA proof (in which case they'd leave off Levi's name) or have paperwork showing that I am married to Levi. Since the only legal way for that to happen would be for him to divorce Brooke and marry me, that was out of the question. When Sam goes to school, we'll make sure I'm listed as one of the parents on all of his documents though.

Being Sam's godfather is cool. And when we had him baptized, the Episcopal priest blessed our three-way union, even if he couldn't legally marry us. That was something at least, and it made us all feel good.

We're hoping eventually Kentucky will join some of the cities in Massachusetts that acknowledge poly families and more than two parents. It may be a long time in coming, but we'll see how it goes. All we can do is love each other to the best of our abilities and raise our kids—yes, we hope there will be more—in a loving, open-minded home.

I suspect you think I've forgotten to tell you about Brooke's birthday present. Don't worry! I was saving that for last. Brooke called Dr. Lassiter's veterinary office to see if he knew of any litters of puppies, but he told her instead about a special program for rehoming dogs in need. This led her to two young dogs who tragically lost their family in a devastating hurricane—poor guys. They definitely needed to be adopted together. Brooke couldn't resist their story, so I borrowed a big van from the garden center, and we drove all day down to a shelter in the Florida panhandle to bring them home. They're both only around a year old. One is a golden retriever named—according to his collar—Teddy Roosevelt and the other a white Clumber spaniel whose tag says he's called George Washington. When Brooke found this out, she figured it was one hundred percent fate that we needed to go adopt those dogs. Teddy and George adore Samuel and look out for each other like it's their job. They're good boys.

Our love keeps multiplying with each new member of the family.

The End

Juni, Jack, and Asher's story is told in the Kentuckiana Romance Writers anthology Double Down on Love (*Jack of Hearts*)

Stay tuned for future Honeybee Hollow stories.

Does handsome Banger keep his shirt on? Or does the

right lucky lady catch the tatters from him? And what is his real name, anyway?

Does grumpy Deputy Sheriff Blake Ogden ever lighten up and find love?

Is there a silver vixen for the silver fox Buford Wallace?

Will there be any more threesomes in Honeybee Hollow?

We'll see…

OR FIND OUT WHERE IT ALL BEGAN WITH THE LASSITER FAMILY from Honeybee Hollow in Savor This and The Rule of 3.

Acknowledgments

Thank you to all the readers out there who keep downloading and purchasing my books every single day. I love each one of you and work hard to create something that will entertain you.

Honeybee Hollow has become so real to me after showing up in several books, I couldn't resist making the town itself like a character and dedicate a new series to it. I hope you've enjoyed your visits to the town with its charms as well as interesting residents. Geographically, I located it where there is an actual town, so I'd have a reference for distances when I needed them. However, the town is completely made up. Too bad. It sounds like a great place to visit or put down roots. Future books will introduce you to more of the population.

I've already thanked her so many times for her wonderful help, but with this book my beta reader Susan proved to be indispensable. Her knowledge as a paralegal kept me from sounding like a complete boob. While I've had *some* experience in the courtroom as a juror and as a spectator in a fascinating case that involved my own father as the defense attorney, preliminary legal procedure is not something I'm at all familiar with. One business law class in grad school did not make me a lawyer—even as much as I loved it. So once again, thank you to Susan for helping me make this story as accurate as possible and for catching other nutty mistakes I made along the way. Her knowledge is incredibly helpful, her attention to detail is amazing, and her friendship is something I cherish.

Thanks once again to my terrific editor Amy Maranville of Kraken Communications who stays flexible when I come up with a "maybe this or maybe that" kind of schedule. She is adaptable, fun to work with, and always full of great ideas. I'm so glad to have her on my team.

My delightful proofreader Mattie Davenport of Davenport Edits is getting to be so busy; I'm always thrilled she can find room for me. I love working with her, and each time is a treat. Who knew submitting a manuscript to be proofread could be a fun experience?

Thank you to Jen DeJong and Olivia Rose of Grey's Promotions who took on the thankless task of promoting my book. They answered about ten million questions—each time quickly and cheerfully—so working with them has been a joy. We're new together, but I foresee a long relationship. I admire their professionalism tremendously.

Dar Albert of Wicked Smart Designs once again created a stunning cover for my book and remained cheerful despite my numerable questions and ideas. She is incredibly talented and professional, and I'm delighted she came into my life to help me along this journey as an author.

My team rocks.

Once again, my husband served as the perfect sounding board for ideas, and he's not afraid to say, "Nope. That's dumb." Sometimes my imagination needs to be reeled in, and other times he challenges me to explore something I've missed. Usually, as soon as I express something out loud, I can tell if it will work or not, so he's heard some pretty crazy stuff. Nevertheless, he remains full of encouragement.

I've met so many wonderful readers and authors this past year at book events, and I have been thrilled to share ideas and learn from them. It's been a blast, and I look forward to many more public appearances and making new friends. In particular, I'd like to mention the members of the Kentuckiana Romance Writers with whom I have collaborated on a book and who have provided hours of fun and encouragement when I've seen them at events.

Thank you to all of my readers who sent in entries to the "Name the Band" contest. I had *hundreds* of names to choose from, so I put the top ten that resonated with me up for a vote via my newsletter. I hope everyone had fun with it. Congratulations to the winner who received a free book! If you're not already receiving my newsletter, this is a good reason to sign up. I try to have a contest like this with each book before it comes out.

Thank you to everyone who wrote a review for the advance copies of the book and to all the bloggers and social media experts who do what I'm hopeless at.

The reviews don't have to stop there, however. If you've read the book and have an opinion to share, please do so on Amazon, Goodreads, BookBub, etc. Tell your book clubs, hairdresser, gym friends, work buddies, anyone you can think of. Ask your local bookstore to carry my books. They're available through IngramSpark to all bookstores. Spread the word, and I'll love you even more than I already do.

It's always fun to hear from readers. Feel free to write to me at ariella@ariellatalix.com, and I'll be sure to answer.

You can sign up for my newsletter here:

https://landing.mailerlite.com/webforms/landing/m6f3i7

Follow me at all the obvious places:

https://www.amazon.com/stores/Ariella-Talix/author/B07MKPB8TN

https://www.facebook.com/ariella.talix.1

https://www.bookbub.com/authors/ariella-talix

https://www.instagram.com/ariellatalix/

https://www.goodreads.com/author/show/18683284.Ariella_Talix

https://x.com/AriellaTalix

https://www.ariellatalix.com

Happy reading!

Ariella Talix

Books by Ariella Talix

Every book is a standalone story with no cliffhanger.

Each series is more fun when read in order, however. Often characters show up again because I can't help myself.

Contemporary Romance

The Drummonds:

Porter the Importer

Make Believe

The Artist

Lovers in Louisville (Spin-off from The Drummonds):

Save Her

Saving Him

Savor This

Contemporary MMF Romance

The Perfect Number (Spin-off from Savor This):

The Rule of 3

The Passion of 3

Living the Fantasy:

Just Curious

Compelling Urges

Standalone:

Group Hug

Honeybee Hollow Series:

Double Down on Love (*Jack of Hearts*) with the Kentuckiana Romance Writers. This introductory MMF novella is the only story in the book related to Honeybee Hollow. It's a spin-off from Group Hug. The rest are small-town Kentucky stories by other romance authors.

Buddy System (Book One is an MMF spin-off from *Jack of Hearts*)

TBD (Book Two is an MF Romance featuring Deputy Sheriff Blake Ogden from this book). Look for this in 2025.

<u>Historical MMF Romance</u>

Hearts of Gold:

The Golden Rush

<u>Fiddle and Fire</u>

Casting Vows

<u>Anthologies</u>

Double Down on Love (*Jack of Hearts*) with the Kentuckiana Romance Writers

The Drummonds

Lovers in Louisville

The Perfect Number

Living the Fantasy